A Jewell Cove Christmas

DONNA ALWARD

Copyright

Contents

Christmas at Seashell Cottage

DONNA ALWARD

Chapter 1

Charlie Yang had never considered herself much of a joiner. So it went without saying that she was surprised to find herself in the middle of setting up a nativity scene in front of the Jewell Cove church, stuffing scratchy straw into a crudely constructed manger. They'd had an early snow, and the layer of white covering the ground and the branches of trees and shrubbery added to the feeling of holiday spirit that had taken over since Thanksgiving.

Like a well-oiled machine, Gloria Henderson and her army of church ladies had taken charge of the volunteers and had assigned jobs to everyone. The men were tasked with anything requiring a ladder and heavy lifting— including lugging three wise men, Mary and Joseph, the shepherds and sheep, and every last bit of the nativity to the front yard. Right now Bill—Charlie had forgotten his last name—from the service station was positioning the figures in the proper places, which were the exact same spots they occupied each and every year, apparently. Charlie gave a dry chuckle. You could always count on small towns, and Jewell Cove, Maine, was no different. It was practically steeped in salt-water traditions.

Still, it stung a little that the committee had taken one look at Charlie's attempt at the red and green velvet bows and suggested she might be better suited to helping with something else. She was a doctor, for heaven's sake. She could suture a wound and leave barely a trace of a scar. Surely her bows weren't that bad...

She'd been sent off to the front of the church with specific instructions: set up the manger, uncoil and string the lights, and put Baby Jesus in place. Charlie huffed. She'd been number three in her graduating class from med school. She could set up a nativity scene with one hand tied behind her back. She shivered against the cold, zipped her puffy jacket up the last three inches, and wished she'd thought to wear a hat to keep her ears warm.

"Manger, check." She wrestled the wooden structure into position by inches until it was in the middle of the nativity. "Straw, check." She took off her gloves for a minute and padded the bottom of the manger with a small brick of synthetic straw, pulling the pieces apart and fluffing them up. As soon as it was done, she hurried to put her gloves back on. "Now for Baby Jesus." Charlie looked around at the boxes of Christmas decorations that surrounded her. "Aha! Baby Jesus, check!" She retrieved a doll from a box, already wrapped and safety-pinned into swaddling clothes, and stared down at the straw padding the bottom of the crude manger. "This doesn't feel right," she murmured to the doll, whose eyes were closed. She looked in the box for a blanket or fabric of some sort. "I can't just put you down on the prickly straw. Surely the new Messiah deserves something softer to lie on."

After a few minutes of digging through the boxes for something that might suit, Charlie sighed. "Well, Baby Jesus, we'll just have to wait to put you in your manger until I can think of something to use to cover the straw. Until then, I need to get these lights untangled."

She sat down on the cold, wooden platform the church had set up to house the nativity scene. It was a lonely, solitary task and she found herself carrying on a one-way conversation with the doll just to break the silence. "I have skills, Baby Jesus. Specific skills. Skills that I should be using right now with my patients. Not sitting in the cold unraveling tangled lights." She sighed in frustration.

God, she was talking to a doll. A doll who was, at this moment, staring at her with unseeing, unblinking eyes. It was a little bit creepy, so she turned her attention back to the task at hand, working away at a stubborn knot, muttering to herself. Once again, the gloves came off; there was no way she could straighten the knotted wires with the material in the way. She blew on her fingers and started again.

"You know," she continued, "when I agreed to help out, I'd thought it would be a good chance be a part of the community. Outside of work, I mean. And here I am alone. As usual."

Charlie cursed under her breath as the knot let go only to reveal another. A burst of laughter drew her attention away for a moment, and she watched as a couple strolled along the sidewalk holding hands.

"Wanna hear something stupid, Baby Jesus? The closest thing to a romantic relationship I have right now is an infatuation with the man who works on the docks. You know?" She paused, studying the glassy eyes of the doll next to her. "Of course you don't know. You're a doll. And the Savior of all mankind, right? You have bigger fish to fry than my non-existent love life." She laughed to herself. "I'm pathetic. But let me tell you, that man is hot. Tall, dark, and rugged." In her mind she could picture the look of him, long legs and broad shoulders, his strength evident even beneath work pants and the navy jacket he typically wore. She sighed. "I don't even know his name. How dumb is that?"

"Um, excuse me, but who are you talking to?"

She jumped at the sound of a deep voice behind her, a muted squeak bursting from her mouth, then spun around to find a giant of a man standing there, feet planted, arms crossed, and an amused expression on his face. Not just any man. The man.

Her cheeks flamed with embarrassment. "Baby Jesus?" she suggested weakly.

Busted talking to a doll. She felt about three years old.

He chuckled. "Really?" He nodded at the bundle in her arms. "What were you going to do? Brain me with him?"

What? It took a few seconds before she realized that she'd grabbed the doll like a weapon and was currently holding it like she was a quarterback ready to go long.

Charlie looked down at the doll's face and then tucked it more securely in her arms.

"You startled me, that's all," she replied, emitting a breathy laugh. Holy crap. From afar he'd looked big, but her dream guy was over six feet for sure, probably closer to six-four, big feet in big boots, faded jeans, and one of those plaid quilted jackets she'd seen a lot of the men around here wear when the weather was cold but not downright frigid.

His arms were crossed, and the stance accentuated the muscles in his arms and shoulders. His hair was thick and dark, highlighting a face that sported a stunning set of brown eyes with long lashes, a strong jaw and good cheekbones.

"I'm Charlene," she offered, only stammering a little, holding the doll in one arm and extending her other hand. "Charlie, actually."

"Dave," he replied, stepping forward to shake her hand. The contact sent a ripple of pleasure down her arm. "Do you always talk to dolls?" He grinned openly now, a slight dimple popping in one cheek.

"Only when I'm trying not to freeze to death." She smiled back, her pulse hammering. Don't say something dumb, she warned herself. Like blurting out that she'd watching him working each day from the wide windows at Breezes Café. The last thing she needed was to seem all... stalkerish.

"You're one of the doctors in town, aren't you?" he asked, dropping her hand. "I've seen you around."

He had? And if he knew she was the doctor, he had to have asked about her, right? As she wrapped her mind around that astounding fact, she tried to remain cool.

"That's me."

"I'm working down at the boat yard for the time being."

"I know."

Damn it. Why couldn't she bite her tongue?

His eyebrows went up and she offered a smile that she hoped wasn't too goofy-looking. "Small town," she reminded him, and he chuckled, sending a warm shiver over her. It seemed her rugged mystery man was just as attractive up close. Lucky for her. Perhaps she'd been neglecting her love life for a little too long.

Dave smiled at her. "I'm pretty new around here. The guy I work for is helping out today and mentioned they needed some help. I thought I'd lend a hand. Maybe meet some people." His eyes were warm. "Looks like I'm off to a good start."

She hoped she wasn't blushing, because she got the feeling he was flirting. She blinked, then smiled back. "I think you're off to a very good start."

Their gazes held for a few moments and Charlie held her breath. This was something she wasn't exactly used to. To have her mystery man standing before her, in the flesh, making conversation...surreal. To say the least.

"Anyway, sorry about the manger," he apologized, breaking the spell. "It's kind of crude, but I didn't have much time to put it together."

She looked down at the rough wood. It wasn't fancy, but it was solidly constructed. "You built this?"

"Apparently the one they had was falling apart. Time to replace it." He shrugged. "I'm more used to working with boats and engines than carpentry, but I borrowed some tools, got some scrap wood from my landlord, and gave it my best shot."

"Aren't we lucky that you're so...handy." And hot. And friendly.

"I'm not sure about that. Anyway, you seemed to be standing around the manger for a long time and I wondered if something needed fixing."

Charlie looked up at him, feeling her cheeks heat again beneath his honest gaze. Good heavens, where was her confidence? "There's nothing wrong with the manger. It's silly, really. I..."

"You?" he prompted.

She swallowed. "I put in the straw, but I was wondering if there was anything to put over top of it before I put down the, uh, baby."

"Over top?"

"You know." She gestured with her free hand. "Like a blanket or something. Because the straw is so scratchy and rough."

His gaze softened and she felt a little bit embarrassed and a little bit melty.

"I don't think it's going to matter to the doll, Charlie."

He finally said her name and it sounded so nice in his deep, smooth voice she wondered if she was really looking at Dave, The Christmas Angel.

She let her eyes meet his, felt the connection to her toes. "It's not just a doll," she said softly. "It's Baby Jesus."

And there was that smile again, and a hint of perfectly white teeth. "You're right," he responded, taking a step forward. Charlie held her breath as he came closer, peering over her shoulder at the wood and straw. He smelled good, too. A little like lumber, but more like man. The kind of scent that made a woman want to burrow her face into the soft fabric of his shirt and just breathe deeply...

He took a step back and she let out her breath. Okay. Granted, her time in Jewell Cove had been a significant dry spell, but this was getting ridiculous.

"I might have something in my car that would work. I'll be back in a minute."

"Okay," she replied, feeling dumb, but enjoying the view as he walked away towards the church parking lot.

Dave strode away towards the parking lot feeling a little bit off balance after the encounter with the good doctor. The men on the dock called her Dr. Pitbull, and Dave thought they must be thinking about two different people. Charlene—Charlie—seemed quiet, and, well, cute. She'd blushed when they'd talked and stammered a little, too. In fact, she'd looked adorable, standing there with the doll and surrounded by tangles of Christmas lights.

He reached his SUV and opened the trunk. Inside the plastic tub containing extra windshield washer, oil, and jumper cables was a crumpled pile of rags, mostly comprised of old T-shirts. He grabbed a beige one, closed the tailgate again, and headed back toward the nativity scene where Charlie waited. She was a tiny little thing, maybe five foot four or five, her build slight. She rather reminded him of a ballerina, with a dainty strength about her. Her black hair was braided precisely, highlighting the porcelain smoothness of her skin, and a set of deep brown eyes that a man could lose himself in. She was absolutely stunning.

The doll was still in her arms when he reached the nativity again, and he grinned at the strange sight. He held out the shirt. "This is clean, and nice and soft. Will it work?"

The smile on her face made the day worthwhile. "That's perfect! Plus, it's almost the same color as the straw. It'll blend in really well."

It was cute how she was worried about authenticity. And the comfort and welfare of a plastic doll.

Dave folded the cotton and draped it over the bumpy straw. He watched as Charlie lay the doll down as carefully as if it were a real baby, then stood back. "That definitely looks better," she said, hands on her hips.

He considered pointing out the cold Maine weather and paltry covering on the doll, but was afraid she'd take that to heart too and insist on covering the manger with heavy blankets, which he was sure wouldn't have been found in Bethlehem.

"Much better," he replied, but he couldn't take his eyes off of her. Petite and pretty, pit bull doctor, sentimentalist. Which was she, or was she all those things? It had been a long time since he'd been this intrigued by a woman. It wasn't exactly an unwelcome feeling.

"Hey, are you all right?"

Charlie's voice interrupted his less-than-pure thoughts. "Yeah, sure. Sorry."

He got the feeling Charlie was going to say something more, but one of the church ladies came bearing down on them like a woman on a mission. "Charlene, we could use your help in the sanctuary. We're putting together the caroling booklets for the tree lighting tomorrow night."

Ah yes. Dave looked at Charlie's face and saw it transform into a polite, welcoming mask, and he nearly laughed. He'd bet ten bucks that she adopted the same expression when she walked into an exam room and greeted a new patient.

"Sure thing, Mrs. Henderson. I think the nativity is all done. I'm still working on the lights..."

The older woman's lips pursed a bit in disapproval. "Well, maybe Bill can finish that up. He knows how we display them."

Mrs. Henderson moved on to fuss about the figures, muscling a shepherd and staff about two inches to the right before declaring herself satisfied. "There. That's wonderful. We're nearly done inside as well. The Ladies' group has provided lunch for the volunteers. Soup and sandwiches, which should be on in exactly" —she checked her watch— "Thirty-six minutes."

Heaven forbid the lunch be a minute early or late.

"Mr...?" Mrs. Henderson looked up at him suddenly, and he got the strange feeling that she was taking stock of him.

"Ricker," he supplied with a nod.

"Yes, you just moved here, didn't you?"

Nosy. Bossy and nosy. She had a way of talking that reminded him of the military. Sharp and precise. "Yes, ma'am. From Virginia." He tried another one of his smiles on her, thinking that perhaps he and Dr. Yang really weren't that different after all. "I built the manger."

"Right." She eyed him curiously. You're working for George Adams down on the docks. Hope he's got enough work to keep you busy."

Now it was his turn to be embarrassed and he hoped the raw bite to the air covered any flush in his cheeks. He wasn't rolling in it, but he could make ends meet.

Besides, this was just a temporary job until he figured out exactly where he wanted to settle.

"I don't know about you, but I think I can smell that soup all the way out here. Are you coming in with us, Dave?" Charlie jumped in with the attempted save.

As much as he might enjoy spending more time with the pretty doctor, he wasn't sure he was up to the sheer volume of hen clucking that was likely to happen over lunch. "No, but thanks for the invite. I've got to get back home. I'm running low on wood and should probably split a bunch to tide me over for a few days."

He waited for lightning to strike through the leaden sky. He'd just flat-out lied, in front of the church with the steeple and cross directly in front of him.

"Well, thank you for all your help," Mrs. Henderson said." You be sure to come to the tree lighting tomorrow night in the square. The choir's leading the caroling and there's free hot chocolate for everyone."

"Sounds great," he responded, giving that automatic smile again.

He looked down at Charlie. She was watching him curiously, as if trying to puzzle him out. Her gaze burned into his, and he thought for a moment he saw a devilish twinkle in their depths. "Oh yes. Everyone comes out for it," Charlie said. "It's one of the highlights of the season." Her voice sounded exactly like an advertisement and he had a hard time not laughing at what he was certain was false enthusiasm.

"Everyone?" he asked.

Mrs. Henderson didn't miss the skeptical tone in his voice. "Oh, the whole town shows up," she insisted. "You'll be there, won't you Charlene?"

"Of course. I wouldn't miss it." Again with the too-bright enthusiasm. Was Charlie also a bit of a wallflower?

"Maybe I'll know someone, then," he offered. Had he really just agreed to go? He had to be off his rocker. Christmas carols? He couldn't carry a tune in a bucket. And hot chocolate? He'd much prefer a couple fingers of whiskey in front of the fire back at the cottage.

"Right. Well, Charlene, we really need those booklets done up. Thanks for your help, Mr. Ricker." Mrs. Henderson got right back to business and began stomping her way to the front steps of the church.

"I'd better go," Charlie said quietly, looking up at him. "That woman means business."

"She'd be a great drill sergeant," he remarked.

Charlie laughed lightly, the sound dancing in the crisp air.

"So will I see you tomorrow night?" she asked, a hopeful note to her voice. "I get the feeling we're both kind of like the new people in town. Welcome to join in, but still a little on the outside. Sometimes I think everyone in Jewell Cove has known each other forever."

"I'll probably make it," he answered. "Not much else to do but sit out at the cabin and stare at the fire."

She laughed again. "That sounds pretty nice to me."

And just like that he imagined her sitting there with him, perhaps a glass of wine in her hand, and that silken black hair loosed from its braid while the fire snapped and crackled behind them...

Get a hold of yourself, man. Dave swallowed and shoved his hands into his pockets. "Aw, it won't kill us to show up, will it?"

"So I guess I'll see you then."

"Guess so." He pulled a hand out of his coat. "Nice to meet you, Charlie."

She took his hand again, but there was more holding than shaking happening and he felt the pull to her through the innocent contact.

"You too." She pulled her hand away. "See you around."

He watched her walk away. She didn't look back at him, just made a straight line through the snow to the church doors. He let out a breath. He'd come to Jewell Cove to start over, to be closer to his daughter, Nora.

Meeting the pretty doctor hadn't been on his agenda, but he wasn't about to complain. After all, he'd learned long ago that sometimes the best things happened when you least expected them.

Chapter 2

Charlie tugged her hat down over her ears a little further and inwardly agreed that her prediction had been bang on. The whole town did come out to the tree lighting—at least it looked that way. Memorial Square was full of people, the scent of fresh snow, evergreen, and chocolate heavy in the air. There was laughter and conversation and happy greetings, but Charlie hung back. She found it awkward, being overly friendly with the townspeople and then having them in her exam room the next week. She tended to isolate herself, maintain that little bit of personal distance. She wasn't sure how her boss, Josh Collins, managed to separate personal from professional, but he did.

Brilliantly. Just like he did everything.

She snagged herself a cup of hot chocolate, both for the comforting heat and to give her something to do with her hands. There was an unoccupied corner by the gazebo, and she made her way there, smiling at people as she went along. There were lots of "Hi, Dr. Yang," and "Merry Christmas, Dr. Yang," greetings, but none to Charlene or Charlie.

This was how she'd wanted it when she first moved here, but now she wasn't so sure. Wouldn't it be nice to be a part of something? To belong and fit in? She leaned back against the gazebo wall and watched the gathering with a bit of longing. Sure, it would be nice, but she had no idea how to go about it. She should call Lizzie, she realized. Her best friend and college roommate did much better with interpersonal relationships. Heck, if it hadn't been for her, Charlie wouldn't have had any social life in college at all.

She sipped at her chocolate. Lizzie had come into their dorm room that first year of med school and had made life bearable. Lizzie went to med school because it was all she'd ever wanted to do. Charlie had gone because it was expected. Study. Succeed. For her parents, it had been about prestige and money and being able to say their only child was a hot shot doctor. One did not merely get by. One strived to be The Best. Otherwise, what was the point?

It really choked them now that she was a simple GP in a small town. She felt the disapproval every time she saw them, which was always at the family home on Beacon Hill. Not once had they driven up to Jewell Cove to see where she was living.

"Hey, is there room for one more to hide over here?"

A delicious shiver ran up her spine. She looked over her shoulder and saw Dave, cradling his own cup of chocolate, a thick knitted hat on his head and a heavy winter jacket making him look even bigger than he had yesterday. She vowed that she would not be as awkward as she'd felt in front of the church.

She smiled. "You realize you're ginormous, right? Good luck hiding anywhere."

He chuckled. "It's in my genes. My dad's six-three and my mom's five-eleven. I was bound to be big."

"Brothers and sisters?"

He raised his eyebrows. "Two of each. I'm smack in the middle of the birth order."

Good heavens. Five of them? "You must be intimidating when you're all together. Any big plans to get together for the holidays?"

"We're all grown. My older brother and sister are both married and have kids. My younger brother Jason is engaged and my baby sister Samantha is just finishing college. We're spread out, too, so having us all together doesn't really happen very often, though we try. This year mom and dad are spending Christmas in Texas at my brother's, spoiling grandkids." He took a sip of his chocolate and then looked down at her. "What about you? Siblings?"

She turned her gaze to the very tall Christmas tree in the center of the square. His family sounded wonderful, even if they were spread out across the country. She focused on the huge star at the top of the tree as she answered. "There's just me. My parents live in Boston."

"So close enough you can all be together for Christmas. Lucky."

He'd think so, wouldn't he? Because that's what families did. But not hers. She forced her voice to be light, nonchalant. "Oh, they're traveling over the holidays. A cruise or something."

She knew how it sounded. The situation was exactly how it appeared. They weren't a warm and fuzzy family. Being together felt like work. She supposed it had been nice of them to invite her along for the trip, but the idea of being stuck on a cruise ship for Christmas, playing third wheel to parents wasn't Charlie's idea of a perfect holiday.

They stopped chatting as the mayor, Luke Pratt, got up to make a short speech.

The elementary school choir then performed three verses of *O Christmas Tree*, their sweet, youthful voices filling the air as a few errant flakes of snow drifted through the darkness. As the last note faded into the night, there was a breathless pause and then the tree came to life, multicolored bulbs lighting up the square and causing a chorus of ooohs and aaahs to wave through the gathering, and then clapping broke out, the sound muffled by heavy mittens and gloves.

"That's pretty impressive," Dave remarked from behind her.

She nodded, staring at the tree, the beautiful colored lights sparkling in the chilly evening. "I've always liked the lights with all the colors." She looked over her shoulder and smiled at him. "White ones are elegant, and I know some people like all red, or green, or whatever. But I think the variety is so cheerful, don't you?"

"Oh, absolutely." He was grinning, and she knew he was teasing her a little bit. She liked it. It was far better than the formal "Dr. Yang" she got when she crossed the square.

They were interrupted by someone from the church, thrusting a carol booklet in Charlie's hand. "We've got a bigger crowd than we expected," the woman explained. "Would you mind sharing?"

"Of course," Dave answered. He stayed where he was, a few steps behind her, even as the church choir led the first carol, easing into the evening with a familiar and rousing rendition of *Jingle Bells.*

Charlie turned around and stared at him. "Either you're incredibly far-sighted, or you're not singing."

He squinted at her—and then laughed.

"Nuh uh," she chided. "If I'm expected to sing, so are you."

"Believe me, you don't want me to."

"Then fake it." She smiled at him sweetly. "Aren't we supposed to be suffering together, here?"

"You'll only suffer if I sing. We could demonstrate our solidarity by abstaining." They were talking during the singing and a few dirty looks were aimed their way.

She shoved the booklet in his hands. "Just mouth the words," she commanded. "And smile."

He held the booklet, but had to hold his arm straight down so it was low enough for her to see. Not that they needed the words to *Jingle Bells.* Charlie joined in, feeling awkward and singing softly. Just enough so she could hear herself, but not loudly enough that anyone nearby could discern her voice from the others.

And then she heard it, a deep rumble an octave below hers, slightly off key, slightly mumbled, as Dave started jingling all the way. She hid a smirk behind a sip of hot chocolate, then joined in for the last chorus.

As the next carol was announced, he leaned over, his mouth ridiculously close to her ear. "I saw you laughing."

She put on an innocent expression. "I swear I didn't."

"I told you I couldn't sing."

"Yes, you can. What you should have said was you can't sing well." And then she did giggle.

And he gave her shoulder a nudge as if to say, Brat.

The next song was more somber, and the crowd started singing *O Little Town of Bethlehem*. That was followed by several others, both religious and secular until Charlie's hot chocolate was long gone and her fingers and toes were starting to get cold.

She shivered and wrapped her arms around her middle, shifting her feet to get warm. How long did these things go, anyway?

And then Dave moved closer behind her, blocking her from the cold with his broad body, putting his left arm around her and pulling her back against his puffy coat while the right one encircled her, holding the lyrics booklet so they could both see.

She should pull away. She should simply say she was getting cold and leave. But she didn't. It felt too good, having the bulk of his body close to hers, barely touching and yet sheltering her just the same. He was near enough she could feel the gentle vibration of his voice through his chest as the crowd started singing *Silent Night*. The mood had turned soft and reverent, the voices blending beautifully as the earlier cloud cover shifted away and left a sky full of twinkling stars. Something stole through Charlie then, a lovely yet wistful sense of contentment. Maybe she wasn't perfect. Maybe she didn't quite fit in here. But right now, the heart of Jewell Cove wasn't such a bad place to be.

Her eyes stung a little and she blinked quickly, picking up the words of the second verse. It had always been her favorite carol, so calm and peaceful and beautiful.

A few voices sang in harmony, and Charlie realized that this was the happiest she'd been in a long time.

The song faded into the night and there was a pause while everyone, by tacit agreement, let the last note linger on the air.

Dave looked down at the warm woman in his arms. Her head didn't quite reach his chin, and she felt tiny and petite as she leaned against his chest. He didn't want to let her go, not yet. And he didn't think she wanted to leave either, because she stayed where she was as Gloria Henderson got up and reminded everyone about the Evergreen Festival coming up. The evening ended with a cheerful version of *We Wish You a Merry Christmas* and then the crowd began to disperse.

She started forward but his arm tightened, pulling her back against his chest. "Hurrying away so soon?" he asked quietly, putting his lips close to her ear. Close enough he could kiss the soft skin just behind her earlobe. He didn't, but he was tempted.

"I should go. It's cold out." Her voice was breathy. She was feeling it, too. But she stopped pushing against his arm and settled back against him once more, in the fleeting moments where they were in the tenuous limbo of the event being over but not yet attracting any attention.

He definitely didn't want the night to end yet.

"I thought you might be interested in that drink. And the fire."

Nerves and anticipation coiled in Charlie's stomach, a delicious blend of "I shouldn't" and "I really want to." Wasn't this what she'd been fantasizing about since she'd first seen him? That he'd show up and proposition her in that smooth, velvety voice?

Charlie slowly turned around and lifted her chin so she could meet his eyes. Just as she suspected, they were serious with a glint of teasing...or was that challenge? She was an achiever. Challenges were her personal kryptonite. It was almost impossible to turn one down. Add into that the fact that she knew exactly what she was looking for in a man, and his invitation became tempting in the extreme. He had a good sense of humor. He was nice, and gentlemanly. Not a bad start, really.

"I'm not looking for a hook-up," she said, casting a quick look around to make sure she couldn't be heard. "Just so you know. It's not really my style." As much as she disliked the rigid structure of her childhood, the end result was that she was constantly weighing pros and cons and making decisions based on logic and not impulse.

Saying yes would definitely be an impulse move.

"Charlie, look at me."

She met his eyes again. The challenge was gone, replaced by something deeper. Something she couldn't help but respond to.

"It's just one drink. I've spent the last few weeks working my butt off. I liked you yesterday. Other than the guys down at the dock, you're the only person I've really met in town." He gave her a little wink. "And you're definitely better looking than they are."

She wasn't beating social engagements off with a stick either. The clinic was small, just her, Josh, and their receptionist-slash-nurse, Robin. There was no office Christmas party, no family, no tight circle of friends. She understood the kind of isolation he was talking about. More than that, she was really attracted to him.

She wavered. "One drink, nothing more." She wanted to sound firm, but her voice had a husky, soft tone she didn't quite recognize.

They'd stepped away from each other, preparing to leave the square when Josh came up behind them. "Charlie, you came to the tree lighting. I wasn't sure you would."

Charlie blinked. So much for slipping away unnoticed.

"And you've got a date." Josh grinned at her and she felt like a little sister at the mercy of a big brother's teasing.

"You're being transparent, Josh."

He actually had the temerity to look innocent and offended. "Me? Transparent? Right." He held out his hand to Dave. "Josh Collins. I'm the other doctor in the Jewell Cove practice."

"Dave Ricker." Dave shook Josh's hand and smiled. "I'm working at the boatyard."

Josh tilted his head and wrinkled his brow. "Hey, are you the guy renting Tom's cottage out at Fiddler's Rock?"

Dave nodded. "Yeah, that's me. You know Tom?"

Josh grinned. "He's my cousin. Welcome to town. Listen, a bunch of us are going to the Rusty Fern for a bite to eat. Come along and I'll buy you a drink," he offered. "You too, Charlie," he added as an afterthought.

"I think we already have plans," Dave replied, his gaze leaving Josh and falling on Charlie.

Charlie looked from Josh to Dave. "You did say you didn't know many people in town," she said, surprisingly grateful for the invitation. "And you mentioned something about a drink. This way you kill two birds with one stone." She let the words hang in the air. It was a chance to spend more time with him without it getting too intimate too fast. Fantasies were one thing. But Charlie was a little more reserved when it came to the actual execution. This might be a chance to get to know him better, rather than being swept away by her Mystery Guy.

Dave sighed. "Sure, why not?" he agreed. He leaned down and whispered in her ear. "But you still owe me a date."

She shivered with anticipation. She had to admit, it felt great being pursued. It had been ages since that had happened.

"Great!" Josh said. "I'll go round up the others."

Before they could answer, he was gone again, melting into the departing crowd.

"Do you get the feeling we were just bulldozed?" Dave asked.

She laughed. "I've learned to pick my battles where Josh Collins is concerned."

"And tonight wasn't one of them?"

She smiled, feeling a little cheeky. "It saved me from having to turn you down later," she explained, and started walking away. "When you would have propositioned me. You coming or not?"

He caught up to her, laughing a little as he looped his arm through hers. "I'd say you assume too much, but you probably don't. Just so you're aware, I haven't given up."

His persistence sent a wave of warmth through her. Their steps slowed and Charlie left her arm linked with his as they ambled down the block. Little flakes of snow were drifting lazily down, settling on the sidewalk with a soft shush. Evergreen wreaths with huge red bows hung from each lamppost, and the businesses that had remained open for late shopping were lit up with Christmas lights. Last Christmas she'd just moved here and hadn't taken the time to really enjoy the holiday season and the sense of community that pervaded the town. This year was different, though. She couldn't help but be swept along in the festive spirit.

"You're awfully quiet," Dave remarked, pulling her arm closer to his side.

She tilted her head and glanced up at him. "Sorry. I'm just enjoying the walk. It's so pretty out tonight."

"It is, isn't it?" He angled a look down at her. "It's been a while since I've seen snow at Christmas."

"Really?"

He nodded. "Yeah. I was deployed a few times, and there's not exactly a lot of Christmas spirit in the Middle East."

Deployed. So he was military—or ex, since he was working on the docks. Now that Charlie thought about it, it fit. There was something in his bearing, the way he carried himself. Confident but not cocky. Respectful and with intent.

He paused, taking a deep breath of cold air as if savoring it. "Before that I was stationed in California. Not much snow there."

"I guess not. How long have you been out, then? I mean, did you resign or get medically discharged or something?"

He stopped in the middle of the sidewalk. "Hmmm. A lot of questions."

"I guess I figured if we're going to get that nightcap at some point, I might want to know a little bit about the man behind the invitation."

His dark eyes searched hers for a moment. A group of teenagers went past them, talking loudly, half of them with their heads buried in their phones.

He shrugged. "I was a SEAL. I'm thirty. I was already older than most of the guys on my team. Besides, it was time to come home. Stop running around the world being Rambo." He smiled. "And now I'm back to where I started. Working on boats and being by the ocean. It suits me."

A SEAL. She couldn't deny the little shiver of excitement that rippled up her spine. Not just a soldier but an elite one. She tried to lighten the mood a little. "I didn't realize SEALS had a best before date."

"Only with some things." His gaze burrowed into hers again, surprising her with its intensity. "I promise, with just about everything else, I'm nowhere near approaching my shelf life."

Oh. My.

They were nearly to the church yard when Dave stopped suddenly, looking over at the nativity. There was a thin film of snow on the tops of the statues, but it really did look lovely, especially with the single small floodlight casting a glow on the scene. She looked up at him and saw a frown marring his face, his brows pulled together in the middle.

"What's the matter?" she asked.

"Stay here. I thought I saw something."

She waited as he stomped through the snow on the church lawn. Down the block, she noticed as a person jogged to a parked car, got in, and wasted no time driving away. She looked back at Dave, whose body blocked her view of the manger. More perplexing was the way he stared at it, his body utterly still.

"What on earth are you doing?" she called out.

A thin, plaintive sound traveled on the cold air, and she looked around to see if anyone was passing close by with a stroller or baby in their arms. But the crowd had dispersed and there was barely anyone on the street now. Her gaze turned back to Dave and her heart thumped against her ribs at the same time as her stomach seemed to drop to her feet.

He was standing in front of the manger. And instead of a T-shirt and plastic doll, he appeared to be holding a baby, wrapped in a red blanket.

Chapter 3

Awake now, the baby cried a bit, a helpless little wail that made Dave hold him or her a little closer to his jacket, tucking the blanket more firmly around the tiny form.

"Dave?"

He stepped forward. "I think we have a big problem, Charlie."

She rushed forward, stirring up snow until she reached him and pulled back a corner of the blanket. "Oh my God. This baby can't be more than a few weeks old. We need to get inside where it's warm."

"The pub?"

She frowned. "I guess. No, wait. My office is only a few blocks over. He...she...needs to be examined. Did you see anyone? What about that car that rushed away?" Without waiting for an answer, she whipped out her cell phone, walking as she talked. Dave followed right at her heels.

"Hi, It's Dr. Yang from the clinic. Who's on duty tonight?" There was a momentary pause as the person on the other end answered. "Can you have him meet me at the clinic right away? I'm on my way now." She ended the call and then automatically dialed again.

"Josh? It's Charlie. I have to take a rain check on tonight. Something's come up." There was another pause and Dave watched as Charlie's face wrinkled with annoyance. "No, not that. We just found...something...at the nativity. I'll explain it all later. I don't have time right now."

She hung up and nodded at him, all business. "Let's hurry. The police are on their way and we have to get this little one inside out of the cold."

The wind had picked up a bit and Dave unzipped his coat part way, then tucked the bundle inside, cozy between his body and the protective nylon shell. Charlie smiled and said, "Great idea" as she led him to the corner and left, going up the street, turning left again at the next corner until they were standing outside a house that had a floodlit signing announcing, "Jewell Cove Medical Clinic."

She dug in her purse for keys, went to the back door and opened up, then quickly disarmed the security system. "Come on in," she invited, flicking on a light.

The reception area was bathed in a welcoming glow. The office was warmer than outside, but still chilly, and Dave stood by feeling helpless as Charlie bustled around, turning up the heat and flicking on lights. She'd gone from sweet, blushing Charlie to super-efficient Dr. Yang in the blink of an eye. Now he understood a little better why she might have earned the nickname Dr. Pitbull.

"Okay," she finally said. "Let's have a look at this little one."

Dave looked down inside his coat. He must have thrown off some good heat because the baby was sleeping, little tiny lips moving in and out as it breathed. As gently as he possibly could, he slid his opposite hand inside and cradled the baby's bottom in his wide palm, using his shoulder and upper arm to assist him in shifting the baby out of his coat.

"You're good with babies," she offered. She reached for the bundle and took it into her hands. They were good hands, he realized. Despite her small size, her hands were strong and capable. Ordinary—no polish, just smooth, rounded nails, and as their fingertips brushed, her skin was soft against his. Yesterday they'd had the thickness of gloves between them. Now, as their hands touched while shifting the baby, the contact felt somehow intimate. It was the damnedest thing.

Cradling the infant in the crook of her elbow, Charlie peeled back the blanket. The baby was dressed in blue fuzzy sleepers and a thin stretchy hat. She smiled up at Dave. "I'm guessing it's a boy."

There was no note tucked in with the baby as far as Dave could see. Instead, he followed Charlie to an exam room with better lighting. She lay the sleeping baby carefully on the exam table and began looking him over. First, checking what she could with the sleepers on, and then she began unsnapping the pajamas. The baby woke then, disturbed by the feeling of being undressed and exposed. At the same time there was a knock at the outer door.

Charlie never looked up from her examination. "Could you get that? It'll be the police."

Dave went to the door and flipped the lock, letting in the other man who was dressed in his uniform and was big enough that Dave figured most men in town would think twice before picking a fight. "Officer," he greeted, holding open the door. "I'm Dave Ricker."

"Is Dr. Yang in trouble?" The cop pushed into the reception area, his eyes sharp.

"No, no of course not." Dave shook his head. "Follow me. She's in here."

The officer followed Dave back to the exam room and brushed by him at the doorway. "Dr. Yang? Are you okay?"

She looked up, keeping one hand on the baby's belly, as if anchoring him in place. "Hello, Todd."

Dave watched as the burly officer's hard gaze softened as he looked at the baby.

"Well. Who have we here?"

"I wish I could tell you." She met Dave's gaze across the room. "Dave, this is Todd Smith. Come on in and tell him what happened, Dave, and I can finish up my exam. This little guy would probably like to be bundled up again."

Dave stepped a little outside the door, the urge to cuddle the infant, to quiet his crying surprisingly strong. He watched as Charlie felt the little one's tummy gently, her concentration focused solely on the baby. "It might be quieter out here," he suggested.

He felt strange now that his arms were empty. He'd gotten used to holding the baby so quickly.

"You said your name's Dave?"

He turned away from the sight. "That's right. David Ricker. I'm renting a cottage in the area and work on the docks. Charlie and I were at the tree lighting tonight."

"Together?"

There was an edge to Todd Smith's voice that Dave recognized. That was another thing he was learning about small towns. People looked out for each other. He was actually really glad that someone had Charlie's back. He got the feeling she felt she was mostly on her own.

"Not together together, if that's what you're getting at." Though they would have been if Dave had any say about it.

"Go on."

"We were walking to the pub—we were going to meet some people there for a bite to eat. I thought I saw someone hanging around the manger, and then they went running off."

Smith's gaze sharpened as he looked up from his notepad. "You saw who left him?"

"Not exactly. I mean I did, but I just saw a person. I couldn't tell you what they looked like. Young, maybe? Slight. Probably a woman. A girl." He let out a breath.

"So you checked it out."

"I did. When I looked in the manger, I couldn't believe it. Who the hell would leave a baby outside, in a nativity scene, on a December night?" His jaw tightened. "What if we hadn't been there? That baby might have frozen to death."

Smith nodded. "Lucky for him you did see. Why didn't you wait there? I would have looked the scene over."

"It was cold. Considering the baby, Charlie wanted to come here where it was warm, and make sure he was okay."

"That's all right. I'll call this in and go back over and see what I can find."

Charlie came back to the reception room, the baby dressed again in his sleepers and wrapped in the blanket. "He's a bit on the small side, but otherwise he looks well enough," she decreed with a smile. The baby was burrowed into her neck, sucking on his fingers. "But he's going to be hungry really soon."

It looked disturbingly right, the way she was holding the child.

"I have to contact child services," Smith said quietly. "He'll have to go into foster care until this is sorted out."

"Of course," Charlie answered, while Dave's gut churned. This poor little thing. Abandoned and then pawned off into foster care. It didn't seem right.

Charlie's hand was on the baby's head now, stroking the fine, blond hair.

"Listen," she said to Smith, "why don't we leave him under my medical care until morning? That's soon enough, don't you think? We've got a stock of diapers and emergency formula here. I can care for him until then, make sure there aren't any other medical issues that weren't immediately apparent. You'll have a better idea of the situation by then, too."

"You're up to it? Because this baby's pretty little. There'll be no sleeping through the night or anything."

Charlie smiled softly. "I'll be fine. I did my neonatal and pediatric rotations and everything." She bounced the baby a little bit. "We'll be fine, won't we buddy?"

Dave jumped in, even though he questioned whether or not he should. "I can help, too."

Smith raised an eyebrow. "What sort of experience do you have with babies?" he asked, laughing a little. "Because believe me, it's harder than it looks. My sister has two. I volunteered to babysit for a weekend once." He shuddered, and Charlie laughed.

Dave paused, annoyed at how easily Charlie seemed charmed by the young officer, annoyed at how he was made to feel left out of their little club. "I have a daughter," he said quietly, his gaze shifting to Charlie, watching has her smile slipped from her lips and her eyes registered confusion.

He probably should have mentioned that before inviting her back to his place.

But it wasn't exactly ice-breaker sort of conversation. It was the kind of thing he'd rather ease into.

"A daughter?" she whispered, and he felt like an absolute heel for springing it on her and for letting himself be baited by his own stupid male pride.

"Yes," he replied. "She lives with her mother in Kennebunkport."

"Oh."

He hated the disappointment he saw in Charlie's face. But now wasn't the time to explain. Instead, he turned his attention to the police officer. "I'll help Charlie get settled, give a statement at the station, whatever you need."

"I appreciate your help, Mr. Ricker." He wrote a phone number on a slip of paper and handed it over to Charlie. "This is my cell number. You call if you need anything or think of something you might have missed." Smith gave her a stern look. "You should program that into your phone, too, so you can avoid calling dispatch."

"I don't think that's necess..."

"You do it. You're part of this town and around here we look out for each other. You'll be getting a call from us too, I expect. I'm sure there will be more questions."

He was gone in a gust of cold air, leaving them alone in the clinic again, the silence loud between them.

Charlie hadn't thought she'd ever be glad to hear a baby cry, but the moment the infant sent up an impatient squall, she finally let out her breath.

She could focus on the baby and not on Dave. Dave with his soulful eyes, helpful nature…and his kid.

He had a child. It seemed to her that was pretty important information.

"I need to fix some formula," she murmured. "Here. You hold him. It'll be faster that way." Without sparing him another glance, Charlie turned away and headed down the hall to a cupboard, where she removed a can of baby formula. Then she marched to the kitchen in the back, putting a kettle on to boil and then taking a bottle and nipple out of the cabinet. She wasn't sure how she felt about this new tidbit of knowledge. Wasn't sure she even had the right to be out of sorts about it.

Dave had followed her down the hall and now stood in the doorway. The baby wasn't soothed at all, even as he jostled his arms up and down a bit. The cries only increased in pitch.

"Do you have everything you need?" he asked, over top of the racket. "He's a hungry little guy."

Charlie nodded, pouring the formula into a bottle and screwing on the top, then immersing the bottle in a cup of hot water to warm the formula. They stood in the small kitchen, the shrill cries rubbing on the edge of Charlie's nerves.

She looked up at Dave. "So. You have a daughter."

He nodded, staring her straight in the eyes. "Yes. And an ex to go with her, of course. You might as well get a complete picture."

He was edgy. Well, too bad. "It might have been nice information to have."

He switched the baby to his other shoulder. "I met you yesterday. Asked you out tonight. I wasn't really sure of the 'when to bring up the ex-and-kid-protocol'."

"I'm not sure either. It just feels weird."

"Why? Because you said yes?"

He started patting the baby on the back as the tension in the small kitchen ratcheted up some more. "So you and Officer Todd. Is there some history there?"

She frowned at the abrupt change in subject. "What?"

"You know. You guys seemed pretty friendly. He was awfully protective of you."

She burst out laughing then, turned back to the sink and took the bottle out of the water. "You think Todd and I have a thing?" It was ludicrous. Todd was a good five years younger than she was, and she was pretty sure he had a girlfriend. "First of all, I wouldn't have flirted with you if I were with Todd. And in case you didn't notice, he was nothing but professional earlier."

His voice was quieter now. "You're right. I guess I just got a little jealous."

Jealous? The idea sent a swirl of something delicious through her tummy. She turned back around and rested her hips on the edge of the counter, determined to keep her composure. The baby's cries had subsided to whimpers now. "Believe me, there's nothing romantic between Todd and me."

"Just so you know, I wouldn't make a move on someone else's girl," he stated, and it made her want to smile. He sounded about sixteen years old. But she supposed it was a good thing. Honor and all that.

"Poor thing," she murmured, taking the baby from his arms so she could offer the bottle. "Can we put a pin in this and talk about it later? Right now I just want to focus on one thing at a time." She laughed a little as the baby began drinking lustily. "And getting this guy fed and comfortable is top priority, don't you agree?"

Dave nodded, and let the matter drop. "I just can't believe it," he said quietly. "Who would leave a baby out in the elements like that? It's barbaric."

Charlie regarded him sadly. "Things like this happen more than you'd think. People can't cope. They get to the end of their ropes, and they do uncharacteristic and terrible things. As a doctor, I can't let myself judge."

"You've seen something like this before?"

Her heart constricted. She tried not to dwell on past cases. Still, there were always a few that she couldn't forget. Ones that haunted her long after they were over.

"Once," she said quietly, "when I was working backshift in New York, the ambulance brought in a preemie. She'd been left in a garbage can. The mother just...didn't know what else to do and she panicked. The baby only lived a few hours after coming in."

One of the hardest things she'd ever done as a doctor was call that time of death.

But then she shook off the heavy feeling of failure. "There are reasons why I chose to be a family doctor in a small town." She didn't want to get into all the reasons why, or how she'd found herself struggling to deal with the traumatic cases she saw on a day-to-day basis. She'd chosen Jewell Cove because it seemed idyllic. Like an East Coast Mayberry, where bad things simply didn't happen. A place where she might find the life she wanted rather than the one that was expected.

Of course bad things did happen, no matter where a person lived. Tonight was a prime example, though at least this one had the potential for a happy ending.

"Anyway," she continued, smiling a little, "thanks to you, we got to this little boy in time. He looks to be full term and hungry as a horse. You saved him tonight, Dave." She smiled up at him. "Let's go to the reception area where it's more comfortable."

There was a beanbag chair in the kid's area, and Charlie held the baby against her shoulder while she lowered herself into it carefully. The form settled around her and she crossed her legs yoga-style. She took the opportunity to burp him and then reintroduced the bottle. The baby took it eagerly, little lips fastening about the tip with a ferocity that made her laugh. "Okay, okay," she soothed, adjusting the angle of her arm for better comfort.

Dave sat in a chair across from the play area and watched her. She couldn't tell what he was thinking, but from the way his mouth was set and the troubled look in his eyes, she guessed it wasn't good.

"You don't have to stay, you know," she said, letting out a breath. "Formula, diapers...I have all I need."

"You're going to stay here all night?"

"It wouldn't be the first time," she said easily. "Seriously, there are worse places to spend a night."

He smiled tightly. "I know. I've stayed in a few myself. But why don't you go home?"

She pulled the bottle away for a minute and wiped a dribble of milk off the baby's chin before letting him have some more. "It's just easier. My car's still down on the waterfront, and I don't have a car seat, either. It's really okay, Dave. It's warm in here, there's a fold out cot in the back and there's even some food in the fridge if I get hungry." She tried to stifle a yawn but failed. The truth was she was dead tired tonight, though she didn't really know why. Maybe it was all the fresh air. Or maybe it was the brief surge of adrenaline from finding the baby. Now that she'd slowed down, relaxation was setting in. Not to mention how warm the baby felt in her arms. He really could throw some decent body heat for an infant.

"You're sure? I could stay if you wanted. So you don't have to stay alone."

It was sweet of him to offer. Charlie was starting to think that despite surprises tonight, Dave was a really decent guy. But she was a big girl, and she didn't need to be rescued. Once more she removed the bottle from the baby's mouth, and then put him on her shoulder and began patting his back, trying to relieve any gas that had built up from his gulping most of his supper.

"I spend every night alone," she answered, blushing a little. "The only difference is I'm here and not at my house."

"I suppose," he answered, and she would swear he looked disappointed.

The sharp crack of a burp echoed through the office and they both laughed.

"There," she said softly, shifting the baby to the crook of her arm again. "That must feel better!"

This time when she put the nipple to his lips, he latched on and his eyes started to drift closed. Her heart shifted a little as one tiny little hand moved to rest along the side of the plastic bottle, willing it to stay in place. What a sweet little treasure he was.

"I guess I'll take off, then," Dave said, rather reluctantly, she thought.

"Thank you for all your help tonight. I mean it. This little guy is so lucky you came along."

To her surprise, Dave got up from his chair and knelt in front of her. "I think he's lucky you came along," he said softly. "You're a real natural with him, you know that?"

"A baby's needs are pretty simple." She brushed off the compliment, disturbed by how touched she was by it. They'd just met. But it was the perfect thing to say.

"Still." He reached out and brushed a little piece of hair away from her face. "I was deployed when my daughter was born. I only got to see her at this age a few times."

Charlie looked away and bit her lip. "Do you see her now?"

He smiled then, and it lit up his face. "Yeah. Janice and her new husband moved to Kennebunkport and opened a little inn. I came here so I could see my baby girl more often. I don't want to miss out on all those important moments, you know? Jewell Cove isn't permanent for me, but this job does let me be close while I figure out what happens next."

If he'd been attractive before, the knowledge that he was trying to be a good father definitely tipped the scales even more in his favor.

He stepped back. "Call me if you need anything, okay?"

"I will," she answered, but she knew she wouldn't. She didn't have his cell number and she didn't know the number for his rental cottage either. Which was okay. She'd be fine here tonight.

He reached the door, but before he opened it, he turned one last time. "Please lock this behind me," he ordered.

"Yes, boss."

He smiled at her once more before slipping out into the cold night, leaving her alone with the baby and the silence. And perhaps what surprised her the most was how, after he was gone, she really wished he'd stayed after all.

Chapter 4

The sky was overcast when Dave crawled out from beneath the covers. He hadn't slept much, though that wasn't entirely surprising after his exciting evening. He might as well get up and get on with his day than lie in bed.

The shower was hot and he dressed quickly in the cold air of the cottage, pulling on jeans and a thick sweater. God, he'd forgotten how raw and unforgiving an east coast winter could be. There wasn't any work today to keep him busy, so he bundled up, scraped the windshield of his SUV, and headed into town.

The only thing open this early on Sunday morning was the café, so Dave stopped and bought two large coffees and a selection of pastries before heading up a street to the clinic. Maybe Charlie wasn't even there anymore, but he felt uncomfortable with how they'd left things last night. He hadn't exactly kept his interest in her a secret. Looking at it now, in hindsight, he could understand why she'd backpedaled when she found out about his kid.

Lights were on inside when he arrived, so he cradled the tray holding the food in one hand and tapped lightly on the door with the other. Moments later Charlie came out of an exam room, the baby on her shoulder and a bottle in her hand. Her usually neat-as-a-pin hair was disheveled and sticking out of a frayed braid, and she had bags under her eyes. Clearly it hadn't been a good night for her, either.

She shifted the bottle, turned the deadbolt, and stood back so he could open the door.

The office was warm, and he hurried in and shut the door behind him before he let in too much icy air. "Good morning," he said softly, peering over her shoulder at the baby. His tiny eyes were closed and his fingers pinched the soft fabric of her sweater. "Rough night?"

"He's asleep now, isn't he?" At his nod, she sighed. "Little bugger. Kept me up most of the night and now he's out. Typical."

Dave let out a soft laugh. "Can't blame a man for wanting your attention all night," he joked, delighted when her cheeks colored a bit. "Here. I brought coffee. And very bad for you white flour and sugary things."

"I take back all the bad things I thought about you last night," she said solemnly, reaching for the bag. "Let's go to the kitchen. I'm not sure if I dare put this guy down or not."

Once in the kitchen, Dave put down the tray and stripped off his jacket. Charlie looked up at him with naked yearning in her eyes. "Can you take him while I have something to eat? I feel like I'm going to keel over, and he can stay nice and cozy. And quiet."

She slid the baby into his arms without waiting for an answer and immediately moved to the counter, grabbing one of the coffees and opening the paper bag, peering down inside before selecting a rather large apple Danish. Her first bite was huge, and glaze clung to the corners of her mouth.

Dave had a lot of thoughts about kissing that glaze from her lips. And if he hadn't been holding a baby in his arms, he might have. But if—when—he kissed Charlie, he wanted to have his hands free so he could put his arms around her and hold her close.

He looked away, taking a deep breath. She wasn't the kind of woman a man played with. He should probably just let well enough alone. Still, thinking about her was better than thinking about the baby in his arms and how the weight felt foreign and familiar at the same time. At least the little guy wasn't crying. Dave figured he'd be okay as long as the baby slept on.

"Let's go into my office," she suggested. "I have my desk chair and there's a decent armchair there, too. I'll bring the stuff and you can have some coffee. It doesn't look like you got much sleep, either."

He frowned, following her down the hall. "It doesn't?"

She shook her head, and he watched the ratty braid move back and forth. "It's in the wrinkles around your eyes. And you showered this morning, but you didn't bother to shave."

He hadn't. He knew a day's growth of stubble was on his cheeks. More than that, she'd noticed. Despite how exhausted she was, she'd noticed all that about him in the space of a few seconds. It was flattering as hell.

Her office was extraordinarily tidy, just as he would have expected, and she pulled the padded chair closer so they could use her desk as a table. He eased himself into the upholstery, careful not to wake the baby, and reached for the thick paper cup.

Charlie sat in her chair, took another healthy bite of Danish, and watched him with keen eyes.

"What?" he asked, after several seconds had ticked by.

"I'm trying to puzzle you out."

"Never a good idea. I'm a complicated man." He grinned at her, trying to dispel her solemn gaze, but it was no good. She was focused now.

"You're good with babies."

"Why is it so important to you?"

She paused then, furrowing her brow a bit. "You mean, your personal life is none of my business."

"I wouldn't put it that bluntly..."

"But that's what you mean."

Awkward silence settled over the room. Finally, he spoke again. "No, I don't mean that at all. It's not an easy thing to talk about. I get that you're curious given that we...that I... started something."

"That's part of it," she agreed.

He wasn't immune to the lovely feeling of warm baby curled up against his sweater. "You're a tough woman, Charlene Yang."

"Thank you." She smiled and took a satisfied sip of her coffee.

"You want the truth? All right. Here it is. Anyone I go on a date with wants to know who Dave Ricker is. Coming right out and admitting I have an ex and a daughter...that can be intimidating. I'm not just a guy. I'm a dad."

"And women are turned off by that?"

He was saved from answering by another tap at the front door.

Charlie looked slightly revived as she said, "That'll be the social worker. Hang tight."

She was back moments later with a middle-aged woman who identified herself as Marissa Longfellow. She looked kindly, like a schoolteacher, and smiled at the sight of Dave holding the baby in his arms.

"He certainly looks contented," she noted.

"He likes Dave," Charlie replied. "He fell asleep right away last night when Dave held him inside his jacket. Then Dave went home, and it seemed like he cried for hours."

Marissa laughed. "Sounds about right. All of mine went through a stage at this age. For three or four weeks they'd be up in the middle of the night and just wouldn't settle. And then poof. One day they got their days and nights the right way around and I'd start getting good sleep. Or at least a good chunk of sleep at a time. Well, let's see to the official paperwork, shall we? I have those papers for you I mentioned, Dr. Yang and then we'll be good to go."

"Dave, are you okay here for a few minutes? He's so contented at the moment."

"No problem. I'll just drink my coffee and we'll have some male bonding time." He smiled up at her.

They left the office, took a sip of coffee, then put the cup back on the desk.

The baby in his arms took a deep breath and let out a sigh. Dave adjusted his hold so the little guy was cradled just right, then slid down in the chair a little so that his head rested against the padded back and his legs stretched out comfortably. He closed his eyes. He'd missed these first moments with his daughter, and he could never get them back. But he didn't regret the choices he'd made since. It had meant giving up being a SEAL, but it also meant being part of his daughter's life as she grew up, and that was more important.

***

Charlie came back for the baby and stopped in the doorway to her office, her heart catching at the sight before her.

The baby was lying on Dave's wide chest, still sound asleep, while Dave's rough hands held him snug and safe. A soft snore broke the silence. Dave had fallen asleep too, and it was as sweet a picture as she'd ever seen.

"Dave," she said softly, stepping into the room. He never moved, not a muscle, and she smiled to herself. He was really out. "Dave," she repeated, louder this time, and he snuffled before opening his eyes slowly.

"I fell asleep."

"You did."

"He's quite the little furnace, isn't he?"

She shrugged. "He didn't exactly settle that well for me."

And there it was. The slow, sexy, slightly smug smile.

"Is it time?"

She nodded, wondering if she was crazy to be taking on this new responsibility. She'd been up all night, been at her wit's end trying to soothe the child, been peed on when she didn't get the diaper on fast enough, and was tired and still hungry. And yet the thought of the tiny bundle going somewhere else felt so wrong. Most of the time she was able to put her desire for a family of her own on the backburner.

Whether it was her ticking clock or what, that talent was getting more and more difficult lately. To her surprise, she'd found herself offering to care for the infant while the police investigated the case.

"Yeah, it's time to get this little man settled." Charlie moved closer.

"If the parents are local, it shouldn't be too hard to find out if he has family. How many baby boys could have been born in the last few weeks, anyway?" Dave asked on a yawn, shifting the baby as he sat up.

Of course, if the family wasn't local, that was a whole other thing. Still, it was a good starting place.

"Here, let me take him." She slid her hands under the warm little body and lifted. His eyes opened as she moved him into her arms, staring at her without really seeing, not crying, but just taking a few moments to wake up from his comfortable nap.

Marissa was waiting with a car seat and warm blanket and strapped him in securely with competent hands. Charlie went forward and put the little cap back on his head. "He needs to keep warm," she murmured. "It's cold out today."

"Are you sure you have everything you need?" Marissa smiled at her. "It's a big thing you're doing."

"I'll go right from here to the drugstore."

"If there's any problem, anything at all, you'll call, won't you? There's lots of support available. And I'm here day or night."

Dave stepped forward. "What? I thought you were taking the baby with you?"

Marissa slid a file into her case. "Dr. Yang is going to watch our little one for a few days. Just temporarily, of course." She smiled. "She's done such great work with our foster care support group. I have complete confidence in her."

Charlie looked over at him, wishing she had the same confidence in herself but determined to do the right thing.

"His weight's a little low, and monitoring his health makes sense right now. Hopefully it's just a case of nutrition and we can get him back on track."

"And we have fewer foster families available every day," Marissa added.

"Ideally, we'll find a family member quickly who can be awarded temporary custody, and if not, then once his weight is up, this little guy will be settled with a good family. Well, I'll be on my way, and let you get home and settled. I'll talk to you soon, Charlie."

She was gone in a gust of wind and left the two of them standing there. Charlie took a deep breath. There was no turning back now. For better or worse, she was temporarily in charge of an infant boy.

Dave came closer and put his hands on her upper arms. She looked up, surprised to find his eyes filled with understanding.

"Feeling overwhelmed?" he asked simply.

"A little," she admitted. "I'm probably just tired. And even though he was fussy, he really is a sweetie. I'm sure we'll be fine."

Dave grinned and squeezed her arms. "Well, he's your little Baby Jesus after all. Kind of difficult to harden your heart to that."

She laughed a little. Come to think of it, she'd had more of those silly little chuckles in the last few days than she'd had in a very long time. "I couldn't bear the thought of him going to strangers this morning. How silly is that? But oh my. I've kind of leaped in with both feet."

"If it makes you feel any better, every parent in the world leaps in with both feet. One minute you're alone, the next you're a parent. It's a big shock."

"Is that how it was with you?"

He chuckled. "Definitely. I'd never changed a diaper or given a bottle or any of those things. At least you know what you're doing. You've got a head start."

His pep talk made her feel better. "Thanks. So why did you come back this morning anyway?" she asked, pulling away. She picked up the carrier and together they headed back to her office where the cold coffee and sweets waited. "I figured you'd be sleeping in after your exciting evening."

"Couldn't sleep, and I worried about you. This isn't the coziest place to spend the night."

"Clearly you've never tried to sleep in an inner-city emergency room," she called out, as she poured the now-cold coffee down the sink.

He came up behind her, balling up a sticky napkin. "No, but I've slept in some nasty places just the same. Like in the desert where you sweat your balls off during the day and then freeze at night and you and your buddies huddle together because you're out of fuel."

She burst out laughing.

"Good times," he confirmed, with a twitch of his lips. "Very...cozy. And you know what? I think that's the first time I've really heard you laugh."

She found that hard to believe. He made her smile a lot. But perhaps she hadn't laughed. It felt good.

"Look," he suggested, "your cottage is on the way to mine. You're dog-tired. Why don't I take you both home and you can pick up your car later?"

Her stomach took that swirly dip again. "That's not necessary. A drop off at the waterfront would be fine."

"We had some snow last night and the roads are a little slick. Maybe I didn't sleep well but I bet I got more than you, plus I just had a nice little cat nap. We can stop by the drugstore for whatever you need first."

It was tempting. She was exhausted. Gosh, how did new parents do it night after night? She was about to find out, wasn't she?

He reached for his coat. "Come on. You know you're dying for a hot shower and a pair of sweats and some sleep."

Oh God, that sounded heavenly.

"All right."

"Get your coat. I'll warm up the truck."

Several minutes later they were loaded down with diapers and formula and back on the road towards Fiddler's Rock. Charlie had her purse and the bag of pastries on her lap as Dave negotiated the winding turns, and hard flakes of snow bit through the air as they left town behind for the relative peace of the seaside road. The baby slept on, comfortable in the car seat, lulled by the motion of the car.

"Which place is yours?" he asked, as they passed the Blackberry Hill intersection.

"About a mile past the curve, on the left."

As they got closer, the flakes started coming down heavier. She motioned for him to turn as they approached the driveway to her place. Even in the gloomy weather, she loved it. The gray shingle siding and white trim were old-fashioned and cozy, and she'd put a big evergreen wreath on her door, complete with a gigantic red bow.

"Nice spot," he remarked, putting the truck in park.

"Isn't it?" She looked over at him and smiled. "The trees make it so cozy, but then you go on the back deck and the bay is spread out for miles. It's even nicer in the summer. I'm not much of a gardener, but I'm trying to expand a few perennial beds."

He'd left the truck running and she asked a little hesitantly, "Do you want to come in?"

His gaze met hers evenly. "Is that what you want? Or are you just being polite?"

"You're very direct, you know."

"Is that a problem?"

"Not really. Takes some getting used to, I think." She bit down on her lip. "I can't eat all these pastries alone. Come in. We'll get this little guy settled and I'll make a decent cup of coffee. It's the least I can do after all your help."

She wasn't as direct as Dave. Her words made it sound like a thank you when it was really an "I'd like to spend more time with you" thing.

He shut off the ignition and pocketed the keys. "I suppose I could do that. You take this stuff in, and I'll bring the baby."

Once inside Charlie immediately went to the thermostat and turned up the heat. "Gosh, it's cold in here." She slid off her boots and hung up her coat. "Make yourself at home. I'm going to start on the coffee."

He came in behind her and shut the door, put down the carrier, took off his boots and placed them precisely beside hers before hanging his jacket on the coat rack. "Are you sure you don't want a hot shower first?"

She wondered if she still smelled of baby spit up. Plus the idea of a shower and comfy, fuzzy clothes was incredibly tempting. "I wouldn't be much of a hostess if I did that." Dave picked up the car seat once more and they walked through to the kitchen.

But Dave stopped at the living room. "Hey, you've got a fireplace. Seriously, go shower. I'll watch the baby and start a fire. When you come out it'll be warmer in here."

Apparently he was taking her *make yourself at home* comments seriously. She put the bakery bag on the butcher block. "It does sound good..."

"Go. We'll be here when you get back."

"I won't be long."

She left them there and headed to the bedroom, gathered a pair of yoga pants and a bulky Harvard hoodie and scooted into the bathroom. The shower felt glorious and she nearly didn't want to get out, except she knew he was waiting. Her heartbeat quickened as she thought of it. She'd invited him in for pastry and coffee, but she was in a steaming shower and he was building a fire and there was clearly an attraction at work here. Was something more going to happen? Did she want it to?

The hot water ran in rivulets over her breasts. God, she did. It had been a very long time since she'd felt like this.

The bigger question was, would she let something happen? Because they barely knew each other. Attraction, desire... were all well and good. But it felt weird, knowing that the mystery man she'd been fantasizing about was flesh and blood, in her house, and unless her radar was way off, interested in her.

Despite the fact that she looked like death warmed over this morning.

"Oh, stop analyzing and get out of the shower already," she muttered to herself, shutting off the spray. There was no rush for anything. They could totally take it one step at a time. Get to know each other better. She did have some self-control, after all.

The air in the bathroom was still cold and she hurried to dry herself and get into her clothes. It would take too long to blow-dry her hair, so she simply squeezed out the water with a towel, brushed it, and held it back off her face with a thin black headband.

She smoothed on some moisturizer, swiped a bit of lip balm over her lips and decided that was enough—she didn't want to appear too obvious. She pressed a hand to her stomach, took a deep breath, and opened the bathroom door.

The cottage was already warming up, thanks to the furnace and the fire she could hear crackling behind the grate. Entering the living room, she saw Dave squatting before the fireplace, adding some small sticks to the dancing flames. She hadn't actually had a man back to her place since moving to Jewell Cove. Her little living room was changed just by having him in it. It felt smaller. More alive. Over by the sofa, the baby slept on, his head at a slight angle, one of Charlie's throw blankets draped over him.

"You're very good at building a fire," she said quietly from the doorway.

He looked over his shoulder. "I could claim it was my military training, but the truth is, I was in the outdoors a lot as a kid. My dad's a fisherman on the Chesapeake."

She went to his side and squatted too, holding her hands out to the warmth of the fire. "Is that where you learned to fix boats?"

He nodded. "Yep."

"But you didn't go back there when you left the navy?"

"I did for a while." He threw two thicker logs on the fire and closed the screen.

Talk about basic answers. Charlie frowned. "And then you moved here to be closer to your daughter?"

He rested his forearms on his knees. "Yes. I did my time, but it's so hard to be a SEAL and a dad at the same time. George Adams is actually an old friend of my dad's. He offered me a job, and that lets me support myself and be close to her."

Charlie was curious about how his ex fit into all of this, but didn't want to ask. Instead she focused on his daughter, who he clearly doted on. "What's her name?"

"Nora. Nora Emily Christensen."

Christensen. Not Ricker. Bit by bit Charlie was beginning to realize that the situation between Dave and his ex was complicated.

"That's a beautiful name," Charlie replied, standing up. "Now, the fire's going, I'm warmed up, and I promised you good coffee."

She left him in front of the fire and went to the kitchen to put on the kettle. While it was heating, she got out coffee beans, her grinder, French press, and frother. She put the remaining pastries on a pretty plate and ground the beans, and then when the water boiled, she heated the press and mugs and put the milk in the microwave to heat.

It was a slightly more finicky process than using a regular coffeemaker, but it was worth it, in Charlie's opinion. Within a few minutes she had freshly pressed coffee with a rich swirl of frothed milk added. She put both cups and the pastries on a small tray and carried it all into the living room.

Dave was still sitting on the floor in front of the fire, staring at the flames.

"Hey," she said, putting the tray down on a small coffee table. "You don't have to sit on the floor, you know."

He looked over at her and smiled, some of the tension gone from his face. "Just watching the fire. You've got a nice place here, Charlie. It suits you."

She liked the light colors—white, with bits of creamy beige and blue and greens. It reminded her of the ocean and sand, very soothing and relaxing. "Thanks. It's the first place I've ever decorated myself, for myself." She'd liked the cottage so much that after her first six months of renting, she'd bought it from the owner.

He laughed. "I'm not much of a decorator. Then again, I didn't need to be. The Navy had it covered. And now I'm renting, which suits me fine."

"Have some coffee while it's hot," she suggested. She nearly sat on the sofa but decided the rug in front of the fire was fine for her too. She sat, cross-legged, handed Dave his mug and grabbed her own, then put the plate of pastries between them.

"This is good," he complimented, taking a sip. "Damn. Really good."

"Fresh beans and a press. Makes all the difference," she replied, taking a sip. She reached for a *pain au chocolat* and a paper napkin. The flaky pastry sent wisps of crumbs flying at her first bite, but she didn't care. Butter and chocolate together was heavenly.

Dave snagged a sugared doughnut from the assortment and bit into it. For a few minutes they munched happily, in comfortable silence. What was amazing was that they didn't feel the need to make small talk or break the stillness.

Her coffee was half-gone when Dave finally re-started the conversation. "So," he said, wiping his sugary fingers on a napkin, "you know a bit about me. How about you? Where did you grow up? Why did you become a doctor?"

The buttery croissant went papery in her mouth. She didn't like talking about herself much. "Oh, my story's pretty boring."

"I doubt that. Especially since you're avoiding the topic." He leaned back on his hands. It made his shoulders look incredibly muscled, she noticed.

"Okay, so here's the short version. I grew up in Boston. My mother teaches at the Berklee School of Music and my father works in clinical research for a pharmaceutical. My dad is the grandson of a Chinese immigrant, and my mom's family probably came over on the Mayflower." She rolled her eyes at him and continued. "They have very busy careers and very high expectations of their one and only child."

"So you became a doctor."

"Sure. After several years of violin and piano lessons, courtesy of my mother, and a lot of pressure to major in BioChem." She let out a breath. "There were good points to that too, though. They were so busy with their own careers and social lives that I stayed under the radar quite often. And I did want to become a doctor."

Eventually, anyway. Lucky for her. She couldn't imagine what might have happened if she'd hated medicine.

He looked at her steadily. "It sounds lonely."

Her heart gave a little thump. "It was, actually. And I know they're disappointed that I'm a family doctor in a small town and not doing important research like my dad or being a top trauma doctor like my best friend, Lizzie. But I'm happy with my choices. I like my job and I like it here."

And maybe she was still lonely at times. But she'd work on it. After all, she'd taken the step of volunteering for the church Christmas decorating, and look what had come from that? Sunday morning coffee and sweets in front of a fire with a gorgeous man. Progress.

She smiled to herself.

"What's so funny?"

"If I told you, you'd get a big fat head, so never mind." She pushed away the plate, her sweet tooth finally satisfied. "You make me laugh, Dave, and that's kind of nice."

He put down his coffee cup, then took hers and put it down too, on the brick hearth in front of the fireplace. Her pulse hammered frantically, beating at the base of her wrists. It was the kind of move she expected a person made before they made a bigger move. When he turned back to her, she swallowed thickly, nervous and excited all at once.

He put his hands on the sides of her thighs and pulled her forward, so she was sitting beside him but facing him, close enough that she could see gold and chocolate flecks in his dark eyes. Her breath shortened, her chest cramped as he lifted his hand and cupped her jaw. His thumb grazed the corner of her mouth and her breath stopped altogether. He removed his hand and put his thumb to his lips, tasting the buttery crumb he'd taken from her mouth.

Oh my.

Charlie was certain her eyes widened as he leaned closer, taking his time, making sure. Half of her was a jittery mess of nerves and the other half wished he'd hurry the hell up already, but she made herself be patient. To wait, to let him take the lead. If things hadn't gone hinky last night, this was where they might have ended up, after all.

He closed the final distance between them, and her eyelids drifted closed as his mouth touched hers for the first time.

His lips were soft, warm, and tasted like coffee and nutmeg and something that was just him. He nudged subtly, prompting her to deepen the kiss, and she did, somewhat shyly but enjoying the slow sweetness of it. One of his hands reached around to cup the back of her head, controlling the contact in a way she wholly approved of.

She liked how he took charge of the kiss without forcing anything. Hesitantly she reached out and placed her palm on his chest in silent approval.

"Mmm," he murmured against her lips, the vibration of the sound sending ripples of desire through her. "You're good at that, Charlie."

"So are you," she replied, a little bit breathless.

"Should we try it again?" he asked.

There was no way she could say no. The combination of suggestion and teasing was impossible to resist.

This time she leaned forward and slid into the kiss, hungering for more. She put her hands on his shoulders and shifted until she was sitting across his lap, her fingers sliding through his hair as the contact deepened and quickened with urgency.

Chapter 5

G od, she was sweet, soft, and pliant beneath his hands. Dave forced himself to go slowly, even though his blood was raging and his desire for her was burning hot. There was something about Charlie that was fragile.

Something that made him want to take his time. For the first time in years, he worried about being careful with a woman.

She was so beautiful today, so approachable in her soft yoga pants and fleecy hoodie. Testing, he slid his hand beneath the waistband of the sweatshirt and touched the silky skin of her belly, gliding upwards until he encountered the satin fabric of her bra. He cupped her small breast in his hand, the point of it pressing against his palm and he reminded himself to not hurry. Even if he did want to. Desperately.

Instead he focused on kissing her, thoroughly, until his mind was clouded with only her.

"We probably shouldn't do this," she murmured.

"I know," he answered, closing his eyes and letting the sensations fill him completely. He kissed her again. She tasted so good. Like rich butter and smooth chocolate and woman.

Panting, she broke the kiss and leaned away a little. "I need to stop."

He did as she asked, even though it damn near killed him. He pulled the hoodie back down and rested his forehead on her shoulder, working on regaining his senses.

Her breath came hard and fast. That and the crackling of the fire were the only sounds in the room for several seconds.

"Wow," she finally breathed. He took it as a good sign she didn't pull away from him. Their legs were still entangled on the rug, though their hands and clothing were all in the right places.

"Wow is right. That's some good coffee, missus."

She giggled, and he loved it. It had been too long since he'd made a woman laugh, and the sound warmed him from the inside out.

"I don't know if it was the caffeine, the sugar rush, or just you," she said softly. Her hand stroked at his hair and he kept his eyes closed, loving the feel of it. "But that was... unexpected."

"Not for me," he admitted. "I've wanted to do that since you nearly threw that doll at me the other day."

She did slide away then, sitting all the way up. He rested his elbows on his knees and grinned up at her surprised face.

"You did?" she asked.

"Do you honestly think I would have gone to that caroling nonsense otherwise?"

The look on her face was priceless. She looked so...pleased with herself. Dave had the sneaking suspicion she had no idea how attractive she was right this moment.

Even in an oversized hoodie with her lip gloss thoroughly kissed off. Especially then.

"You are very good for my self-esteem," she admitted.

"And you're good for my self-control," he replied, and then chuckled. "Don't mind me if I don't thank you for it."

She tugged at the hem of her hoodie. "I, uh... help me out here. Is there a way to transition from this gracefully?"

And then he laughed. He couldn't help it. Neither one of them was particularly smooth, were they? And he liked that about her. A lot. She seemed incapable of playing games. That was damned refreshing.

"I'm no good at this either," he admitted. "It's probably really bad form to talk about exes at this particular moment, but it's been a while since I had to navigate..." He paused, scrambling for the right word. "Dating," he finished, not sure if that was the right choice or not, but relationships seemed premature.

"You guys were together a long time?"

"Not too long. We were friends." He felt his cheeks heat. "Friends with, uh...well, anyway, Nora was a surprise. I haven't dated much since then. I was away, then figuring out what was next, and being Dad..." He raised an eyebrow. "You?"

She laughed. "Are you kidding? I had med school and then crazy, crazy hours. Hard on relationships."

"And there's been no one here in Jewell Cove? I find that hard to believe."

She shrugged. "It's a small town. There's not always a huge selection on the dating market. And then there's the fact that everyone is a potential patient. Awkward..." She looked at him earnestly. "I spent most of my childhood studying or practicing. I had friends, sure, but social skills didn't come naturally to me. I swear, if it wasn't for my college roommate, I'd be a hermit."

"You're no hermit," he confirmed, and he slid over closer to her. "Hermits are old and wrinkly and hairy."

"I think you're confusing them with trolls."

He laughed, then kissed her quickly. "Maybe."

"So if I make a confession, you won't laugh at me?"

"Cross my heart." He made the motion across his chest and she smiled sweetly.

"I'm not good at the fling thing. I'm more of a slow mover. Just so you know..."

"Hey," he offered gently, realizing that the more he got to know her, the more he liked her. "We only just met. There's no hurry. Besides, last night was the most unusual first date I've ever had. There's something different about you, Charlie."

"Um, is that a good thing or a bad thing?"

It took all his willpower not to kiss her again. "I like being with you," he said. "And I'd like to see you again. Let's start there."

"Like living in the moment? Keeping it simple?"

"Yeah. Like that." He halted, considered before he spoke again. "I'm not really the jump in headfirst kind of guy when it comes to relationships, either."

She looked up and her lips curved the slightest bit. "I wouldn't be opposed to getting to know you a little better, too."

The attraction hummed between them again and Dave considered whether or not he wanted to start over...or pick up where they'd left off. He looked over his shoulder, saw the baby still sleeping, and debated. He decided to wait. Charlie needed to nap when she could, and he shouldn't get in the way of that. "I should probably go," he decided. "You really do need some sleep. I'll call you?"

"I'd like that."

She walked him to the door and waited while he shoved on his boots and put on his jacket. "Drive safe," she advised, and he nodded.

"I'm only a couple more miles up the road. But I will. Don't worry."

"And thanks for the drive home."

"You're welcome."

There was an awkward pause where he had his hand on the doorknob, not quite out the door, but almost. He wanted to kiss her. Finally he leaned in a bit and dropped a small kiss on her lips. Not too much. Just enough to let her know that he was interested.

"I'll call you," he repeated, and went out the door into the snow and ice.

***

Charlie was already at work the next morning when her cell phone vibrated with a new text. Her heart gave a little thump when she saw the short message.

It's Dave. Do you need a lift to pick up your car? I can pick you up on my way to work.

She'd deliberately set the alarm for a half hour earlier than normal and called one of the two taxis that Jewell Cove offered. With the added time required to get the baby ready, the last thing she wanted was to be late to work. She knew everything would take her longer and she was still trying to figure out how she was going to manage appointments. By seven-fifteen she'd been on her way to the waterfront where she'd warmed up her car and scraped the ice and snow from the windows, and by seven-thirty she was in her office tackling her e-mail as best she could.

She'd had a lot of time to think since yesterday morning, and had decided to take a step back from whatever had been developing between her and Dave. Looking back at the last few days, she realized she'd been dealing with two different situations, neither of which was conducive to clear thinking. First, there'd been the whole fantasy-in-the-flesh thing when he'd shown up at the church and then at the tree lighting. She'd been, as Thumper said in Bambi, "twitterpated."

And then there was the whole baby in the manger thing. It had been an extreme situation, and at the end of it she'd been exhausted.

She put down her coffee and quickly tapped a reply.

I'm already here. But thanks for the offer. I appreciate it.

There was a long pause before he answered again.

Okay. Talk soon.

That was it. Short and sweet. No suggestion on when they might get together next. She was relieved. Wasn't she? She should be. She'd given herself a firm talking to after she'd gotten some sleep. Put things in perspective. Did she even have time for dating right now? She looked down at the carrier which doubled as a seat. The baby was awake and staring up at her with big blue eyes. She'd been up twice throughout the night to feed him. Babies took up a lot of time.

The truth was, she was nearly thirty. She figured that any man she got involved with pretty much had to be keeper potential. It was simply the way she was wired. She'd never wasted time on things that were going nowhere. Sometimes she wondered what that would be like. Pointless? Or liberating? Either way, she had her laundry list of attributes for her future partner. Top of it were marriage and father material. Dave certainly seemed devoted to his daughter, but how long would he stay in Jewell Cove?

She enlisted Robin's help in caring for the baby, putting his seat in the office area, taking turns changing him or carrying him around when he was fussy. Mid-morning, two cups of coffee and four patients later, Robin came back and let her know that Todd Smith was in the waiting room and wanted to talk to her. Figuring it could only be about the baby, she checked her watch and nodded. "Bring him back here, Robin. If it's about the investigation, we won't want to talk where everyone can hear."

"Sure thing, Charlie." Robin smiled and scooted out, returning only seconds later with Officer Smith trailing behind her.

Next to the petite receptionist, Todd Smith looked big and imposing, especially in his uniform. He'd removed his hat and had it tucked under his arm, and she realized some of his bulk came from the impressive array of gear on his belt as well as the probability of a flak jacket beneath his clothing.

"Morning, Doctor Yang," he greeted.

She smiled. "You can call me Charlie," she offered. "Unless you prefer the title for official business."

He smiled back. "Too bad I am on official business." Before she could dissect that particular comment, he motioned towards a chair. "May I?"

"Oh, of course. Do you want a coffee or anything?"

There was a tap on the door frame and Robin came in, carrying a steaming mug.

"Here you go, Todd. Heavy on the cream, no sugar."

"Thanks, Robin." He smiled at the receptionist and then grinned at Charlie.

"Robin already asked when I arrived. Thanks for the offer, though." He took a sip and sighed. "That's way better than what Bryce makes up at the station."

Charlie sat in her chair and crossed her ankles. "So. I take it you have news?"

He took another drink of coffee and then put the cup down on the corner of her desk. "Well, yes. But not the kind we hoped for." His gaze met hers. "We did a records check. Couldn't find any unaccounted-for babies from any of the nearby hospitals. We went back over three weeks."

She frowned. "Huh. I really thought that would work, you know?" She thought for a second and then voiced an idea. "What if the baby was born at home? It happens. Not often, but it happens."

"You mean with a midwife or something?"

"Sure, that too. Couldn't you cross check birth certificate registrations against the hospital records?"

He nodded and smiled. "Actually, we've already started on that."

Charlie sat back in her chair and pondered. It was hard to hide a pregnancy, or any record of it if the mom had been receiving regular prenatal care. Surely it would only be a matter of time until they found the baby's mother. "Well, something will hopefully turn up."

"It takes time. The wheels of bureaucracy and all that. I just wanted to give you an update, seeing as how you've got a stake in this too. I was surprised to see him with you today."

She gave a little laugh. "I couldn't resist. He's sweet. Even though he kept me up all night."

Smith shuddered. "Yuck. Been there done that during a few of my Uncle of the Year moments." He laughed. "I like my sister's kids much better now that they're mobile. It'll be even better when they hit Little League."

She looked at the officer closely, took quick stock of him. Tall, handsome, stable job, liked kids, settled...he ticked all the right boxes. But she didn't get that tummy-lifting, butterfly sensation that she did when she saw Dave. How inconvenient.

"Charlie, would you mind stopping by the station, maybe tomorrow? It might be good to go over your statement from Saturday night. See if you remember anything else that might help us out."

"I don't work until one. I can probably pop in tomorrow morning."

"That'd be great. Well, I'd better be going." He hesitated for a minute, then caught her gaze and held it. "This Ricker guy that was here on Saturday. Are you...?"

"No." It wasn't exactly a lie. But she couldn't deny that Todd looked relieved at her answer.

"Oh. It seemed like you were."

"We were merely walking to meet Josh and some others at the pub. He didn't want me to be alone is all."

Liar.

She checked her watch. "Listen, thanks for stopping by. I do have another patient waiting, though."

He stood and nodded. "And I've got to get back to work. Take care, Charlie." His smile was warm enough to melt icicles.

"Thanks, Todd. You too."

When he was gone, she took a minute to sit and recover. Unless she was greatly mistaken, and she could be—her romantic radar wasn't the best—Officer Smith had been sending out some signals. On Saturday night he'd been rather protective of her too, she remembered. She didn't know him well, but they'd met on several occasions...

"Charlie? Exam room one is waiting." Robin appeared in the doorway with a smile. "Can't blame you for needing to sit down, though. Todd Smith in uniform is..." She stopped talking and merely made the motion of fanning herself.

Charlie couldn't help but laugh. "Don't let Josh hear you talking like that."

"I suppose we shouldn't let on that we call him Dr. Hottie then?"

Charlie nearly choked. "Oh my God. He'd die."

With a cheeky grin, Robin disappeared, and Charlie made her way to the exam room, grabbing the chart off the door. Enough fun—it was time to get back to work.

Chapter 6

Charlie wished this wasn't the first time she'd had to give a police statement, but she'd done her share during her ER rotation. Then there was the time she'd stopped at a gas station for a pint of ice cream and had found herself in the middle of a domestic dispute. As the boyfriend had come charging across the parking lot, the cashier had locked the outside door. Charlie hadn't thought twice. She'd taken the girl into the storage closet and locked them in until police arrived, spending several minutes trying to calm the girl down.

Her parents had been livid that she'd inserted herself into a potentially dangerous situation. That had been the day that she'd realized that she simply did not think the same way as her mother and father did and she'd known exactly what she was going to do. She asked herself why she'd become a doctor and the answer had been clear—she'd done it to help people. That was the marker of her success— not acclaim or status or money. She didn't give a rat's ass about becoming chief of anything or top of her field. Prestige meant nothing to her. She'd been around it her whole life and found it to be an empty ambition. And so she'd stood up for herself for the first time ever, put her foot down, and found herself part of a small practice here in Jewell Cove. No regrets. Not one.

Now here she was again, in the middle of a situation that wasn't her doing, sitting, waiting. Drinking terrible police station coffee while the baby sat in his car seat, his bright eyes open and staring at a colorful toy bar she'd bought during a very necessary trip to shop for the necessities like clothing and a proper snowsuit. An additional surprise had been Josh's sister, Sarah, who had arrived at the office with baby items from when she'd had her children, like a playpen with a thick pad at the bottom that Charlie could use as a makeshift crib.

Absently she checked her e-mail on her phone—nothing major other than a couple of e-bills that required paying and a few newsletters she'd read later. She picked up a magazine and flipped through it, but nothing really grabbed her interest. She was about to resort to a game of spider solitaire when the office door opened, and she looked up.

And saw Dave.

She was immediately transported to two days earlier, sitting on her floor and kissing him. Her face had to be turning red even as she tried a friendly smile. The look he gave her was sweet, as if they shared a secret, and she melted a little bit. Why was it he could turn her to mush with just an expression?

"Good morning, Dr. Yang," he said easily. "I guess you're here for the same reason I am."

"I guess so." She pushed on the arms of the chair and stood. Her heels increased her height by a few inches, but she was still a good five inches or more shorter than he was. She tugged at her black skirt, brushing her hands over the fabric.

"Dr. Yang? Come on in." The officer on duty called her into the office and she picked up the car seat. She was starting to get used to the weight of it.

"It's good to see you, Dave."

She moved to pass him and he caught her arm. "How about an early lunch when you're done?" He leaned close, his words soft. "I don't have to be to work until one."

"Me either," she confessed, and then wondered why she'd been so quick to answer. Hadn't she decided yesterday that it was better to just let things go? Besides, he'd been the one to say talk soon and then hadn't texted again. Clearly it was much easier to put him off with a text message than it was face to face.

"So we're on? You can fill me in on how this little guy is doing." He peered down into the seat, a goofy smile on his face.

She hesitated. It was just lunch, after all. Perfectly platonic and public, right? And she did have to eat before doing her stint as the walk-in doctor this afternoon.

"The Tuesday special at Breezes is meatloaf and mashed potatoes," he urged.

"That sounds fine to me. I'll see you when you're done."

She didn't want to keep the officer waiting, so she slipped inside the office and took a chair to answer any lingering questions about Saturday night.

It didn't take as long as she expected, and she was out thirty minutes later. Dave was sitting in the chair she'd vacated, flipping through the same magazine. "Ready?" he asked, standing.

"I guess." She put her scarf around her neck and then went to put on her coat. In an instant, Dave was there, helping her slip her arms into the sleeves and balance the baby. "Thanks," she murmured, buttoning the buttons and taking her gloves from the pockets.

"It's a cold one," he observed as he held the door and they stepped outside into the police station parking lot. "Did you walk over from the clinic?"

"No, I drove here straight from home." She looked around and didn't see his truck. "You walked up, didn't you?"

"I did."

"Guess you're riding with me, then."

He took the carrier from her hands and they started across the parking lot. Dave was right, it was bitterly cold, the kind of aching cold that seeped through clothing right into the bones. She hadn't worn boots today either, and her heels and nylons gave no protection against the weather. Halfway across the lot, her shoe slipped on a sheen of ice and she felt herself careening backwards.

"Oopsie Daisies!" The funny expression slipped from Dave's lips as his hand caught her elbow, keeping her upright. "Careful there."

She could feel the strength of his fingers through the thick wool coat. "Thanks. I should have worn boots today."

"No kidding. Don't get me wrong, your legs look great. But those shoes are not made for ice and snow."

She got out her keys, feeling a bit fluttery from the compliment. "I know. I figured with just four hours at the office today, I'd skip the boots."

The heater took a minute or two to kick in, and the drive was so short that Charlie's toes had barely started to thaw when they parked on the street outside the café. It was only eleven-thirty; they'd arrived before the lunch rush. This time, when Charlie got out of the car, Dave took her arm securely so she wouldn't slip on any black ice on the sidewalk.

Breezes was toasty warm and smelled heavenly when they walked in. A local radio station played over the speakers and despite the cold outside, it was cheery and bright on the inside. It had already been decorated for Christmas, with gaudy tinsel draped along the lunch counter and silk poinsettias on every table. Above the wide window overlooking the harbor, a gold and red and green shiny sign said, "Merry Christmas" and in the corner, an artificial tree was up and lit with colorful lights and red and green ornaments.

"Lunch for two today, Charlie?" the waitress, Linda, called out from the kitchen. "I'll be right out. Just putting up a takeout order. Sit where you like."

Charlie chose her usual table without thinking; a table for two with comfortable wood Captain's chairs and an unimpeded view of the docks. "Hey," Dave said as he hung his coat on the back of his chair and then sat down. "I can see the boat yard from here. Cool." He pulled a spare chair over and put the car seat on it. "There you go. You get a chair like everyone else."

She was very aware that the boat yard was visible, and instead of meeting his gaze or responding, she kept her eyes down and reached for the menu tucked in a wire holder on the table.

Linda didn't waste any time bustling over with two glasses of ice water. "You beat the rush today, folks. And oh my soul, who is this adorable boy?" Linda peered into the car seat and smiled. "Aren't you handsome," she cooed, and Charlie couldn't help but smile.

"I'm watching him for a few days. He's our baby in the manger." Charlie knew the grapevine would spread the news anyway, so she filled Linda in on the details. "Dave and I were just at the station, answering a few last questions, and thought we'd grab lunch before going to work."

"Oh, of course. What can I get you? The special's meatloaf and your choice of potato with carrots, and we've got a holiday special happening all month long. Stuffed turkey breast with mashed potatoes and gravy, peas and carrots, cranberry sauce and dessert."

"I'll have that," Dave said quickly. "Sounds perfect."

"And you, Charlie?"

Dave's meal sounded like an awful lot of food. Usually, she went for a salad or a bowl of soup, but today she was starving.

"I'll have the meatloaf with mashed," she answered, smiling. "Thanks, Linda."

"It'll be right up," she answered. "I'll bring you some coffee while you wait. It's wicked cold today."

The radio station was interspersing holiday songs with their regular playlist, and Charlie caught herself tapping her toe to a country version of *Santa Claus is Coming to Town*.

"Not to be corny," she suggested, "But it's beginning to look a lot like Christmas around here."

He nodded. "I know. Now that the tree's up in the square, every single window is lit up and decorated. I mean, a lot of stuff went up right after Thanksgiving, but it's a full-court press now."

She smiled, waited while Linda poured their coffee and then replied as she added milk to her cup. "So, are you a Santa or a Scrooge?" she asked.

He grinned. "Maybe a little of both. Sometimes it can get to be a bit much. The hoopla and the crowds and how it can all seem like a competition. But then there are other things I like about it, too. We always had good Christmases growing up. There wasn't always a lot of money to go around, but with the five of us there was always something fun. There was always a new board game every Christmas, and sports equipment. One year the three of us boys all got new ball gloves. We took them outside to play and I swear I couldn't feel my fingers when I came back in, they were so cold. We used to have New Year's Eve movie nights too, with all of us crowded around the TV and my mom would make popcorn and Kool Aid. It was the only time we were ever allowed to stay up past midnight."

"That sounds so fun. It was only me at home, so the only time anything like that happened was if I had a friend over or I went to their house."

"And that didn't happen very often?"

She shook her head. "Not really. My parents always threw a Christmas Eve cocktail party. It was not really...kid friendly. And they went out for New Year's, and I had a sitter until I was old enough to stay alone." She shrugged.

"Wow. You missed out on a lot."

She shrugged again. "It was what it was."

Linda came back bearing two huge plates of food. "Oh my word," Charlie exclaimed, but the aroma was so good that her mouth was already watering. "That smells so good, Linda."

"You just holler if you need anything else. I'll be back with dessert and more coffee in a bit."

The café was starting to fill up now, the lunch regulars filtering in, chafing their hands together to keep warm. The tunes on the radio were drowned out by conversation as Charlie and Dave dipped into their meals. Gus, the main cook at the café, hadn't let them down. Charlie's meatloaf was moist and flavorful, the potatoes smooth, the carrots sweetened with just a hint of something.

"If I could cook like Gus, I'd never eat out," Charlie admitted. "I do okay in the kitchen, but the guy is a master of comfort food."

"I agree. His crab cakes are almost as good as my mother's." Dave dipped a piece of turkey in cranberry sauce and popped it in his mouth. "And this sauce is not from a can."

"I think Gus would rather die than cook anything that wasn't from scratch."

Charlie laughed. "So, what are your plans for this Christmas?"

It was a simple, harmless question but it dampened the good mood considerably. "I haven't decided. I need to talk to Janice about that. I'm sure they have plans."

"Plans that don't include you?"

He smiled. "That might be awkward. I'm just, well, at loose ends a bit. Missing my family. So." He lightened his voice and smiled down at the baby, who was surprisingly content. "Our baby Jesus. Still no sign of the Virgin Mary."

"Or Joseph," Charlie added, letting the matter of Christmas drop. "I honestly thought someone would have come forward by now."

"I'm thinking someone would have to be in a pretty bad situation to abandon their kid."

"Well, I'm sure we'll hear something soon." She met his gaze. "I think he's very lucky we happened by at that moment. It couldn't have been planned any better. I mean, the night of the tree lighting. Everyone in the square for a good hour or more, and then tons of foot traffic. It was almost as if whoever left him wanted him to be found."

What she said sank in and they stared at each other. Maybe the manger wasn't that random after all. "I'm sure the police have thought of that." Dave nodded at her. "But you're right. I mean...remember you said about that case you handled. Someone trying to" —his voice tightened— "dispose of a baby wouldn't put him in a church manger on the busiest night of the season. Know what I mean?"

Charlie swirled the last bite of meatloaf in rich gravy. "Right. They'd put him somewhere he wouldn't be found."

"Still," he argued, "It's winter. What if we hadn't come along? In these temperatures he wouldn't have survived very long. Even if the intention was to have him found, there would always be a chance he wouldn't be." Dave's face darkened. "Hell of a big gamble to take with your baby's life."

"I agree." She looked up at him and asked the question that had been bothering her for the last thirty-six hours. "Dave, I can't go on calling him 'the baby'. Is it wrong to want to give him a name?"

Dave chuckled. "Not at all. It's been getting kind of awkward, actually." They both looked down at the baby, who's lids were drooping sleepily.

"He looks like an angel," Charlie whispered. "Even if he does keep me up most of the night. I can't resist that little face."

"Then name him after an angel."

"Gabriel?"

Dave grimaced. "Too predictable."

"Raphael?"

"The painter or the Ninja Turtle?"

She made a face, then pulled out her phone and Googled angel names. "Maybe this wasn't such a good idea. Most of the names have 'iel' at the end. Jophiel. Hesediel."

Dave laughed and ate a forkful of mashed potatoes and gravy. "Yuck."

"Wait. There are gospels here, though. Paul. John. And... ooh. Daniel."

"I like that."

"Me too." She looked up at Dave with surprise. "Hey, did we just name a baby together?"

"Well, temporarily. His birth certificate probably says something else."

Right. Reality. Not her baby. Not her life. She had to be careful she didn't start pretending it was. She put her fork and knife on her plate and wiped her lips with her napkin. "I should get back, I suppose. It'll give me time to feed Daniel" —she tested the name on for size— "before I start my appointments."

Dave frowned at her. "You're going now? Without pie? Is it possible to have a meal here without pie?"

Charlie laughed. "Oh, it's possible, otherwise I'd be the size of a house. I eat here most noon hours."

She realized what she'd just said and hoped he didn't pick up on it. But then, why would he? It was her own embarrassment speaking, that was all.

"Your loss," he said easily. "Pie comes with my meal and I'm going to take full advantage."

She opened up her purse to grab her wallet but Dave reached across the table and put his fingers on her wrist.

"Lunch is on me," he said quietly. "I invited you, remember?"

"I don't mind paying my share," she replied, still startled by the intimate touch.

It was made worse when she looked up and into his dark, chocolaty eyes. They were so beautiful. The kind of eyes a girl could get lost in if she weren't careful.

"Would that make you feel better? So you wouldn't have to call this a date?"

Her lips fell open, and she tried to respond but didn't know what to say.

"It's just lunch," he finally said, slipping his fingers off her wrist. "Falls under the getting-to-know-you-better category. No biggie, okay? You can get the next one."

Assuming there would be a next one.

"Then...thank you for lunch."

"Anytime."

Why was this so easy for him and so hard for her?

With a parting smile, she hefted the car seat and made her way to the doors, out into the wintery air. If anything, it had only gotten colder outside.

Keeping her distance from Dave was proving to be a challenge. As she started the car and felt the cold blast of air as the fan kicked in, she sighed. It would be easier to avoid him if her heart were really in it...

***

By Thursday night Charlie was going a little crazy. The last text from Dave sat on her phone, mocking her. *Thanks for lunch and talk soon*, it said. But there was no talking.

He'd gotten her message loud and clear.

Charlie plumped the pillow she held in her lap and stared, unseeing, at the evening news. She couldn't make up her mind what she wanted to do. She'd always been a planner, with the future mapped out in front of her. Things fit into tidy little boxes and that was comforting. Reassuring. And Dave Ricker didn't fit in a tidy box. He was a nice guy. He liked her, and she liked him. Which, if she were being honest, was frustrating as hell. He was definitely a more go-with-the-flow kind of guy, unsure of what came next or where he'd go. He wasn't a long-term thinker. His relaxed attitude drove Type A people like her a little crazy.

She reached for the glass of merlot she'd poured and took a restorative sip. If Lizzie were here, she'd have some definite opinions...

Charlie snagged the cordless phone from the base and hit the speed dial. It only rang twice when Lizzie answered. "Dr. Howard."

"Hello, Dr. Howard."

"Charlie! Hey, girl!"

Charlie laughed. This was so what she'd needed. Lizzie was driven and borderline workaholic, but she was Charlie's best friend and always knew how to make her laugh, even with a simple greeting. "Hey yourself. Where are you?"

"Driving home."

"I'll call you back."

"Don't be silly. Bluetooth, baby."

Charlie chuckled. "You're in a good mood."

"I guess. I'm off shift for three days. That works for me."

Charlie sank down into the cushions and sipped her wine again. "What? You haven't taken on extra shifts?" She raised her eyebrows. "There must be a man involved."

There was a beat of silence.

"Liiiizzziieeee!"

The warm laughter on the other end made Charlie feel so much better. "Okay. But I'm not spilling because I don't want to jinx it. Soon."

"Killjoy."

"How's Mystery Man? Still watching him from the café?"

"Funny you should mention that." Charlie stared into the crackling fire, swirled the wine in the glass. "We, uh, actually met."

"Oooh, do tell!"

Charlie heard the blare of a horn through the phone. "You sure you don't want to talk later?"

"I'm sure. I'm on my way to pick up my dad and go see my mom. I could use the distraction."

Charlie got a lump in her throat. Mrs. Howard had always been good to her, and her early onset Alzheimer's had hit the family hard. If Lizzie wanted distraction, Charlie would give it to her.

"We met when I was decorating the church yard for the holidays."

Lizzie let out a hoot that made Charlie grin. "Wait, you were decorating the church?"

"I know. Do you want to hear the story or not?"

Lizzie's laughter mellowed and Charlie grinned to herself. "Anyway, the next night we hung out at the tree lighting ceremony and we were going to go get a drink after when we found a baby."

The line went quiet for several seconds. "You found a baby? Did I hear that right?"

"Yep. An abandoned baby. So our date turned into calling the cops and dealing with social workers."

"Well, that'll be a story to tell the grandkids." Lizzie's good humor was back.

"I'm not so sure, Liz." Charlie put down the glass and sighed. "I was so stupid, having this crush on someone I'd never met. It's totally different now I know him in person."

"Different good or different bad?"

"Both?" She picked at a thread on the pillow. "You know me, Liz. I see men as candidates with potential."

"Yeah. You do. Which is no fun at all."

Charlie giggled a little. "Right. And this guy? I don't know if he's a candidate. He's got a kid and just moved to town, and I'm not sure he's even staying or if he even wants to be a father again..."

The sharp bark of laughter on the other end cut Charlie off. "You already talked about that stuff? Honey, you're more involved than you realize."

That's what she was afraid of.

"Crappy thing is, Liz, that I want to spend more time with him. He....he floats my boat, if you know what I mean."

Lizzie laughed again. "Yeah, I know what you mean." Charlie wondered what the heck her friend was being so close-lipped about. Maybe this developing romance of hers was serious. If Charlie had learned anything, it was that Liz would tell her when she was ready. She always did.

"Charlie?"

"Hmmm?"

"I think you should have a torrid affair. I mean, you never have. A no-strings, great sex, live in the moment affair. That's assuming this guy is torrid affair material?"

She thought back to Sunday morning on the living room floor and how badly she'd wanted to rip his clothes off even though they'd kept it strictly to kissing. "He is." The words came out slightly strangled.

"Sister, you are leaving out some pertinent details."

"You could always come for a visit. Maybe over the holidays."

There was a beat of silence. "Tempting, but I think I'll be kind of occupied over Christmas. It's Dad's first one without mom at home and Ian will be around..."

"Ian. So that's his name."

"Long story."

"Whenever you're ready."

Lizzie chuckled. "Damn, I'm glad you called. Really glad."

"Me too."

"Listen. You do what you're comfortable with as far as things go with Mystery Man. I'm just saying, not every guy needs to have a wedding registry above his head and tick all the right boxes, know what I mean? Sometimes you can just go with it. In fact, this might be better because you could go into it without any expectations from each other. For Pete's sake, have a fling, Charlie. You've never done anything spontaneous in your life, other than moving to Jewell Cove.

And look how that's turned out for you. It's a little slow for my speed, but I know you love it there."

She did, and she was glad Lizzie recognized it. Her family certainly didn't.

"The torrid affair might have to take a back seat. I'm looking after the baby temporarily. He's a bit small, and it's not for very long."

"You're looking after a baby?" Liz's voice came across the line loud and clear. "Are you crazy?"

Charlie laughed. "I'm exhausted. But it's good practice."

"Better you than me, sister."

"I'll think about what you said," Charlie promised. "Thanks for the pep talk. I needed it."

"Next time I want better details. But I'm here at Dad's, so I'd better go."

"Love you," Charlie said, missing her friend desperately.

"Love you back. Text me a pic of Mystery Man. I want visuals."

Charlie was laughing as she clicked off the phone.

Lizzie had certainly given her something to think about. She was right. Charlie had never done anything spontaneous. Plus they were attracted to each other. It could work.

Or...not. Things were rarely that straight forward, were they? Besides, as alluring as the idea was, Charlie wasn't sure she knew how to go about having a "torrid affair," as Lizzie put it.

Chapter 7

It was all going fine until Friday at eleven o'clock. Routinely she and Josh closed up shop on Friday afternoons, with one of them remaining reachable during the afternoon through the answering service in case of a patient emergency. That rarely happened, since anything urgent automatically went to the hospital in Rockland or the nearby walk-in clinics. Today their last appointment was at eleven-thirty, which meant they might actually wrap things up by twelve-thirty or one. She'd thought to do some Christmas shopping at the town shops, maybe grab some decorations for the cottage.

Instead Josh poked his head inside her door when she was between patients.

"Hey. It's Robin's birthday today. I said we'd take her to lunch once we wrap up here."

Charlie liked Robin. She was even impressed that Josh knew it was her birthday and was making an effort. But she really, really didn't feel like going to lunch and having to make small talk.

"Where?" she asked, knowing she couldn't really say no.

"Breezes?"

Right. And she'd find herself watching the waterfront, looking for Dave. He hadn't called or texted again this week. Whatever interest he'd had, it had clearly waned.

"We always go there. If we're knocking off for the week, what about the pub?" At this time of day, the pub catered to the lunch crowd, and she could take Daniel along with her.

"I'll ask. There's something to be said for Friday night nachos and wings." He smiled at her. "So you're in?"

How could she say no? "Yeah, I'm in." She'd just go do the dutiful lunch thing and then her shopping. On Fridays the stores remained open until nine. She'd have lots of time, even if she had to stop and give the baby a bottle somewhere. Truthfully, she could really use some sleep, but she could stand to get out a little, too. How did new moms manage?

But fate stepped in once more, with a last-minute appointment that Josh felt he couldn't put off. And indeed he couldn't. The patient was all of five years old, and her mother didn't have a car for driving to a hospital. While Josh waited for them to arrive and then treated the child for bronchitis, Robin got out the small box of holiday decorations and spruced up the waiting area a bit, adding a small rope of lights along the front of the reception desk, putting a tiny bottle-brush tree on the magazine table in the corner, and hanging a battered synthetic evergreen wreath on the door. Meanwhile, Charlie supervised from the comfy chair in the waiting area, feeding Daniel his bottle and sitting with her feet up for a few minutes. It put them behind schedule, but it was relaxing just the same.

By the time Josh had sent the patient's prescription to the pharmacy, Charlie and Robin were waiting, stomachs growling. It was nearly two o'clock.

The weather had been cold the last few days, but today it had turned sunny and milder, a welcome reprieve from the bitter, raw wind that seemed to seep through the bones. Charlie parked the car in the lot next to the pub, in one of the last available spots. She put Daniel in a borrowed stroller before they all made their way inside, into the welcoming warmth of the bar.

Their food had just been served when the door swung open on a gust of wind and a group of five blew in with it. Five big, burly men in heavy jackets and thick knitted hats, one with a particular set of dark eyes that immediately found Charlie and made her traitorous body respond with a jolt of pure electricity. What was with the crazy physical attraction, anyway? All Dave had to do was show up and she got this jacked up, excited feeling racing through her veins. She had to get a grip.

It had been easier to put off the impact of her attraction when he was out of sight, to pretend it was all in her head. Not so easy when he was standing there, larger than life, reminding her of exactly what it was like to be in his arms. He kissed like a freaking angel, that's what. Made her forget all her good intentions.

"Charlie, you okay?" Robin nudged her arm. "I just asked you to pass the ketchup."

"Oh. Sorry." She offered a weak smile and reached for the squeeze bottle. Her wrap and sweet potato fries smelled delicious, but she wasn't sure she could eat.

For heaven's sake. He was just a man. Mortal. Imperfect.

She looked up. Caught his eye. Held her breath.

Josh nudged her elbow. "What's going on?"

She hadn't realized she was biting on her lip until Josh spoke to her. She released it and pasted on a bright smile. "What do you mean?" She picked up a fry, dipped it in sauce and took a definitive bite.

"Last time I saw you with that guy, you were at the tree lighting. Then the whole thing with the mystery baby happened. Now he walks in and you're wound tighter than a watch. What am I missing?"

"Nothing." She deliberately ignored looking over at the corner where Dave and his buddies had taken a seat. "Once the cops left, Dave went home. He came back to the office the next morning and gave me a lift back to my place. That's all."

Josh was so quiet she stopped dipping her fry and put it on her plate before turning to face him. "What?"

"Did he do something he shouldn't have?"

There was a protective note in Josh's voice that grated on her nerves. She frowned at him. "What is it with the men in this town, anyway? You sound as bad as Todd Smith."

But her sharp reply and frown did nothing to deter Josh. "I work with you. I care about you. You're a single woman. I just like to protect my friends, that's all. And if this guy is bothering you, I've got your back."

"Me too," Robin piped up from across the table.

"It's not like that," she answered, laughing tightly. "Besides, I can handle myself, I promise. Right now I just need something to eat. Like my sweet potato fries that are getting cold."

The topic was set aside as they finished their meal, even though Charlie was always aware of Dave back in the far corner, talking and laughing with his pals. Charlie actually thought she might be able to scoot out of the pub and tackle her shopping, and when Josh paid their bill for lunch, she stood and reached for her coat and scarf while Robin excused herself to go to the bathroom.

Charlie's hand was nearly in the second sleeve when the weight of her coat disappeared and the hole of her sleeve shifted into a more accessible position. Her tummy flipped over as she realized it had to be Dave, standing close behind her. She shrugged the coat over her shoulders and took a breath. She could do this. She could have a conversation with him without wanting to rip his clothes off.

She turned around and realized she was wrong. He was just so... everything.

"Hey," he said quietly, and her tongue felt thick in her mouth as she struggled to find something cool to say.

"Hi."

It could have been worse. What was it about him that turned her into an idiot?

"How've you been?"

"Fine. You?"

"Not so great, as it happens."

"Oh?" She relaxed a little. "Did you get the cold that's going around? I've been seeing people in the office all week."

"No," he said quietly, his gaze locked on hers. "I've been wanting to call you since Tuesday and keep convincing myself I shouldn't."

Boom. Forget relaxed. All her senses went on high alert again.

"Dave, I..."

"And that's why. I didn't want to hear you turn me down or scramble to find an excuse to say no."

She wanted to explain, but it would sound so terribly juvenile to admit to him that she'd watched him for weeks during her lunch hour. That he'd been her guilty little pleasure, a kind of escape from the day-to-day real world. It would sound creepy.

Neither was it possible to bring up the other reason— that she was looking for a husband and father to her as yet unborn children and didn't think he was that guy. Talk about putting the cart before the horse... That would be enough to send any man running for the hills.

"Anyway, have a nice weekend, Charlie. It was good to see you." He peeked into the stroller and a soft smile curved his lips. "You too, sprout," he said quietly, and she melted all over again.

And that should have been the end of it. Except she didn't want him to walk away. What she wanted to do was break free for once from the only kind of existence she'd ever known. One based on pros and cons and logic and safety and security. The one that never took risks. She'd bought the requisite dollhouse cottage on the sea in an idyllic small town with the perfect job, putting all the pieces of the puzzle together to find the life she craved.

Which, she was quickly realizing, was simply setting herself up for failure.

"Dave?"

He turned back.

"Look, uh..." Wow, she sounded so eloquent and composed. She tried a weak smile. "Do you want to take a walk or something?"

His gaze warmed. "I thought you'd never ask. Let me ditch the guys and grab my jacket."

Robin came from the bathroom. "Oh, you're ready. Shall we go?"

"You go ahead," Charlie said. "Daniel and I are going to catch up on some shopping."

Which might have been a good excuse if Dave hadn't returned in record time. "I'm back."

Robin's grin was wide and her eyes twinkled. "Yes, you are. Well, Charlie, you have fun shopping." To make matters worse, she winked at them. "I'll see you Monday morning."

"I hate small towns," Charlie muttered, and Dave chuckled behind her.

"Oh, come on. They have a certain charm."

Charlie pulled on her gloves as they made their way to the door. She wasn't quite prepared for the blast of cold air that smacked her in the face as they stepped outside, though, and she adjusted the blanket tucked around the baby. "It's funny," she said, huddling into her coat. "This is considered a mild day. And it really is so much better than earlier in the week. But you know what? It's still damned cold."

Dave laughed beside her. "There's a lot of winter left. You should get used to it. Personally, I can handle the cold if we still get sun, you know?"

She did know. There was something about dull, gray, dreary days that made her want to sleep and eat carbs all day long. She was always glad when the time changed in spring.

"So, was that a late lunch or early dinner?" she asked, as they started to stroll along the boardwalk.

"We decided to knock off early today," Dave said in reply. "Friday afternoon, and we had a good week. We brought Jim

Williams's boat into dock this afternoon, but there wasn't much sense in starting anything until Monday morning." His big body sheltered her from a bit of the wind. "Know what always amazes me? Lobstermen this time of year. What a thankless, cold job. You think it's cold here, imagine being out on the water, checking traps. Brrr."

They wandered along the boardwalk for a minute. Finally Dave spoke again, his voice deeper than it had been only moments before. More private, intimate.

"You've been avoiding me, haven't you?"

"No!" The answer came out before she could consider what best to say. "I mean...damn. I just did some thinking after our lunch the other day."

"Did you sit down and make a checklist?"

Her cheeks flamed, despite the cold. "Look, Dave, I've had relationships before. And they were..."

She broke off the sentence and considered. What made this different? "They were people I already knew. That I had something in common with."

"Doctors and med students, then."

She nodded. "Well, yes." She looked over at him and tried being as transparent as she could. "We already had something in common, so no shortage of things to talk about. We ran in the same circles, knew the same people."

"Wow, Charlie," he said, shaking his head a little. "I totally didn't have you pegged as a snob. I'm just a guy who works on the docks, right?"

She stopped walking, shocked by his assumption, belatedly realizing how it sounded. "God no! That's not it. It's more..." She struggled to explain. "I guess it was more that we all had similar lives. Crazy schedules, goals, expectations for the future."

"Safe," he supplied.

"I suppose so," she agreed, though she'd never considered that before. It made complete sense now that he'd said it, though. She'd dated within that sphere because it was comfortable. Expectations were managed. There was little ambiguity.

"The thing you have to understand about me is that I don't really know how to be...I don't know, spontaneous. I've always based decisions on logic, common sense. There's always a plan and a goal."

"Good God, that sounds terrible."

She couldn't help it, she laughed, and he chuckled too. Their boots made scuffing noises on the boardwalk and gulls wheeled and cried above the harbor. The tension between her shoulders began to let go. Maybe this was what she'd needed, too. Some fresh air and relaxation.

"It isn't as terrible as it sounds." Not always, anyway. "It probably comes from having two very driven parents. We didn't do anything on a whim or for sheer pleasure. It had to have a purpose. I don't even remember them going out just for fun. Dinner dates and social events were for networking. Course selection was based on advancement. Medical school provided me with security..."

"I'm getting the picture. Sounds like you had a very... productive upbringing."

That was it exactly.

"I don't really know how to do anything else. And I don't mean to scare you, but I've never looked at relationships as simply a way to pass the time. I know I said we should enjoy the now but honestly I don't know how to do that. Everything fits into a bigger plan, you see."

He stopped walking and faced her. "Like a house with a white picket fence and a husband and dog and two-point-five kids?"

Nailed it. She was afraid to admit it but she nodded anyway. "Yeah. Like that."

"And I'm not keeper material."

She let her silence answer. And yet there was this stupid, crazy physical attraction thing she felt whenever he was near. What the heck was that about, anyway?

They were now standing in the middle of the sidewalk on Main Street. It wasn't the best place to be having this kind of conversation. Her hands were shoved into her pockets and his nose was red from the cold and she said what was on her mind anyway. "If I hadn't taken a taxi to work that morning, would this have gone differently?"

His gaze held hers. "I certainly hope so."

He had a way of saying things that sent a delicious shiver rippling through her body. She recognized it for what it was: anticipation. Pure, simple, in-the-moment, desire and possibility.

"Nothing's changed for me, Charlie." His gaze dropped to her lips. "I enjoy your company. I'd like to enjoy it more, but I can't put a label on it or make it part of a bigger plan. Hell, I don't even know if I'm going to be staying in Jewell Cove, you know that. But that doesn't mean we can't try."

The ball was clearly in her court. She knew the rules, and the only question was if she could abide by them. Part of her balked and said to listen to reason. It cautioned her not to waste her time on something that was probably going nowhere. But a bigger part of her was tired of being reasonable, and safe, and predictable. Not once in her life had she done anything wild or risky. She never threw caution to the wind or acted in a way that was less than sensible. Daniel started to fuss a little, so she started walking again, Dave taking his cue and joining her. She hoped the movement of the stroller would soothe the baby for a little while longer.

"By enjoy my company, you mean..." She asked the leading question, not sure how she wanted him to answer.

"I don't know. I'd be lying if I didn't say I was crazy attracted to you."

Zing went the arousal meter.

"But I can see you're not a 'leap into it headfirst and deal with the consequences later' kind of person."

No, she wasn't.

"A date," he suggested. "A real date. Something casual that we can do together. No commitments, no pressure. Just a single date on a Saturday. What do you say?"

A date. What would be the harm? Besides, with a date, things were planned. There wasn't as much chance of getting caught off guard, was there? A date had a basic itinerary. Dinner. A movie, something. "What did you have in mind?"

He thought for a moment. "You said you had shopping to do," he finally said, looking down at her. "But I think I kept you from it. The Evergreen Festival is tomorrow and I've never experienced one. We could go together, take Daniel too, of course. That's pretty low-key and casual."

It certainly was. In fact, it didn't sound very date-ish at all. She should be relieved, so why was she slightly disappointed?

"You want to spend your day shopping?"

He shrugged. "Why not? Besides, I was thinking about getting something for Nora for Christmas. I'm clueless when it comes to little girls. Maybe you could help me."

Oh, that was playing dirty.

"We could have lunch and finish our shopping. The weather's supposed to be fine. It'll be a great day for it."

Wow. When he said low key, he meant it. How on earth could she refuse? Never mind she was planning on attending the festival anyway.

"It sounds like a nice day," she agreed.

"Then it's a date." He dropped his shoulders and looked supremely pleased with himself. "I can stop by your place and pick you up."

They'd wandered back along the dock now, nearly to the public lot where her car waited. Dave lifted a hand to George Adams at the boat works, then shoved his hands back in his coat. "He's a good boss," Dave said. "Fair. Good sense of humor."

"Do you think he'll keep you on?"

"I don't know. I guess I'll cross that bridge when I come to it. I spent a lot of years being told where I was going and what I was doing. It was all about the mission and my orders. Now that I'm a civilian, I get to figure all that out for myself. I don't see any point in rushing into anything."

Charlie couldn't imagine not having a firm plan. But she was starting to realize that maybe that wasn't such a bad thing. People could become too attached to plans. And then what happened when they didn't work out?

***

Dave stared up at the ceiling, resisting the urge to flip and flop around in the bed. He'd awakened early and his thoughts ran to Charlie and what he was doing with her. He honestly hadn't planned on staying in Jewell Cove that long —it was a temporary fix until he could make some decisions, a way to stay close to Nora in the meantime. But something about the good doctor had knocked him for a bit of a loop. Enough that he was losing sleep over it.

He knew he was up for good now. Rather than toss and turn, he slipped out of bed, grabbed some clothes and his phone, and went out to stoke the fire in the stove that had died overnight.

He added a couple birch logs, hoping the papery bark would ignite from the coals and get things going again. He'd just checked the weather on his phone when it vibrated in his hand, indicating an incoming message.

He exited and went to look, and his heart jumped up in his throat as the latest picture of Nora showed in a little block in the conversation. Janice had sent through another picture.

He touched the thumbnail with his finger and his daughter's face filled the screen, all light curls and brown eyes and bewitching smile. Lord, she was beautiful.

The eyes were his, but everything else was her mother. It was disconcerting.

His throat tightened.

He closed the pic and went back to the conversation. Janice had typed something with the attachment.

Latest of Nora, when we put up the Christmas tree. She's asleep but looking forward to next weekend.

His thumbs hovered over the keyboard. Finally, he typed in a reply.

Me too. What are you doing up so early?

The answer came back immediately.

Nora has a cold. I've been up to give her medication and cuddles. Now I can't sleep.

You and me both, he thought, but in his case it was thinking about the woman he'd be spending the day with and there was no way in hell he'd type that message to his ex.

There were days—a lot of them—that he felt badly he hadn't given Nora a two-parent home. The truth was, he hadn't really, truly been in love with Janice. He'd been trying to make a romance out of a friendship, and that just didn't work. He thanked God that they were able to maintain an amicable relationship.

I was thinking of getting Nora a Christmas present today. Any suggestions?

He didn't even know his own kid well enough to shop for a Christmas gift.

A few minutes later a reply came.

She's going through a puppy stage. DO NOT GET HER A PUPPY. The stuffed kind would be nice though.

He gave a huff of laughter at the all caps. Oh, wouldn't that leave Janice fit to be tied, if he got a real dog? But he wouldn't pull that kind of trick.

Good to know, he typed. *Do you need anything?*

This time the answer was quick to come back. *Brian and I are managing fine, Dave. Don't worry.*

Better go. See ya.

He got out of the conversation and put the phone on the coffee table. He was glad she'd sent the picture. Glad they'd chatted—even if it was just texting back and forth.

Then he thought about Charlie, and the way that she kissed, and his pulse leapt.

That was all it took. Just a thought and his body reacted. He wondered why. Wondered if it was just a symptom of his long dry spell, or if it was something more. Something that was distinctly Charlie that caused him to get the automatic sense of urgency and protectiveness. And how much he should act on it.

Maybe first he should figure out if it was really real.

He sat in the corner of the sofa until daylight began to filter through the windows, and then he got up and started making coffee.

***

The sun was out and the air was crisp and cool as they made their way down the hill to where the main shops were. Already crowds of people were milling about, carrying shopping bags, bundled up in winter clothes and sipping from paper cups of coffee or hot cider. Charlie nudged Dave's elbow and grinned. "Every store has a themed Christmas tree, see?"

They were at the far end of Main, where the shops began, and the first store was the bakery. A fat pine tree sat in the corner of the veranda, and it was decorated with ornaments shaped like cupcakes, cookies, loaves of bread, and kitchen utensils. Today, instead of wheeling the stroller through the crowds and packed stores, she had Daniel tucked into a Snuggli carrier where he stayed warm and secure against her chest. The weight felt foreign but somehow nice, too, and it left both hands free for shopping bags and browsing. Not to mention the baby seemed to love being snuggled as she carried him around.

"Shortbread," Charlie announced. "I'm fueling this shopping trip with shortbread." She grabbed Dave's hand and dragged him along, into the full shop that was noisy and squished and smelled like vanilla and fresh bread and cinnamon.

Decisively she approached the counter and ordered a plastic container of two dozen shortbread nuggets. "We can share," she said, paying for the cookies and tucking them into a cloth shopping bag. The cashier gave her a pamphlet and put a cookie-shaped stamp on a square next to the shop name. "Get all the stamps and you can enter to win a shopping spree," the chirpy cashier said, and Charlie called out her thanks and tucked the paper into her purse.

They stopped next door at the Shear Bliss salon, where the tree was decorated with sample bottles of hair products. She was really getting into the spirit now, especially when people she recognized lifted a hand in a wave or stopped to say hello. Maybe she hadn't realized it until lately, but she was finally starting to feel like a part of this community. But as she went outside and rejoined Dave, she held back a little too, not holding his hand or walking too closely. A part of her wanted to keep that private part of her life private. She'd never much been into PDAs.

Charlie's shopping bag was starting to fill up, with a tin of hibiscus tea from The Leaf and Grind added to her purchases as well as a box set of bubble bath and lotion from Bubbles. Dave, though, was still empty-handed. "Come on," Charlie chided. "There must be something you need to buy. You have sisters and stuff, right? Plus you said you wanted to find something for Nora."

He smiled down at her. "I think you're shopping enough for the both of us."

"Oh, this is hardly anything." She pulled him along to the bookstore, past a sparkly artificial tree adorned with paper ornaments. On closer examination, she realized that each round ball was constructed of strips of paper...strips of book pages…overlapping each other. It was a clever idea, and she paused briefly before the tree, reaching out to touch one of the fragile balls.

"Oh, look at this one," she said wistfully. "It's all Shakespeare." There were random lines from several plays, and as she turned the ornament in her fingers a line jumped out at her. Whoever loved that loved not at first sight? She couldn't name the play, but it gave her a little shiver just the same. Of course, she and Dave weren't in love. But still. She'd been the one to look down over the docks and get that silly swirly feeling whenever she saw him.

Dave peered over her shoulder. "I didn't know you were a fan."

She nodded, scanning the strips for more familiar words. "My parents used to assign reading to me. It was no big deal. I read the first one and I was hooked. Though some plays I enjoy more than others."

"Like Romeo and Juliet?"

"Are you kidding?" She turned her head and laughed up at him. "Young love meets tragic ending. Not my favorite. But it did provide some great romantic lines." She let the ornament fall back among the boughs and turned all the way round so that she faced him completely. "My bounty is as boundless as the sea, My love as deep; the more I give to thee, The more I have, for both are infinite." She hadn't meant for it to be so serious, but the way he was looking down at her made her shift and slide away towards the door. "Anyway, let's go inside."

The store was crammed full of people, filling the narrow aisles. "Go browse," she instructed him, moving away. She hadn't shopped in a while, and she knew there were several titles she was waiting to add to her shelf.

He disappeared into the non-fiction section.

It took no time at all for Charlie to pick out a couple of the latest thrillers for Lizzie for Christmas. She hadn't mentioned it to Dave, but half the stuff she'd already bought today was for Lizzie. Buying for her parents was like buying for the people who had everything, so Charlie had already sent gift certificates for her parents to do some shopping before their holiday cruise. Other than token gifts for Robin and Josh at the clinic, she had no one else to buy for.

She found Dave in the kids section, a frown on his face. "Find anything you like?" she asked, holding her volumes in her arms.

"I don't know what's good. What's popular." His dark eyes pleaded with her for help. "I mean I've read to her, but I'm overwhelmed by bunnies and ducks and princesses. She's almost three. Is that too young to really appreciate a book for Christmas?"

Charlie took pity on him. "It's never too early for books," she decreed.

Holding her books tightly against her chest, Charlie leaned forward and pulled a good-sized hardcover from the shelf. "I'd get her something she can have as a keepsake. When I was little, my grandmother gave me a copy of The Night Before Christmas, and I read it every Christmas Eve." She didn't mention that she read it alone in her room, while her parents entertained downstairs, or that it was still packed away in her things. "How about The Polar Express? The illustrations are beautiful and it's a classic." She handed him the book.

He ran his hand over the glossy cover. "That's a good idea."

"I do have them occasionally. Are you ready to go? I'd like to hit Treasures before we make our way down to the gallery."

"Sure. I'm ready."

At the checkout Charlie got her "passport" stamped and collected a free bookmark on the way out the door. She was waiting outside, talking to someone who'd stopped to admire a very cute sleeping Daniel, when Dave finally came out.

"That took a while," she said, waving goodbye to the woman who'd stopped.

He shrugged. "They had to change the register tape."

They made their way one street up to Treasures, a beautiful old house on the corner of Lilac Lane. Once in the door, they were assaulted by sounds and colors and activity. A middle-aged woman worked the till while someone else bagged and wrapped, and Charlie saw two children disappear into a back room where a sign said "Workshop in Progress."

"This place is crazy."

Charlie laughed. "Josh's sister owns it. She runs classes here sometimes, too. I've been meaning to take one, but somehow I never sign up."

He looked over at her as they moved out of the way of some browsing women.

"Afraid of looking silly? That maybe there's something you're not good at?"

She thought about that for a moment, then shook her head. "No, that's not it. It's more...I'm not sure how useful it would be. I'd end up making candles or a pair of earrings or something, and it seems a bit—"

"Frivolous," he finished. "And maybe fun. Charlie, you think everything has to have a purpose or fit into a bigger picture. But sometimes fun really is enough. It's a purpose all on its own. To enjoy life just for the sake of enjoyment."

"I'm learning," she said, leaning closer to him.

His eyes delved into hers and she felt a delicious shiver run down her spine.

"I'm always willing to help. I'm a very good teacher."

She just bet he was and it sent a thrill rippling over her. She changed the subject, particularly since the crowd was growing larger in the store and she didn't want to be overheard. "Come on, let's browse around. Maybe you can find something for your mom and sisters, hmmm?"

They shopped for several minutes. Though she'd already sent the gift cards, Charlie found a gorgeous hand-painted candle-and-holder set for her mother and bought another hand-painted glass ornament for Lizzie. She treated herself to a new knitted infinity scarf, and on impulse grabbed a thick wool hat and mitten set for Dave, just in case they ended up exchanging presents. She was admiring a rack of sterling silver and crystal earrings when Dave came over, a huge smile on his face.

"What did you find?" she asked.

He held out a large plastic case. She looked at the cardboard insert. "It's a puppet show. Oh, how sweet!"

He beamed. "Finger puppets, which should be easier for little fingers, right? There's one set up over there. The wings fold out so it stands on its own, and the puppets store in little pockets on the back. There are little curtains with Velcro and everything."

"You're excited."

"I'm happy I found something that I'm certain about, I think. I mean, little girls would love something like this, right?"

"I think so. And no little parts to worry about. It's really lovely, Dave." He looked down at her and she got that swirly feeling again.

"Are you ready? We can hit the last few shops and then get lunch."

"I'm ready. If I buy anything more, I won't have arms to carry it." She kept the mitts and hat beneath the thick infinity scarf, out of sight.

Their parcels were bagged and wrapped and paid for and they stepped outside into the bright winter sunlight. They decided to walk back to the clinic and stow their parcels in his truck before grabbing lunch at Gino's. Gino was doing a brisk business selling pizza by the slice with a can of soda as a festival lunch special.

The sun chased some of the chill out of the day, and they found an empty bench along the dock where they could eat. Daniel was awake but content, and Charlie lifted her pizza slice high and took a bite, sighing with pleasure as the flavors exploded on her tongue. "It's been a good morning."

"Yes, it has. Thanks, Charlie."

"For what?" She squinted in the sunlight as she looked over at him. He had a little piece of cheese stuck to the corner of his mouth and she reached over and wiped it off with the side of her thumb.

"For taking me shopping."

"You asked me, remember?" She popped the last piece of tender crust into her mouth and took a gulp of soda.

"Well, I wouldn't have if we hadn't..." He reached over and took her hand. "If we hadn't talked yesterday."

Fling, she reminded herself. This would be a fling and nothing more. She would not get her hopes up. She would not read more into this than there was. Dave was a live-life-as-it-comes kind of guy, not someone to plan a future with. Live in the moment. Be spontaneous. Why was she finding it so difficult? For heaven's sake, it was a simple date.

"It was fun," she answered, trying to adopt a flirtatious tone.

"How fun?" he asked, and he wiggled his eyebrows, making her laugh. She leaned sideways and jostled him with her shoulder.

"So," he said, when the last crumb of pizza was eaten, "are there any more stores you'd like visit?"

She shook her head. "I think we made it through most of Jewell Cove already."

"That's too bad."

"It is?" She turned on the seat and looked at him. His gaze caught hers and she was momentarily spellbound as the seconds drew out.

"Charlie," he whispered, leaning forward.

She caught herself leaning in too, her heart pounding like crazy as he kissed her, the baby between them. Nothing major, just a soft, sweet, mingling of lips before he sat back again. She was sure there must be stars in her eyes when she looked at him, but she couldn't help it. That was possibly the sweetest, nicest thing to happen to her, maybe ever.

"I don't want the day to end so soon," he said quietly, "and I'm trying to come up with something to do."

She was feeling the same way. There'd been no pressure in that last kiss, just a really nice moment between two people who were enjoying each other and their date.

The whole day had put her in the holiday spirit, far more than she'd expected. "Well, you do have the SUV. There is one thing we could do this afternoon."

"What's that?"

"Have you bought a Christmas tree yet?"

He leaned against the back of the bench. "I wasn't actually going to put one up."

"You have to." She put her hand on his knee. "It's not Christmas without a tree. I wasn't going to, either, but I changed my mind. It seemed pointless if I were going to be by myself, but if I have Daniel much longer... it's his first Christmas. All kids should have a Christmas tree, no matter how old they are."

He laughed. "You're sentimental. Go figure."

She smiled at him. "Maybe I am."

Daniel started to squirm and she knew she'd been lucky for him to stay quiet for this long. "Someone's selling trees in the gas station lot. Do you want to check it out? I need to change the baby, too. Give him a bottle before he turns into Mr. Crankypants."

In some ways this was the strangest date she'd ever been on. How many people took a newborn on a first date?

"Okay, but there might be another problem you haven't thought of."

"Oh?"

He tilted his head and regarded her lazily. "Sugar, if I wasn't going to put up a tree, chances are I don't have any decorations to put on it."

Right.

She looked at her watch. "We could hit the department stores in Rockland first. Stock up on lights and ornaments and pick up the trees on the way back."

"I dunno. That seems like quite a commitment."

She laughed. "The afternoon, or the tree?"

"Both. You sure you're both up to it?"

She raised an eyebrow. "Seriously. What else are we going to get up to on the weekend? A pit stop for some hot water to heat a bottle and we'll be good to go. Consider this me, learning to do something on a whim."

He grinned. "I'm game if you are."

"Let's hit the road then. I'm betting the tree guy packs up by five."

Chapter 8

As a rule, any big chain department store was a cacophony of Christmas music, impatient children, and intercom announcements this close to the holidays. Today was no exception. Charlie stepped inside and immediately felt overwhelmed. There was a reason she did most of her shopping in small specialty stores or before the Christmas rush. Right now, it felt as if everyone on the midcoast was crammed into this one store, hungry for bargains and frantic for deals and short on patience and goodwill toward men.

"It's Saturday," Dave remarked, grabbing them a metal cart. "And you thought the crowds at the festival were bad."

"Then we need to be strategic." Charlie adjusted the straps of the Snuggli and looked down into Daniel's face to be sure he was okay. His eyes were alert but he was contented after his bottle and changing. They started down the widest aisle as Charlie began ticking items off on her fingers. "You need a tree stand, skirt, lights, and ornaments at the very least."

"That sounds like a lot."

"Just think how much money you'll save next year." She smiled up at him. "Anyway, if we head to the seasonal section we should be able to find everything we need there."

She led the way while Dave wheeled the cart behind them. Before long they found themselves in the middle of a Christmas wonderland, full of lights and tinsel and ornaments that sparkled. Charlie ignored the crush of people and simply enjoyed the bright colors. Truthfully, she loved the idea of Christmas. Maybe growing up she hadn't had the warm, intimate down-home family holiday that she saw on all those Christmas specials, but she still liked the schmaltz. It had been better, too, when she'd started visiting Lizzie at the holidays. Her family really knew how to do it up right.

She turned around to say something to Dave and burst out laughing. He'd put a Santa hat on his head, one of the plushier ones with the big white pompom on the end.

With his dark eyes and slight shadow of stubble, he looked both adorable and mischievous and very, very dangerous to her willpower.

"Very nice," she complimented.

He held out his hand. In it was a green striped hat with white fluff around the edge. "Here. You can be my elf," he suggested.

She put it on her head and felt ridiculous. They were actually in the middle of a department store wearing the childish things and while she tugged hers off, Dave left his on. He grabbed her discarded hat and tossed it into the cart. "You never know," he said, wheeling along the aisle.

She wasn't sure what she'd never know, but she followed him anyway, marveling at how he just took things in stride. He was perfectly okay being silly, wasn't afraid to look a little foolish. Not so damn serious all the time...

She stopped mid-aisle as what she'd just thought truly sank in. She'd been describing herself, hadn't she? Was she really that uptight and boring? She didn't try to be.

Dave stopped to pick out a tree stand and she caught up to him, reached into the cart, and took out the hat. When he turned around, she had it on with the peak of it flopped over at a jaunty angle, the tiny bell at the end making a faint dinging noise.

"What are you doing?" he asked.

"Trying to remove the stick from my butt," she replied. "Is it working?"

He burst out laughing so suddenly that she couldn't help but grin. The smile was wiped clean off her face though as he took a step forward and planted a smacking kiss on her lips. "I dunno," he answered. "But it's a good start." He let his fingers graze the top of Daniel's head in a little caress before stepping back.

They moved along the aisle and then Charlie asked the question that had been on her mind for quite some time. "Do I really have a stick up my bum? Am I really that boring?"

Dave had his hand on a soft, velvety tree skirt, but he put it back on the shelf and faced her. "What? No! What made you ask that? You are not boring. You're smart and you have a great sense of humor—when you let it out to play. Listen," he said, coming forward so he was only a few inches away from her. She looked up at him and saw he was dead serious. "I like that you're focused and driven. I like that you're smart and you're quick in a tight spot, like you were the night with the baby. There's nothing wrong with you, Charlie. I think once you figure that out, you'll loosen up more and worry about things less."

Her throat had tightened painfully during that little speech. His insight was so bang on she didn't quite know how to respond. A few nearby shoppers were glancing over at him and her stomach tightened, reminding her of a frequent feeling when she was a child.

"Can I tell you something personal?"

The grin slid from his face and he gave her his full attention. "Of course."

She rested her hand on Daniel's head, then met Dave's gaze. "When I was a kid, it wasn't just parental expectation that put pressure on me. It was being Asian. Everyone expected me to be a whiz at math and science. I always felt like I was somehow one test away from being a failure."

His gaze softened. "And you never wanted to disappoint anyone."

"Kids liked asking for my help with stuff or wanted me in their group projects because I would do all the work rather than risk a low mark. I didn't think they'd like me anymore if I failed." She swallowed the next words. She'd felt her parents' love was conditional that way, too.

"What about in Jewell Cove?"

She shrugged. "It hasn't been like that. Josh is a great boss but easy going, too. And I was accepted there far quicker than I expected."

"You can be yourself."

She nodded. "No one seems to mind that I'm partly Chinese. Which surprised me." Her fingers played with Daniel's downy hair. "I faced my share of anti-Asian sentiment in Boston."

He put a hand on her cheek, his thumb rubbing softly over her cheekbone. "You can be yourself with me, too, you know."

She nodded, touched and a bit verklempt. Daniel squirmed in the Snuggli and her attention was momentarily diverted. "Thank you," she said, moving away a little and focusing on some ornaments.

"Thank you for sharing that with me," he said. "And for what it's worth, I'm sorry that people can be such asshats."

She snorted unexpectedly, and just like that, they were back to being easy with each other, a feeling she was coming to appreciate more and more. He turned his attention back to the tree skirts. "Now help me decide on this thing. This red fuzzy stuff or the green shiny stuff?"

Charlie huffed out a little laugh at his descriptors for velour and sateen, and put her hand on the red. As they continued through the section, picking up strings of lights and packs of ornaments, Charlie realized that she could really get to like Dave. A lot. So much that it was starting to get harder to remember why she was so opposed to being with him in the first place. She'd never shared that bit of herself with anyone other than Lizzie. That must mean something, right?

By the time they started the downhill slope into Jewell Cove, Charlie was asleep. Dave looked over at her and felt a warm sort of protectiveness steal over him. She'd definitely enchanted him in the store today, wearing the goofy elf hat right up to the cash register, where she'd taken it off so that the cashier could ring it in. He liked that she had a bit of a silly side and that she'd felt safe enough with him to let it show, even for just a little while. And she'd opened up to him, too, which had been really unexpected. Truth was, there wasn't much he didn't like about Charlene Yang and that was equally pleasant and disconcerting. Pleasant because he liked being with her. She made him smile, laugh. Made him think and didn't let him off the hook easily. But it scared him a bit too, because he'd enjoyed kissing her a lot.

She woke as they rolled to a stop just before the service station. "Oh my gosh! I slept the whole way back!"

He nodded. "You must have had a long week. I didn't want to wake you."

She pointed to the station. "Well, pull in. We haven't bought trees yet. They're still open."

It must be the doctor in her, he thought, appreciating the way she could go from sleep to fully alert in such a short amount of time. He was the same way, had been that way since he started soldiering. You slept during sleep time and when it was time to get up you hit the ground running. Old habits were hard to break.

The lot was just about to close up for the night, but they each managed to get a tree and strapped them on to the top of Dave's SUV with the help of the lot owner. It was dark by the time they left town limits and headed toward her cottage. When he turned in, his headlights swept across the front yard. With no lights on, inside or out, the place felt lonely.

"I didn't think we'd be gone so long," she explained. "I'll go turn on some lights and then we can get the tree down."

She took Daniel inside, along with the first of her bags and Dave followed with the rest of the decorations. He left her settling the baby in a playpen, then went to work on the straps holding the trees in place, making sure to release hers but leave his securely fastened. The outside lights came on, casting a circle of light around her front step, and he saw a glow come from the front windows as she turned on a few lamps. By the time she managed to get outside again, he had the tree standing up and was waiting for instructions on where to put it.

"Wow, that was fast." Charlie grabbed the final bag and slammed the tailgate. "Bring it in. I'll get the stand ready."

"You know where you want it?"

"Of course." She shrugged. "I made room in the living room. I took so long because I was settling Daniel in the bedroom. I'm not sure how long he's going to hold out. It's been a long day and he's been really good. It can't last forever."

He followed her inside, got her to hold the tree as he took off his boots, then carried it through to the living room. She hustled ahead of him carrying the tree stand, and then put it down before shrugging out of her coat. As he waited, she deftly set it up and loosened the bolts that would hold the tree in place. "Okay," she said, looking up as she stood on her knees. "Bring that sucker over and we'll get it in place."

He lifted, she guided, and within seconds the trunk slid into the hole. "Keep it straight!" Charlie called out, her voice muffled from beneath the branches. She was lying on her stomach now, reaching in under the tree to tighten all the wingnuts.

"Okay! Let it go!"

He cautiously let go of the top of the tree and it stayed steady. Charlie scooted backwards on her belly and then popped up, her shirt mussed and spruce needles decorating her hair. "So? What do you think?" she asked.

"Perfect. Just the right size."

"I think so too." Her eyes dancing, she disappeared into another room and came back with a box. She plunked it on the sofa and started rooting around. "Aha. Here it is." She withdrew her own tree skirt, a cute felt thing with sewn-on reindeer faces and antlers that were puffed out from the base fabric.

She was back down on her stomach again, sliding forward until she could put the skirt around the base. When she appeared again, he noticed a smudge of dust down the side of her breast.

He had to get out of here. The last time he spent any time in her living room they'd started kissing. It was about to go that way again if he wasn't careful. He thought spending the day together would be easy and fun. And it had been. A little too easy and a little too fun. Silence settled around them, heavy with potential. Waiting.

Waiting for one of them to make a first move. Or not.

"Well," Dave said, "I should be going. I have to unload my tree and get my stuff inside."

"Oh, right. Of course." His words seemed to have broken the spell and Charlie smiled at him. "It turned out to be a longer day than we planned, but a fun one. I think I have my Christmas shopping all done!"

Her voice was a little too bright; was she disappointed, or relieved?

"I got a start on mine, for sure," he admitted. He still hadn't purchased anything for his parents, or his siblings and nieces and nephews.

She walked him to the door, their steps meandering a little as he waited for an invitation. Which was stupid since he'd been the one to suggest leaving. It was for the best, right? And yet the day had been so nice, so fun and easy, that he was disappointed it was over. All that waited at home was whatever he could throw together for a meal and a hockey game on TV.

"Thanks for everything," Charlie said quietly as they reached the tiny foyer. "It was a really great date."

"Even though our plans changed?"

She smiled up at him. "I think, especially because our plans changed," she answered.

"Are you going to decorate your tree tonight?" Dave asked, his hand on the doorknob, putting off leaving for just a few moments longer.

"I don't think so. I'm too tired. Besides, it'll give me something to do tomorrow."

Right. Normally the idea of a quiet Sunday afternoon was alluring, but the idea of putting his tree up alone seemed rather depressing. And yet the ebullient Charlie seemed excited about the prospect.

"Sure." He knew it was a lackluster reply. He really should go. But then there was the fact that this marked the official end of their date and he had to decide how exactly he wanted to leave things. With a simple goodnight? A hug?

A kiss?

She was standing close enough he only had to reach out a little to put his arm along her back and pull her close. She put up her hands and they stopped her progress into his arms, pressed against his chest as her chin tilted up...

There was no way he could not kiss that pert little mouth. He didn't want to come on too strong, so he tempered the heat that flared in him simply from holding her close, and took his time, sweetly exploring her lips as he held her body against his.

He let it end after a single kiss. He'd promised a date and nothing more, and he tried to keep his promises. Which was why he rarely made them.

"Thank you for the wonderful day," he murmured, his voice husky in the silence of the foyer. "I hope we can do it again, Charlie."

He nearly reconsidered as she ran her tongue over her lower lip, and he wondered if she could taste him there. "I hope so too, Dave. I had a good time."

He was moving in for a second kiss when the baby started crying. They both froze, mid-move, and he was gratified to hear Charlie sigh. Did that mean she was as disappointed as he was?

"I'd better go," she said quietly, stepping away. "Somebody's not very happy."

He got out of there while he still could, with the picture of her dark eyes and soft, kissable lips still in his mind. The whole drive home he wasn't sure if he was happy for the first time in months or if he'd just made a huge mistake and if Daniel hadn't just done him a huge favor.

Despite Dave's best intentions, he was falling for her.

***

Charlie stared at her decorated tree and frowned. The lights were fine, the garland looped perfectly, the ornaments sparkling in the sun that filtered through the windows.

She should be happy with it, but she wasn't.

She couldn't stop thinking about Dave, the way he'd looked at her yesterday, how he'd kissed her goodnight, all soft and swoony. He was over at his place now, with his own tree and brand-new decorations. Was he feeling as lonely as she was?

It was the first Christmas she didn't have any plans of any sort. Up until this morning she thought she was okay with it. But now, staring at the tree, she knew she wasn't. There would be a present from her parents and one from Lizzie. She'd open them all by herself. And then she'd heat up a takeout turkey dinner from Breezes.

Tears stung her eyes.

"Enough of feeling sorry for yourself!" She said the words out loud and reminded herself that she was cozy and comfortable in a snug little cottage while there were others out there far worse off. She looked over at Daniel, on his back on a blanket, waving his little arms and legs, and smiled. Well, maybe she wasn't completely alone.

She was falling for this little baby head over heels, and she had to remind herself that this was only a temporary situation. She couldn't let herself get too attached...and yet she couldn't seem to help it, either.

She knelt on the blanket and played with the tiny fingers and toes, cooing to him in nonsensical syllables. He was still too little to laugh, and she kept looking for a smile. It wouldn't be long. Days, maybe a week or two, and he'd show her that first smile.

She'd looked it up...

Definitely getting too attached, but she couldn't find it in herself to be sorry.

It was a beautiful afternoon, so after they'd both had lunch, she decided they'd take a walk. The sun was out, and it made the snow and trees glitter like a fairyland.

There was no self-delusion at work. As she pulled on her heavy boots and retrieved a hat and scarf from the tiny entry closet, she knew she was heading toward Dave's place, probably with an idea of giving him a hand with his tree if he hadn't finished it already.

The road to her cottage and on to Fiddler's Rock was a side road that ran mostly parallel to the main highway and hugged the shoreline of the cove. As such, most of the traffic was local traffic, and Charlie only met maybe a dozen cars on the half hour walk to Dave's place, the stroller wheels making gritty noises on the asphalt. Chickadees had taken up residence on the snow-covered branches and alternated their chirpy calls with the throatier "dee dee dee" sounds, and Charlie took deep breaths of the crisp air. By the time she reached Dave's, she was warmed up from the exercise and the sun that had seeped through her winter clothing. The motion and fresh air had lulled Daniel back to sleep.

With a soft laugh, she wished he dropped off to sleep this easily at night.

She knocked on his door and waited, but there was no answer. Surprising, because his truck was in the yard. She hopped down the steps and peered around the corner into the back yard. It didn't take long to find him. The lot sloped down to the beach, and she caught sight of his plaid jacket through the shrubs. He was sitting on a boulder, tossing rocks into the water, the *lap lap* of the gentle waves soothing and rhythmic.

She often found it too cold on her deck, but she understood the allure. In warmer weather she spent a lot of time looking out over the bay, listening the waves and the gulls, letting the sounds ease her mind.

She took Daniel from the stroller and snuggled him against her shoulder. "Hey, stranger," she called, announcing her arrival. She sauntered closer, taking her time as she picked her way down the rocky path to the beach. "Is this a bad time? I got my tree up. It was feeling a little empty at my place. I thought a walk in the sun would do me good. And...I wondered how you were getting on with your tree."

"It's in the stand."

"I see."

They sat for a few minutes in silence.

"Sorry," he apologized. "I'm in a cranky mood and not the best company, I guess."

"It's okay." She smiled softly. "Everyone's entitled to a bad day. Anything I can do to help?"

He huffed out a humorless chuckle. "The doctor is in?"

"I figure if you want me to know anything more, you'll tell me. If not, I'll mind my own business."

He sighed. "I was supposed to have Nora next weekend. But Janice called and said her husband's family has invited them all to Boston for some big holiday event. I feel like an ogre saying no, but I missed my last weekend because she was down with the flu."

"That's rough." Charlie covered his gloved hand with hers, repositioning Daniel on her shoulder. "But Nora knows you're a good father, so does Janice."

"I guess it just bugs me to think that I'm letting my family down. And I know it doesn't make sense. I'm not the one changing plans. But still." He met her gaze. "This is the first Christmas I get to spend with her, and I feel like I'm missing out."

There was no reason why Charlie should feel jealous, but she did. She had no claim on Dave, and she wasn't sure she wanted to have either. All they'd shared were a few kisses, a lunch, and a first date. But hearing him talk about his family was like a shot to her irrational heart. He already had what she wanted so badly.

"She's bringing Nora by later this afternoon," he added, and Charlie swallowed thickly. "Kind of a consolation for me losing my visitation time."

"I see." It was the only response she could come up with. She knew she was being petty, but she wondered if Dave wanted to see his ex. If he still had feelings for her. And there was no way on earth Charlie would ask those questions.

"Okay," she said, taking a breath and scrabbling off the rock. "I'll get out of your way." It seemed Daniel had had enough too, because he squirmed against her chest, fussing. She patted his back with her mittened hand.

"You're not in my way."

"Are you sure?" He definitely hadn't invited her in, or to stay, or anything else. She was feeling worse and worse, just when she'd thought maybe she should put her misgivings aside and take a chance on them. "I get it, Dave. You would rather we weren't around when your daughter visits."

He ran his hands over his hair as she turned to go. She'd only taken a few steps when his voice stopped her again.

"Charlie, when Janice and I parted ways...."

She turned back. Faced him head on.

"...I think both of us were relieved. We'd always been better friends than lovers. We tried for Nora's sake, but there was no point."

"You're telling me this why?"

"Because you seem to think I don't want you around. It's not that. It's just...I only have a few hours. I want to talk to Janice about visitation and it's probably better if I do that without an audience."

"It's fine, really. I should get Daniel home anyway."

He took his hands out of his pockets again and reached for her, pulling her into a warm hug. Daniel squirmed in the close quarters but they both ignored him, focusing on each other instead.

"Are you jealous?" he whispered.

She smelled the clean, woodsy smell she was getting used to, the softness of the flannel of his quilted jacket. "Of course not," she lied.

"Charlie?"

"Hmmm?" Why was she getting so lost in his eyes? Daniel whimpered, the sound muffled in his plushy snowsuit.

"Are we starting something here? Because it feels like we are."

"Do you want to be?" she asked, and held her breath. The more she got to know him, the more her misgivings melted away. He had potential. He was a good man making his way through a complicated situation. Surely that was reason enough to curb her usual need to define and categorize and just chill. Take it one step at a time.

"How can you ask that? Ever since we met, I've been trying to find ways to spend time with you. You make me laugh, which is something I haven't done much of recently. You're kind and a little bit shy and..." He paused and framed her face with his other hand, too. "And you're beautiful. I'd be crazy not to want to see you again."

She pushed away the little voice that insisted that nowhere was a possible destination for the two of them. Charlie was getting thoroughly sick of hearing that voice, and she was starting to understand why. It was because every time she'd tried to make a decision for herself, her parents had insisted that it would take her nowhere.

That their way was better. Safer. They knew best way more than she did.

She swallowed. Told herself this wasn't about rebellion but about finally, finally trusting herself to make good decisions. To know what was best for herself. Like she had when she'd made the move to Jewell Cove.

"Me too," she whispered.

His lips were cold as they kissed, but she didn't mind in the least. With a slight groan of pleasure, she twined one arm around his neck, and he squeezed his around her waist, their bodies angled so they fit together without crushing the baby. The wind made a shushing sound in the fir trees around them, cocooning them from the outside world.

When they finally broke apart and Charlie's heels were back on solid ground, Dave gave a little chuckle. "Phew," he said.

"Phew is right. But I'd better go, let you get ready. I'll talk to you later?"

"I'll call. Let you know how it went."

She gave him a final peck on the lips and then stepped back, lifting a mittened hand in a wave. "Good luck."

"Thanks." He nodded at her. "And thanks for understanding, Charlie."

"Of course."

It only took a few moments to fasten Daniel back into the stroller and start home to the cottage, her thoughts whirling with Dave, his kiss, their conversation.

Chapter 9

When Charlie didn't hear from Dave on Sunday night, she pretty much reconciled herself to the fact that she'd been constructing sandcastles in the sky where he was concerned. A few dates and a few kisses did not a relationship make. Even if he had said it was something more. Obviously, it wasn't enough to get him to pick up the phone.

Reality check, Yang, she reminded herself early Monday morning as she cradled Daniel in one arm and poured herself a cup of Josh's high-test sludge from the office pot with her opposite hand. It had been a rough night. Daniel had fussed and she'd been up every two hours trying to get him to settle.

It was Josh who finally stepped into her office between patients and told her to sit for five minutes.

"You look like death warmed over. You need some time off?"

"Of course not." She was managing okay. It was just a bad day was all. "We had a rough night. Nothing serious."

He crossed his ankle over his knee. "Charlie, it's a big thing taking on a newborn. There's a reason why women take maternity leave."

"Is his being here a problem?"

Josh's face softened. "Of course not. The practice isn't that busy, and I don't mind covering a little bit. It's a good thing you're doing."

"Thanks, Josh." She let out a breath of relief. "I appreciate the support. You've been really understanding."

Josh smiled. "Hey, I'm not a scrooge. Besides, I know it's only temporary."

The words left a gaping hole in her heart. "I don't want to give him back," she confessed. Every maternal instinct she'd tamped down for the last few days came roaring back. She did want this. She wanted a family of her own, to love and to be loved. To be needed. She swallowed as she rubbed her hand over Daniel's tiny back.

Boy, Dave was right about one thing. Life didn't come with a perfect blueprint for happiness.

"Are you planning to adopt him?"

She swallowed. Was she? "I don't know. I want a family, but one thing I've learned the last few days is that being a single parent is really hard. I'm just enjoying him while I have him and trying not to worry too much about the future."

She sat back, surprised at the words that came out of her mouth. Her, the super planner, who had everything mapped out and on schedule. She was living in the here and now. Wouldn't Dave have something to say about that?

She wished she hadn't thought of Dave at this moment... Dave, who already had a child of his own. She wanted him to have a relationship with Nora, but she wondered how much room there was for her in that scenario. It had been nice spending time with him on the weekend. Wonderful, in fact. She wasn't a fast mover, but she'd definitely let her mind wander to certain places, wondering if they were headed in that direction.

But the reality was that the weekend was a little like a vacation. They'd shopped and ate pizza and kissed and flirted, but it was an anomaly. A nice memory. This, right here, was who she was. Anything else was just...

Vacation.

Josh tapped his chin, and she could tell he was considering his next words. Her stomach twisted with nerves. He was her boss, after all. And she knew she'd been juggling trying to care for Daniel and still see all her patients. She didn't want to let him down. And this morning she was just so tired....

"I was thinking," he said, his voice soft but firm, letting her know what was coming next wasn't exactly a suggestion. "Maybe you could find someone to help with Daniel while you're working, if you're so determined to not take time off."

Leave him home? With a sitter? At his age?

"He's bottle fed, which makes things much more convenient. You could use your office, set up a playpen, bring in a comfy chair. I even have the perfect candidate."

"You do?"

He nodded. "My mom. She's going crazy, waiting for more grandkids."

"Josh, I don't know what to say. You've asked her already, haven't you?"

He smiled. "I might have put a bug in her ear. You're not superwoman, Charlie. Just think about it and let me know. And when your last appointment happens this morning, go home. I'll cover walk-in today."

"But it's my shift..."

"Consider it a Christmas present. Or an order from your boss, if that doesn't work."

She was touched. Josh wasn't always touchy-feely, but his gesture was so thoughtful. After he left her office, Charlie grabbed the chart for her next patient.

She found herself wondering about Daniel's mother. In her job, she tried to keep an open mind, because she was generally shown time and again that unless you walked in someone else's shoes, you just didn't know what they had been through. But still, even if leaving him in the manger had been planned as they suspected, it was dangerous. Desperate.

Clearly, she wasn't entirely objective about this situation. But that was what she loved about this job, too. When she'd first moved here, she'd been so professional, able to distance herself from her patients. But slowly she'd started caring about them in more than just an empathetic way. They weren't family, but they were community.

The thought was comforting somehow. Maybe Josh was so good at it because he'd been here all his life. Maybe, just maybe, this was starting to be her home, too.

Shortly after eleven Dave texted to ask if she wanted to meet for lunch. She waited until her current appointment was finished, and then considered. Did she want to see him again? Hell, yes. She was dying to know what had happened between him and Janice.

When she caught her next break, she called him instead of texting, and asked if he was busy for dinner. When he said he wasn't, she offered to bring dinner to his place after work. She'd grab some takeout and meet him at the cottage.

She was afraid she might be falling for him, and how stupid was that? He wasn't even sure if he was staying in Jewell Cove, and she called herself ten times the fool for letting her imagination get the best of her.

Chapter 10

C harlie sat back in her chair and put her hand on her stomach. "Oh my God. I'm so stuffed I think I'm going to blow up." Dave was still polishing off his mountain of cashew chicken and fried rice, but Charlie was so full of Lo Mein that she couldn't think of eating another bite. "That was good."

It was extra nice to have a night out without the baby...in some ways, this felt like more of a date than their official date had. Tonight Meggie Collins was at Charlie's house, getting to know Daniel and crocheting something pretty out of pink yarn. Josh's idea had been a good one. Charlie loved looking after Daniel, but the break was lovely, too.

Dave nodded. "I haven't had takeout like that in ages. When I was stationed at Little Creek, there was this place we used to go to that had the best hot and spicy beef thing. It was perfect with a cold beer." He grinned at her. "Or two."

"Do you miss that life?" she asked. "Being in the Navy?"

"I wasn't just in the Navy, Charlie. I was a SEAL."

His smile had faded. "I know," she answered quietly. Just as she knew there was a difference. She'd never asked him what he'd done or seen or anything more about his job. She figured a man couldn't do a job like that without facing a few ugly truths about the world.

They sat in silence for a few more moments and then Charlie couldn't stand it.

She got up and started clearing away the mess. Maybe this hadn't been such a good idea after all. Dave didn't seem his usual happy-go-lucky self. He was...broody.

She rinsed the plates and started running water in the sink to wash the few dishes they'd dirtied. His chair scraped against the floor as he pushed it back and stood, and her heartbeat quickened a little when he came up behind her and reached around for the drying cloth.

"You didn't ask me about yesterday," he said. "It must be killing you."

Annoyance flared. "Don't flatter yourself."

He gave a little laugh at her sharp reply. "Easy, tiger. I just meant that you aren't always patient when it comes to wanting answers. I figure you're either not interested in what happened or you're too afraid to ask."

She hoped her expression portrayed calm and perhaps a touch of ennui. "Why on earth would I be afraid?"

"Charlie," he said quietly, and her heart knocked against her ribs.

"Don't say my name in that kind of voice. I've been an idiot, okay? We can just go back to being friends, like we said."

She scrubbed at a plate and put it in the drying rack. He instantly picked it up and dried it. "Whoever said we were just friends?"

She didn't reply. Damn, he was patient. More patient than she was. They continued washing the dishes until there was nothing left to wash, and then Charlie finally said what had been on the tip of her tongue ever since she walked in the door.

"You promised you'd call."

He put down the towel. "Okay…"

"When I left. You promised to call to let me know how it went. And then you didn't." She looked up at him.

"Charlie…"

She waved the rest of whatever he was going to say away.

"I know I'm being stupid. But you were right, I was jealous. You were talking about your family, and I kept thinking about you and Janice talking, bonding. And it's stupid, but when you didn't call. . ."

His lips curved the slightest bit. "Charlie, sweetheart." There was such warmth in his voice that it cut into Charlie. "Janice is pregnant again."

The words made Charlie look up at him quickly. To her surprise, he didn't look upset by the information. "She and her husband?" Charlie asked, then realized it was a stupid question. Dave and Janice had been over for a long time, right?

He nodded. "Yep. She's happy. Far happier than she was with me."

"And that bothers you?"

"That she's happy? Of course not. I'm happy for her, and happy for them. I guess if I was looking for a sign that Janice and I were wrong for each other, this is really it."

Charlie didn't even realize she'd been holding her breath until she let it out again in a long, measured exhale.

"I'm going to take a few days before Christmas and drive down. Take Nora her gifts and spend some time with her. That's what Janice wanted to talk about."

"Are you thinking of moving closer? It's not a huge drive from here to there, but it's long enough."

"Would it bother you if I did?" he asked, and silence fell in the room. What was he asking?

"Why would it bother me?" Why couldn't she come right out and ask what she wanted to ask? Say what she wanted to say? She didn't usually have a hard time speaking her mind. Maybe it was because she was afraid to hear the answer. "I've seen you with Daniel." She met his gaze. "I would never want to do anything to stand in the way of your relationship with your daughter."

She smiled up at him, feeling completely false. She wasn't cheerful. Wasn't happy. She was let down. Mad at herself for getting her hopes up. For pretending that it didn't matter that he wasn't looking for a relationship. "Anyway, I should go."

"So soon?" He came closer, close enough she had trouble breathing. "But I haven't decorated the tree yet. I thought we could do that together. It looks so naked, sitting in the stand with nothing on it."

She took a step back. "And then what? I don't think I can do this." Her insides trembled. Why was it so hard to say the truth? To verbalize her own needs? She would do it this time. She would.

"Do what?"

"This!" She gestured with her finger, moving it between the two of them. "I know what you said from the beginning. About seeing where all this goes, no pressure or anything. I know all this in my head, Dave. My head is not the problem."

"Then what the hell is?" he asked, his voice brittle. "I thought we were just going to enjoy being together, no strings, no demands."

"The problem," she said, her throat tight, "is that I'm not built that way. I want to be. I want to be that carefree, easy kind of person who can accept something at face value, who can live in the moment and enjoy it. And I've tried but it doesn't work, because that's not who I am. When you smile at me...when you kiss me..."

"You want more?"

"I want more. I want all of you and I know all of you isn't available."

He cursed. His dark gaze heated as they stared at each other, both breathing heavily as the tension closed in on them.

"You know I want you, right?"

God, how could he make his voice so smooth, so deep and sexy and filled with promise? This was what she was fighting against. Fighting and losing. When they were apart she could be rational. But when he was close, the moment he said or did something like this, she lost all perspective.

"Don't," she whispered. And wished the word had come out stronger.

"We've been doing this dance," he said, ignoring her plea. "Keeping things easy. You think your voice of reason is giving you trouble?" He was so close now she could almost feel the heat of his body against hers. "I find myself calling or texting and wanting to be with you and then when I'm with you I just want to touch you. Dammit, Charlie, it's been killing me to leave it at a few kisses and then walking away."

She swallowed. Hard. He was right before her now. Big, strong, former SEAL confessing to wanting her. Her, little Charlene Yang who always stayed in the background and never caused any trouble. Charlene Yang who had found it so difficult to make friends here that up until a few weeks ago she'd made do with watching him from a restaurant window and the most illuminating conversation she'd had was with a doll at the church nativity scene.

He wanted her. And she wanted him so badly she was nearly dying with it. The only thing holding her back was knowing that she would be giving him the power to really and truly hurt her. If she took one step in his direction, she'd be taking responsibility for that.

"Charlie," he murmured. "Look at me."

His eyes were so intense she stopped breathing for a second.

The anticipation was so strong that she would swear she could already feel him touching her even though they were inches apart.

"I used to see you working on the docks and wondered who you were," she admitted, her voice soft. She swallowed against a lump of nervousness in her throat. "I would imagine that you would show up somewhere and...and...and sweep me off my feet."

It should have sounded stupid but instead the words fanned the flames of attraction, ramping up the tension between them. "I just..." She bit down on her lip, realizing she was probably doing this badly, but stumbling along anyway. "I just want you to sweep me away. Can you do that?"

His breath came out in a rush and he reached down and clasped her hand, gripping it tightly. "You're sure? I'm asking because you'd better be damned sure you know what you're doing."

"Yes," she answered meekly. "Please."

He muttered something incomprehensible, stared at her for a long moment. The air snapped and sizzled between them and she licked her lips, watched his pupils widen, felt her muscles tighten with delicious anticipation. No one had ever looked at her that way. Not ever. Not with such desire and intent and all it did was fuel her own longings.

For once in her life she was not going to think or dissect or weigh the ramifications. She was going to feel and she'd let the cards fall where they may.

He reached over and pulled her straight into his arms. His mouth fused to hers, fierce in its intent, all-consuming and wonderful, his tongue sweeping into her mouth as his strong arm lifted her against his body, hard in all the right places. She loved his sheer physicality, and she wrapped her arms around his shoulders and held him tight.

His hands circled around and cupped her bottom, and she wrapped her legs around his waist. Dave made a raw sound in his throat and took a single step backward, which put her hips up against the kitchen counter, and she pressed her core against him, letting the pleasure of the moment soak in.

He backed off, breaking the kiss, running his tongue over his lower lip as if tasting her there. Her body was feeling jacked up and liquidy all at once. He reached for the neck of his T-shirt and pulled it over his head, revealing a muscled body that up to this moment, she'd only seen in pictures. For the first time in her life, any thoughts of anything beyond the next few minutes didn't exist. He'd succeeded in wiping them all away.

This time he took a little more time with her. He dropped the shirt on the floor and stepped back in the v of legs, kissing her again, slowly and persuasively. She slid her hands over the hard curves of his shoulders, loving the feel of his warm skin beneath her fingertips. Encouraged, she reached down and slid her hand along the curve of his ass, pulling him closer against her.

His breathing grew ragged, all from her simple touch. It amazed her that she had that sort of effect on him, and it fed her female vanity.

"You drive me crazy," he said, sliding his lips over her cheek and pulling her earlobe into his mouth. When making out in the kitchen was no longer enough, he wrenched his mouth from hers and picked her up in his arms as if she weighed nothing.

Swoonworthy. The guy had gone into total alpha mode and she loved it. She linked her arms around his neck and let him carry her down the hall to his bedroom.

"You took the 'sweep me away' thing seriously," she said softly, looking up at him as he laid her gently on the bed.

"I'm just getting started," he answered, flicking on the bedside lamp, reaching into the night table drawer for a condom.

Oh God. They were really doing this. And she was going to get to enjoy that body, have it all to herself. What a giddy thought.

Dave sat on the edge of the bed and reached for her. She sat up and moved into his arms, losing herself in the feeling of having him surround her. He gently pulled the elastic from her hair and sank his hands into the heavy mass of it, pulling her head back as he undid the braid, the weight of it falling over her shoulders. With her head tipped back, he took full advantage and dipped his head, running his tongue over the sensitive flesh of her neck. When his fingers slid from her hair and traced a gentle path down the side of her face, goose bumps broke out over her skin.

"You're sure?" he asked, and she loved the way his gaze searched her face. Hungry, but not reckless. She was hungry too. Hungry for him.

"I'm sure." Slowly, she reached for the buttons of her shirt. One by one she undid them, slipping them from the buttonholes, pulling the tails out of her trousers.

Dave took over then, pushing the soft fabric off her shoulders until she was sitting before him in her bra. She was doubly glad she'd worn the black one today, with the scalloped lace around the edges. Her breasts strained against the material, the peaks hard and pointed in anticipation of his touch.

"Wow." His grin slipped sideways, teasing her. "You drive me crazy, you know that?"

"Likewise," she answered, and this time he pushed her back into the comforter and she got to feel the heat of his skin pressed against hers. She was pretty sure it was the most erotic feeling on earth, this skin-to-skin thing.

He reached behind her and undid the clasp of her bra with one hand, then pulled it down her arms and dropped it on the floor. "It's pretty," he murmured. "But not as pretty as this." He cupped a breast in his hand and then let his mouth follow.

She was going to die, she was sure of it. But if this is what it felt like, she was totally okay with it. When he licked her nipple, a moan slid from her throat.

After that everything seemed to speed up. Hands hurried, stripping off the last of the clothing, scattering it on the floor until they were both naked on the bed. His hands and mouth seemed to be everywhere, igniting her senses until her whole body was on fire. Charlie reached out and took him in her fingers and he groaned. "We need to slow down," he said, his breath hot in her ear. "Or I swear to God it's going to be over before it gets started."

She giggled with the sheer elation of pure feminine power.

He reached for the condom. "You're prepared." Her heart hammered against her ribs. This was where all the foreplay was leading. To him. Inside her. She didn't want to wait. She wanted to grab the packet, rip the foil and get on with it. Never in her life had she felt this pounding need for fulfillment.

"After what happened at your place...I wasn't going to take any chances. I knew this day was coming."

She watched, intrigued, as he took care of putting it on. Then all she could do was lose herself in the overwhelming sensations of being completely and thoroughly pleasured by a lover, once, twice, and a third time that left her so weak and sated she could barely move. Then, and only then, did he release the hold on his control, growling her name as he pushed her up the bed until she felt the headboard against her skull.

Moments later, the harsh sounds of their breathing began to temper and the sweat on their bodies cooled. Charlie lay on her side, looking over at him, marveling that they'd just done everything they'd done.

There'd been no choice to make once he'd touched her. She'd been incapable of stopping. They had simply lost themselves in each other. He'd possessed every square inch of her body and now she felt gloriously limp in the afterglow.

Then she heard it... a low, satisfied chuckle that reached in and warmed her from the inside out.

"What's so funny?" she asked, unable to keep the smile from her face.

"Nothing's funny." He rolled over to his side and opened his eyes. "That was just...spectacular." He grinned at her. "Who knew you were so bendy, Chuckles?"

She should take him to task with calling her Chuckles right now. And she would, except...well, she liked it. From him, anyway. "I've done a lot of yoga."

"I hear it's supposed to be good for stress."

If he only knew.

She raised an eyebrow. "Anytime you want to try. Naked yoga is liberating." His eyes widened and she laughed as she teased him. "Nothing like getting in touch with your spirituality when it's just you and the mat."

"Eeeew."

Her lips twitched.

"You're teasing."

"I am."

He reached over and grazed his fingers over her hip. "I like it."

She did, too. He was the most comfortable-in-his-own-skin man she'd ever met. It was more than the boneless bliss she was feeling after a thorough love-making. It was a freedom, a lightness that she suspected came from living in the moment rather than from an agenda.

She shivered and Dave reached towards the bottom of the bed, pulling up a blanket to cover them. Then he lay on his back and opened his arm wide. "Come here," he said quietly. "We can huddle up to keep warm."

She was still naked. She suspected she should be feeling if not bashful, at least a little self-conscious. But she wasn't. She slid over next to him and rested her head along the curve of his shoulder, draped one arm over his ribs and lifted her knee, settling it along the length of his leg.

"God, you're a cuddler," he murmured, squeezing her close.

She never used to be.

"Is that okay?"

"Yeah." There was this texture to his voice that she would never tire of. A bit deep, a bit husky, one-hundred percent sexy. She closed her eyes and let out a breath.

"You know, I'm kind of sorry I stopped things that first morning. If I'd known this was waiting for me..."

He chuckled and the vibration rippled through her. "I'll take that as a compliment."

"You should."

"You're not so bad yourself."

Her hand ran up his back and encountered smooth scar tissue. It reminded her of what he'd been through...the parts she knew about and the parts she didn't. She traced her finger along its path. "What is this from?"

He shrugged. "Oh, one of my many badges of honor. No big deal."

"It doesn't hurt?"

"Not anymore." Then he smiled wickedly. "Wait. If I said it did, would you kiss it better?"

She swatted his shoulder.

"You want to talk about it?"

"I've just had mind-blowing sex and a gorgeous woman is naked in my arms. What do you think?"

She smiled in the darkness. "Obvious distraction, but I still have to ask. You think I'm gorgeous?"

"Are you kidding?" His wide palm curved over her hip. "Have you looked in a mirror lately?"

She relaxed further, sinking into his embrace, twining her legs with his and running her toes up one of his calves. "Hey, Dave?"

"Hmm?"

"I needed that." After she said it she realized it was a bit ambiguous. She could have been talking about the sex or the compliment. Truthfully, she thought she rather needed them both.

He kissed her forehead. "I know."

She wasn't quite sure what he meant, but she was too mellow to ask. He felt so good. Warm and strong. The blanket was soft on her skin and he'd turned off the light, so the room was gray and dim. The wood stove in the next room had been stoked and the heat of it made her feel lazy. She was going to doze off and she was completely okay with it.

She curled into his embrace. "It's so warm and toasty in here. I never realized how great wood heat was. So much nicer than a furnace or radiator."

He nodded against her hair. "A stove can really crank it out. Plus, if the power goes out, I can stay warm. Cook. It's a bit rudimentary, but convenient."

She imagined being snowbound here with him and the idea held some merit.

The stove meant he had to split wood, she thought. She took a moment to appreciate the image in her mind of him with an axe, his muscles bulging and shifting as he split logs. When had she started going for the physical labor kind of guy?

She snuggled in closer. She supposed that happened when she'd first seen him on the docks in the fall, all work boots and broad shoulders and a ball cap.

"Charlie?" His voice was soft in her ear, sending ripples of pleasure down her spine.

"Mmm?" She answered lazily.

"Stay a while?"

She turned in his arms so she could look up at him. His hair, just a touch on the shaggy side, was ruffled and mussed, and his jaw held a hint of stubble after the long day. He was so attractive. So...virile.

"I wish I could. But Daniel's staying with Josh's mom and I should get back soon."

"Right. Damn." His fingers slid along the soft skin of her arm. "Maybe just a little while longer?"

"A little while," she agreed.

She hadn't realized he was tense until his shoulders relaxed. "Cool." His fingers ran up and down her arm, an absent-minded gesture that Charlie reveled in.

Good heavens, what would her mother say? Her mom had always pushed her to "guard her sexuality like a priceless treasure." Charlie rolled her eyes. Mother probably expected Charlie to have remained a virgin, too. She sobered. Well, it had been long enough she wondered if she could reclaim virgin status. Up until tonight, that is.

Dave's fingers traced a slow, gentle line up the outside of her arm and she gave in, letting out one last deep breath before sliding into sleep.

Chapter 11

H er breathing was deep and even.
Her skin was soft, and a scent like vanilla and flowers filled his nostrils; soft and light and mingled with the scent of sex.

He hadn't expected it to be so...consuming. So possessive. But from the moment he'd put her on the bed and stripped her of her jeans, something had clicked.

He'd never been a dominating man and it wasn't like that now, either. But there'd been a crushing need to possess her and, conversely, to be possessed by her. To know that he was capable of bringing her to ecstasy over and over again and to hear his name on her lips as she shuddered around him. And then...not to take her, but to lose himself inside her.

And that scared the shit out of him. Big time. Despite the spontaneity of the moment, being with her hadn't been thoughtless or fun or careless. It had been fast and sometimes rough and other times inspired, but he'd made sure to protect her and when their eyes had met as he climaxed something had shifted painfully inside him. A connection he hadn't been prepared for. If he wasn't careful, he might fall in love with her.

A delicate snuffle came from beside him. She was really and truly asleep in his arms and it filled him with a sweetness he'd forgotten existed. There was trust in making love, but it was fueled by desire and lust and need. The real trust was now, afterwards. And clearly Charlie trusted him.

The idea made him panic just a little bit. He hadn't planned on staying in Jewell Cove. His dad had hooked him up with the job at George's, something to keep him going until he found a permanent situation. Except, he admitted to himself, he hadn't been looking for a different situation. Charlie made staying seem...possible. Perfect, maybe.

Charlie wasn't the kind of woman a man fooled around with. He'd understood that from the start. So he either had to break it off with her and let her go, or really be involved. They'd been fooling themselves, thinking they could keep things casual.

But being open to the possibility of "them" meant opening himself up to the chance of loving...or being hurt. Or worse—hurting her. Because deep down he knew they were two very different people. She loved plans and charts and lists, and he knew life involved a certain measure of improvisation. She had a day planner, and he went with the flow. Wouldn't they end up driving each other crazy?

Her arm tightened and his eyes slammed closed, loving the feel of her wrapped around him so damn much it scared him. He'd forgotten what it was like to be the center of someone's world, even for five minutes.

She was the center of his, too. At least for a little while. So he left his eyes closed and let his muscles relax, shifting a little so they were entwined together. He'd wake her soon, but not yet. He wanted to hold on to the perfection of this moment as long as he could. Then he'd do what he had to do.

***

Charlie woke slowly, then lifted her arms and executed a long, limber stretch. She couldn't remember a time when she felt this relaxed. The soft fleece blanket slid over her skin and she realized she was still naked.

Her cheeks heated and her stomach did a little flip. Oh my. They'd done it.

Charlie, who planned everything, who examined every angle of a situation before making a decision, had taken a huge leap and had sex with Dave Ricker.

It had been amazing. Stupendous.

And she was alone in the bed.

She crawled out from beneath the blankets and shivered in the cool air. Draped over a chair was a flannel shirt, and she picked it up and put her arms in the big sleeves, buttoning it up the front. It was huge. The cuffs came down over her hands and the tails covered her to mid-thigh. Charlie lifted a handful of the fabric and drew a long breath, her head filling with his scent. As an afterthought, she snagged her panties from the floor and stepped into them. Barefoot, she left the bedroom and went in search of him.

He was in the kitchen. Dressed in plaid pyjama pants and a t-shirt, he looked both adorably cuddly and casually sexy. He was whisking something in a pan on the stove, and there was a hint of chocolate in the air.

"That smells good," she said softly, and he spun around.

"You are some quiet," he said, smiling at her. "I didn't hear you get up."

She went forward to see what he was concocting. "Oooh, hot cocoa. Yum."

"Made with real milk, none of that powdered stuff." He smiled at her, but she got the slippery feeling that something was wrong. He was too nice. Too polite. "I was going to wake you soon. It's nearly ten. I thought some hot cocoa before you had to relieve your sitter."

"At least it's a bit warmer out here," she said, wrapping her arms around her middle.

"I brought in some wood for the fire, too." His gaze dropped to her improvised nightshirt. "Nice," he added.

Not that she'd say it out loud, but she'd watched lots of movies where the confident, sexy woman wore her lover's shirt after sex, and wondered what it would be like to be that girl. It felt fantastic, if she were being honest. Who knew she could be that woman, anyway? It's not like she had a history of hookups and men certainly hadn't been beating down her door. She suspected, however, if she said anything of the sort she'd sound silly and awkward, so she met his gaze evenly. "You don't mind?"

"Of course not."

But there was no innuendo, no shared intimate look or smile. Unless she was totally off base, Dave was backing off. Big time. Why? Maybe tonight hadn't been as good for him as it had been for her...

"Dave, did I do something wrong?"

He spared her a glance. "Of course not." It seemed to be his stock answer. His gaze slipped back to the pan and grabbed a ladle. "Hand me a mug, will you?"

Mechanically she took a cup from the cupboard and handed it to him. He poured the rich cocoa into the mug and handed it to her, then repeated the process with his own cup.

She perched on a chair at the table, unsettled, and sipped. "What's wrong?" she asked.

She knew whatever he was about to say was a lie because his face took on an expression of innocent denial. "Nothing. Why would something be wrong?"

"Because you're acting strangely. Because I woke up and you weren't there, and you've brought in wood and made cocoa. Something's on your mind, I can tell."

He sighed. Stared into his cup. "We can talk about it later. You need to get home soon."

Classic avoidance. Charlie tried taking a drink to simply be doing something but the moment it touched her tongue her stomach twisted.

There were times Charlie deeply resented her upbringing, but today she totally understood what her mother had meant when she said that sex had the power to change everything. In this case, it hadn't changed in a fairy-tale-come-true way, had it?

She didn't trust herself to speak. Thought back to that first moment that they'd met, how unsettled and awkward she'd been. The man before her wasn't some fantasy guy from the docks anymore. That seemed like another time and place. He was real, flesh and blood, and currently pulling away from her.

And then she looked across the table at Dave and knew that she couldn't pretend forever. She was tired of feeling like she always had to please people. That if she was just quiet and went along with everyone else's plans for her everything would be fine.

She'd come to Jewell Cove to get away from that. Trouble was, she was still accepting it in her personal relationships and that wasn't okay.

"I have a few minutes. If something's wrong, I want to know."

He shifted in his chair. Charlie frowned. Difficult conversations were so not her strength.

"It's fine."

"No, it's not. Dave, we made love. You asked me to stay. Now you're treating me like nothing happened." Encouraged by the steadiness of her voice, she lifted her chin. "Honestly, I don't think I did anything wrong. Which means you're running scared. What I want to know is why."

He pushed back his chair and took his mug—his cocoa unfinished—to the counter.

"Hey," she said. "Avoidance is my party trick. For God's sake, Dave, just be honest with me. If you think we made a mistake, just say so."

He turned around and met her gaze. "Being with you was great," he answered, his voice rough. "But yeah, it was probably a mistake. My mistake, Charlie, not yours. I got involved with you when I knew I shouldn't have."

She gave a quiet snort. "That makes two of us."

"See? That's what I mean. We were both pretty honest from the beginning about what we did and didn't want.

Then we ignored it. Convinced ourselves it didn't matter. I told myself it was nothing serious. That we were just enjoying each other's company."

"Until tonight. Because sex changes things."

He nodded slowly. "Yeah, it does. And all the things I'd been ignoring were suddenly there in front of me again. I'm not sure I can be the perfect man for your perfect plan."

Her body felt strangely heavy. Perhaps it was the weight of disappointment. She thought it was more likely that it was inevitability, because she knew, deep down, that he was right. She'd always thought so.

He ran his hand through his hair. "I told you from the beginning that I wasn't staying in Jewell Cove. That I'm not sure what the future holds. Shit, Charlie. I've tried a serious relationship and I'm terrible at it. The idea of marriage..."

"Who said anything about marriage?" she interrupted, turning in her chair so she was facing him, and crossed her left knee over her right. "Aren't you getting a little ahead of yourself?"

"Am I?" He stared at her. "Come on, Charlie. You're not a fling sort of person. You're a lifer. You want the whole enchilada. The husband and the kids and the little house in the 'burbs. You're a liar if you say otherwise."

"I never asked any of that from you."

He paced through the tiny kitchen. "I know that. That's what I'm saying. We knew this about each other, but we pretended not to notice. I told myself it would be okay. That you knew what you were getting into. That it was only a few dates and a handful of kisses and it was no big deal. Until..."

Silence fell over the kitchen.

"Until?" she finally prompted.

He let out a breath. "Until tonight. Tonight was a big deal. It wasn't just a kiss goodnight. It was..."

Again he paused and she met his gaze evenly. She knew what he wasn't saying.

There'd been a connection between them that had been far more potent than either of them had expected.

"It was too much for you," she said quietly. "You're right, you know. I do want those things. I always have. And I told myself I didn't and I conveniently forgot I did when we were together because I like being with you. I like kissing you and I loved making love with you. You're absolutely right, Dave. I want the whole enchilada."

She deserved better. "I spent my whole childhood feeling like I was in the way. I took what attention I could get. Dressed in what I was supposed to, showed up at events when it was requested, got good marks. Tried to please them, anything to get a smidgen of genuine affection. To mean as much to them as their precious jobs and precious itineraries. And you know what? It never worked. And you know what that made me? Afraid. Timid. Unable to stand up for myself. Do you know what happened when I took this job? I had already signed the contract and rental agreement before I told my parents. I didn't even tell them until I was already here in Jewell Cove. Even when I was rebelling, I was afraid to confront them. Afraid to disappoint them."

"Jesus, Charlie."

"Yeah. And I was afraid to disappoint you, too, so I told myself I'd just go along with whatever you wanted. Not interested in a relationship or a family? That was okay. We'd just have fun. But you are so right. I'm not built that way. I want a man who loves me, and a family of my own and children who can be whatever the hell they want when they grow up as long as they're happy. I want them to feel love and acceptance and I want smiles and laughter. I want it all, Dave. And tonight, for about five minutes, I caught a glimpse of what it could be like if you gave us half a chance."

"I told you..."

"I know. I didn't listen. I heard what I wanted to and ignored the rest."

She was slightly out of breath, amazed that she'd said all that, wondering how she'd kept it inside all these years.

Dave was staring at her in shock.

"What the hell are you so scared of?" she asked. "Or is it that you don't have the capacity to care at all? Is that it?"

"Maybe I don't. Maybe I'm just a selfish prick who only thinks about himself. Maybe I've got a huge ego and the world revolves around me. That's what you're saying, isn't it? Or is it that I'm a coward? Which option is most appealing to you?" His words were hard, brittle. The heat in his eyes had cooled, dulled. "We both pretended for a while, but I'd just hurt you in the end, Charlie."

Once again silence fell over the room. There was something he wasn't saying. Something more than his marriage. He'd been pretty forthcoming about that, so she guessed whatever it was had to be important. Hurtful.

"Shit," he said, quieter now. "It wasn't supposed to be this way. I thought I could handle it. Tonight was amazing. You need to understand that. But this has to stop now, before someone gets hurt. Before I hurt you."

She blinked a couple of times. She would not babble, or cry, or be an emotional wreck. She would also be honest, because wrong or right, she'd started to believe they had a chance. "Don't you get it? You already hurt me."

"Don't say that."

"What, and lie?" She went to him, put her hand flat on his chest. "You're a good man, you know. Somehow, somewhere, I think someone made you feel like you weren't. And I think that's not because you let someone down but because someone let you down. Until you figure that out, you're never going to be happy."

"You'd better get home to Daniel."

There was no emotion in his words, just dismissal and finality. She retreated to the bedroom and pulled on her clothes, braided her hair, and went back to the kitchen, where Dave was sitting at the table, staring into his cup of cold cocoa.

Wordlessly she put on her boots and her jacket and picked up her handbag. She went out and shut the door behind her, latching it with a quiet click, wondering how she could have been so stupid as to let herself fall in love with the wrong man.

Chapter 12

Charlie ended up putting in extra hours at the clinic. A flu outbreak swept through the schools, and she and Josh doubled up their hours so that whenever one was taking appointments, the other was working walk in or administering flu shots. The lead up to Christmas was anything but relaxing, and it was only Meggie's help with babysitting that kept her afloat. She managed to package Lizzie's presents and ship them off, with a promise to visit for a weekend in the new year. As the virus spread, Josh and Charlie saw increased numbers of senior citizens presenting with the same symptoms that often progressed to bronchitis or pneumonia, both of which required more than simple rest and fluids.

By December eighteenth, it hit Charlie and laid her flat for three days of fever, chills, and a hoarse cough. She spent her down time on the sofa with a soft blanket, drinking hot lemon and honey and sleeping whenever Daniel saw fit to nap too. Because he was so small, she took particular care with hand washing, praying he didn't come down with it too. And during her waking hours she spent way too much time thinking.

Thinking about Dave, and how everything had gone wrong, and how for the first time in several years she'd fancied herself in love.

How could that be? She'd always believed a big component of being in love was being loved in return. That it wasn't one-sided. But he certainly hadn't loved her. Liked her, yes. Enjoyed her company, yes.

But he hadn't been a fool like her. She replayed moments in her mind; how they'd look into each other's eyes, the way he kissed, how he laugh at something and tilt his head back just a little bit. The way he raised one eyebrow just a little before he said something sarcastic, and the way only one dimple popped when he smiled.

She'd been smitten. No doubt about it. And she missed him. She could tell herself she didn't, but what purpose did that serve? No sense lying to herself. He was up the road at his cottage or working in town and going about his day completely and absolutely without her. Like she didn't even matter.

Charlie's bout of self-pity was interrupted by a knock on the door. It was Josh, and he carried a box in his arms.

She tugged her blanket closer around herself, blinked at him blearily, and held open the door. "What on earth is that?"

"Word got around town that you came down with this bug. It's a care package."

She stepped aside as he came in and stomped off his boots. "A care package?"

He nodded. "Today I'm your delivery boy. Can you take this?"

She took the box from his arms, shocked at how weak she felt. Once he'd removed his boots, he took the box back. "Let's put this in your kitchen."

She followed behind him, her slippers scuffing against the floor as she sniffled and then reached for a tissue from the box on the counter. Josh put everything down on her table and started taking things out.

An ice cream container which he handed over. "My mom's chicken soup. Her not-so-secret ingredient is a dash of curry powder. You look like hell. I recommend a bowl of it, stat."

She laughed a little, which started her coughing. Without saying a word, Josh found a glass and got her some water.

Then he took a bowl from the cupboard, poured some of the soup into it and shoved it in the microwave.

"Right. Next...Shirley at the Leaf and Grind sent over some tea." He put the little tin on the table. "She recommends honey to sweeten it. Jess sent eucalyptus candles to help with congestion." Those went beside the tea. "Mary at the bakery brought in a dozen cinnamon rolls, which annoys the hell out of me because no one ever gives me cinnamon rolls and they're my favorite." The rolls were added to the assortment on the tabletop.

Josh handed over a small plastic bottle. "Robin says to take a hot bath with some of this in it and you'll feel lots better."

Charlie was overwhelmed. Good heavens, homemade soup and tea and aromatherapy...just for coming down with the flu? "What about you, Josh?" she joked, as the microwave beeped, indicating her soup was done. "What did you bring me?"

She opened the door and caught a little of the scent, even through her plugged nose.

Her stomach rumbled and she realized she couldn't remember when she'd put anything other than fluids in her tummy.

Josh held up a bottle. "I'm not much of a cook. But codeine cough syrup will do. You should at least get some sleep." He grinned at her. "You really do look like hell, Charlie. Do you need someone to take Daniel for a day or two?"

"Thanks for this," she grumbled, but then she looked up at him and smiled a bit. "Thank you, Josh. And Dan and I will be fine. He's been sleeping better lately, only up once in the night. I just put him down. I should be good until about one in the morning." She took a sip of water. ""This is pretty amazing and a real surprise."

He gave a shrug. "That's what happens in a place like Jewell Cove. People help each other out. Sometimes it's suffocating, but everyone means well. Almost everyone, anyway," he amended with a crooked smile.

She sat down at the table with her soup. "You want to join me? There's lots here."

"I'm good. I'll sit for a minute though, if you don't mind."

"Okay." It seemed odd that he'd hang around, but her head was pretty fuzzy. She might not be the best judge of what was weird and normal at the moment. The first taste of soup made her close her eyes in gratitude. The broth was hot and rich and filled with vegetables and chicken and soft noodles. "Oh, tell Meggie that this is delicious and just what I needed."

"I will." He hesitated for a minute and then leaned on the table on his elbows. "Charlie, are you okay?"

"It's just the flu, Josh."

"That's not what I mean." He looked slightly uncomfortable. "Look, I don't like to pry into people's private lives, but you've been burning the candle at both ends for the last week and now you're sick and it looked like things were heating up with that Dave guy. Did something happen there?"

"There's nothing happening there, don't worry," she replied, scooping up more soup to keep busy, to keep her from thinking too much.

"Do I need to have a talk with him?"

She swallowed and looked up in surprise. "What?"

"You're my business partner now. And my friend. And if you need help, I hope you know you can ask me."

A silly grin broke out over her face. "Are you saying you'd beat up Dave Ricker if he hurt my feelings, Josh?"

Josh looked at her evenly. "He's a big boy. Not sure I'd beat him up, but I'd give it a good try."

Her eyes stung with unexpected tears. "That's sweet. I never had a big brother, you know. But this feels like something a big brother would say."

He smiled at her. "Look around you, Charlie. You're part of this community. People care about you. I know it's hard at first, coming to a place where it seems everyone has known each other forever, and have all this shared past stuff. It's hard to come back to that too, you know. I didn't find it easy last year. People get in your business. But they're also there when you need them. I guess what I'm saying is, don't let this get you down. There are people who care about you."

"Wow, Josh, this is pretty touchy-feely for you."

He chuckled. "Don't I know it. My sisters are much better at this kind of thing, but since you and I share an office, I put on my big girl panties."

Josh could be really businesslike, or so charismatic that Charlie often felt outmatched. But he was really approachable today, relaxed and cracking jokes.

"I'll be fine. Dave and I just want different things. We kind of ignored it for a while, but there it is. It wouldn't have worked out anyway."

"Bummer," Josh replied.

She laughed, coughed, and then sighed. "Yeah. Bummer."

"Well, listen, I should go and let you get your rest. We miss you back at the office. I was run off my feet today."

"Now I know why you brought this stuff over. So you can get me back in the office and go back to your cushy hours."

He laughed. She saw him to the door, and when he was ready to go, she thanked him again. Once he was gone, she returned to the kitchen, finished her soup, and decided to run a bath using some of Robin's bubbles.

It wasn't until she sank into the hot water that she let the emotions in. She'd been holding them back for days now, but the virus, added to her long work hours and then the unexpected generosity of friends had her protective shields down. The steam made a peppermint and eucalyptus scented cloud in the bathroom as she finally cried.

She'd trusted him. She'd believed in him. Wrong or right, foolish or not, she had. And for a brief, wonderful moment, she'd lain in his arms and believed in the possibility of forever.

But that moment was gone. It was time she let it all out and then moved on.

***

December 23rd rolled around. Charlie had received a huge parcel from Lizzie and placed it beside the Christmas tree since it was too big to fit underneath. She'd mostly recovered from her flu, though by the time she got home at night she was exhausted.

Honestly, she was looking forward to having the two extra days off for Christmas and Boxing Day. With nothing planned, she'd eat her take out, talk to Lizzie, watch a few movies and drink hot cocoa. To her surprise, several other packages made an appearance. Not so much for her, but for Daniel. There was something from Meggie, which wasn't a huge surprise, but also packages from Josh's sisters with Daniel's name on them. Robin gave her a care package for pampering herself and there was a little gift bag with something for Daniel. She sat in front of the tree with him, watching the curiosity in his eyes as the colorful lights lit up the room, and kissed his soft, downy head. She wasn't alone. And maybe he wouldn't understand what was going on or remember a thing, but she was determined to have a real Christmas for his sake.

Even though the outbreak was winding down, the clinic was still busy. Between regular appointments and walk-ins, both Josh and Charlie were run off their feet. It was mid-afternoon when Charlie stepped into the exam room to meet a new patient. The chart said she was a walk-in and her name was Michelle Green.

"Hi, Michelle." She smiled at the young girl sitting next to the bed. "I'm Dr. Yang. What can I help you with today?"

The girl didn't look particularly sick, though her color was a bit pale and her hair was limp. Mostly she looked tired. No, not tired. Worn. Charlie smiled reassuringly.

"I, uh..." The girl suddenly looked down. Lifted her hand and started chewing on a fingernail.

Charlie's heart softened. She couldn't be more than eighteen, maybe nineteen, and something was clearly bothering her. Charlie sat on her rolling stool and edged her way closer to Michelle, so they were sitting facing each other at equal heights.

"Are you ill? Or is there a problem I can help you with?" Charlie touched Michelle's knee lightly. "I'm here to help. Everything is confidential."

Michelle looked up, her blue eyes swimming with tears. "Are you the Dr. Yang who found that baby a few weeks ago?"

It was a strange question to ask, and Charlie's heart started beating faster. Oh my. She was going to have to tread very, very carefully. Could this be Daniel's mother?

"I am."

Michelle looked down again and Charlie saw a tear streak down the girl's cheek. "Is he okay?" she whispered.

Charlie nodded, a lump in her throat. She was sure now. No one else would come into her office, asking these questions, their emotions so raw. "He's doing just fine."

She nodded again. "Okay. Thanks. I should go..." Awkwardly, the girl got up and reached for an old winter jacket hanging on the back of her chair.

"Don't go yet," Charlie said, alarmed but trying to adopt a soothing tone. "Michelle, have you seen a doctor since you delivered? You're a little pale. It wouldn't hurt to have a checkup, make sure everything's okay."

"I don't know what you mean." She gripped the jacket tightly, and her face took on a belligerent expression. But Charlie could see beyond it to the fear. This poor kid.

Charlie reached out and rubbed Michelle's arm reassuringly. "It's okay. I promise you it'll be okay."

"I just... Oh God." She sank back down into the chair and covered her face with her hands.

Charlie kept her voice soft. "You put him in the manger on purpose, didn't you?"

Michelle nodded, moved her hands so they were in her lap, twisting together nervously. "I knew everyone would be at the tree lighting and I saw you and your husband walking by. I waited to make sure..."

At that point she dissolved into tears. Charlie squatted in front of her and held her hands. "You waited to make sure..."

Michelle hiccupped. "That you noticed. I wouldn't have left him there alone. If no one had come I would have gone back for him. I wouldn't have let him die." She sobbed again. "I wouldn't have done that. I just didn't know what else to do. I couldn't look after him...I didn't want anyone to know..."

"Of course. It's all right. We're going to make everything all right, okay?"

"I just wanted to know he was okay."

"And he is. Michelle, can you tell me where and when you had your baby? Were you in a hospital?"

She nodded. "Yes, in Dover, on November nineteenth."

Across the state line in New Hampshire. Which was why nothing had turned up when they checked Maine hospitals.

"And everything went all right?"

She nodded again. "I was discharged the next morning. A friend came to pick me up and take me...home."

"No complications since?"

The pale pallor of her skin made way for a slight blush. "Um, I bled a lot."

"Are you still bleeding?"

She shook her head. "Not for the past couple of days."

That was a relief, then. She really did need a thorough exam, but Charlie wanted to keep her talking as much as she could. "Michelle? Do you want to tell me why you left your baby here in Jewell Cove?"

Charlie could see Michelle swallow. The girl wouldn't meet her eyes again and Charlie could understand why. Michelle was fighting a battle within herself...wanting to know about the welfare of her child while at the same time probably feeling ashamed and embarrassed and scared.

"It's okay. I'm not here to judge you."

Another pause, and then Michelle spoke. "I couldn't look after him. When I got pregnant, my parents kicked me out. I was working at the mall and living on my own, but I could barely make the rent. I didn't qualify for any maternity leave and I couldn't go back to work because I couldn't afford day care. All he did was cry. All I did was cry. I couldn't think of what else to do. A friend of mine lent me her car and I just...drove. When I was in Portland, I heard some people in the store talking about driving up to Jewell Cove for the weekend, that there was some big tree lighting event every year. I thought it would be pretty. I didn't even think about what I was going to do until I drove by the church and saw the manger there, all lit up."

Her tears had stopped, and she finally met Charlie's gaze again. "I was stupid. I know that now. I'm not equipped to be a mom, Dr. Yang. And Jewell Cove...it's nice here. It seemed like a place where a kid could be happy, you know?" Her voice caught. "I thought it was just better if I... disappeared."

"But it wasn't better, was it?"

She shook her head. "I wanted him to have a better life than I could give him. I let him down. So I parked behind the church. And then you guys came along and I knew he'd be okay."

Michelle broke down again, and Charlie let her cry it out. She snagged the stool again and sat down, staying close to the overwrought girl. "Are you feeling a little better now? What do you say we give you that exam?"

Michelle screwed up her face and Charlie laughed a little, trying to lighten the mood. "I know. Not your favorite thing in the world. But making sure you're healthy is number one right now, okay?"

She nodded. "Okay."

Charlie went to the cupboard and took a gown out of the drawer, a real cotton one rather than the paper they normally used. She would treat this girl with kid gloves. It was a sensitive situation that was going to get worse before it got better. "I'll leave you for a minute to change."

"Dr. Yang?"

Charlie put her hand on the doorknob, and then turned back.

"What's going to happen to me now?"

Charlie smiled reassuringly. "Let's get this exam over with first. Then we'll worry about the rest, okay?"

She slid out of the room and shut the door behind her, then rested her head against the wall for a moment.

"Charlie?"

Josh's worried voice came from his office across the hall. She opened her eyes and let out a sigh.

"Make sure she doesn't leave, okay?" Charlie poked her head into his office. "Daniel's mom is in there."

"Holy shit."

"I know. She's scared to death. I'm going to give her an exam."

"Do you want me to call Bryce?"

She thought for a moment. If Michelle had left the baby at a hospital, or a police station, it would have been better for her. But she hadn't. She'd abandoned the baby in a church yard.

"I've got her talking. Give me some time. I may be able to get her to come around to turning herself in. It would be the right thing to do. She needs help. She's just a kid, Josh."

Josh nodded. "You've got a good heart, Charlie. I'll hang around a bit, though, in case you need me to make that call."

"Thanks."

She took a moment to go to the reception desk and quietly asked Robin to cancel the rest of her afternoon appointments. The whole time she fought against the sinking feeling that she might lose Daniel. What had initially been a situation lasting a few days had been weeks and she couldn't imagine the cottage without him. But he wasn't hers, and she had to remember that. Steeling her spine, she gathered what she needed and re-entered the exam room, pasting on a new smile.

While the exam was uncomfortable, Charlie was reassured that Michelle was doing fine. Rather than give her a requisition for blood work that would never get done, Charlie did it right then and there. She expected they'd find some slight anemia, and figured what Michelle really needed was a few good meals, some rest, and counseling sessions. Michelle had gotten dressed again and Charlie pulled a chair over next to the girl's.

"So. What do you want to do now?"

"I don't know. I could go back to Dover..."

Charlie was relieved that going home didn't seem too appealing. "What do you really want?" she prodded gently.

"I want to see him." Michelle looked up at her and she seemed so young, too young, to be dealing with something this huge.

"In order to see him, you're going to have to tell people who you are. And even then, I can't promise it'll happen."

"Can't you just... I don't know, help me see him somehow? I promise I won't even say who I am. I just want to see him."

Charlie closed her eyes and prayed for the right words. "I can't do that, Michelle. I can't lie for you. I can help you, absolutely, but not by lying." She thanked God that today

Meggie had offered to look after Daniel at the cottage. How awkward it would be if he were here, like he normally was, and started crying.

She saw Michelle's hands start to shake. "You mean I have to turn myself into the police?"

"Yes." Charlie nodded. "But I'll help you with that. I'll be with you the whole time."

"But what if they put me in jail?" Michelle's eyes were wild now. "I made a mistake. I don't want to go to jail. I just want to see my baby. Be sure he's okay. I never meant for any of this to happen!"

Charlie reached out and rubbed Michelle's knee, hoping it was calming and reassuring. "I know." She'd seen people with no remorse before, with no conscience.

This wasn't like that. Michelle was as much in need of a social worker as her baby. Her records said she was only nineteen. Barely out of high school and alone and pregnant with no support. Desperation could drive people to do strange things. "I promise I'll help you. And I know for sure that coming forward will make things easier on you. You need to do this, Michelle. For yourself and for your son."

Michelle nodded a little, and a few tears trembled on her lashes. "I'm just scared."

"I know. But you don't have to do this alone now. We can help you get some support, okay?"

"Dr. Yang?"

"Yes?"

"You're a very kind person."

Charlie's heart softened even farther. She was nearly tempted to explain that she knew he was doing well because she was looking after the baby, but that might cause more trouble than solutions, so she held her tongue. The situation was complicated enough as it was.

Michelle took a deep breath and let it out, almost as if fortifying herself for what was to come. "Do you think I could talk to them here instead of having to walk into the police station? I'd feel like such a...a criminal." Her cheeks flushed.

"You're welcome to use the room here, no problem," Charlie replied, hugely relieved.

Michelle nodded.

"Okay. I'll be back in a bit, once I make a few calls. You'll wait here?"

She nodded again. "I promise."

Charlie left and went straight to her office to make the necessary calls, and then grabbed a juice box and a couple of granola bars from the kitchen. Michelle looked like she could use something to eat, and while it wasn't much, it might put some color back in her cheeks. She delivered the snack and gave Josh an update, then met with Todd Smith and a female officer who had come along on the call and filled them in on what she knew. By that time the social worker had arrived, and it was time to get the ball rolling.

Charlie entered the exam room once more. "Michelle, this is Marissa Longfellow. She's your baby's case worker."

"Hi, Michelle. It's very good to meet you."

"I don't want to go to jail," Michelle stated quickly. "I just wanted to know he was okay, you know?"

"He's perfectly fine, so you don't have to worry about that. Right now I'm here to help you. Together we're going to sort everything out, okay?"

Charlie put her hand on Michelle's shoulder. "The two of you can use the room for as long as you want. I'll be in my office if you need anything."

She left, took a precious five minutes to pour herself a cup of coffee, and then retreated to her office to make sense of the afternoon's events.

***

In some ways, Dave wished he could have stayed in Kennebunkport longer. He'd taken three days off work and stayed in a room at Janice and Brian's small inn. It had been awkward at times, but the truly odd thing was that Dave liked Brian. He was good for Janice, and he was also a great dad to Dave's daughter. Dave wanted Nora to be raised in a happy home. That was the most important thing, and thankfully everyone was willing to work together. Nora's next visit would be to Jewell Cove, for New Year's, and Dave couldn't wait. He wiped his hands on a rag, trying to rub off the grease on his knuckles. He didn't have much time coming to him, but he'd ask George for a few extra days, particularly as they'd talked about him staying on indefinitely. It was time to stop running and make a home.

And so while that part of his life was great, his romantic life had ground to a complete halt. He'd ruined things between him and Charlie, probably for good. She'd walked out and never called, not once. Not a text message, not a peep. He'd known from the beginning she was a strong woman. Stubborn. It was part of what he loved about her.

He was just punching out for the day when Josh pulled into the parking lot next to the boat yard. Which perhaps wasn't that noteworthy except Josh hopped out of his truck and made straight for George's small office. Dave's stomach twisted. He hoped nothing had happened to Charlie...

He pulled on his gloves and greeted Josh cordially, if not cautiously. "Hey, Josh. What're you doing here?"

"Probably pissing my partner off. She didn't call you, did she?"

"No." The nagging feeling of dread persisted. "Is she okay?"

"If you mean, is she physically okay, I'd have to say yes, although I think she's still beat from her go-round with the flu."

She'd had the flu?

"It's not that," Josh continued. "It's Daniel. His mother showed up at the clinic today. First of all, since you found him, I thought you might want to know before it gets all around town. And secondly, Charlie's had a hell of an afternoon. I don't know what happened between the two of you, but she's been moping around for the last week and a half. She's tired and it's been a rough few hours. She could use a friend today."

"I doubt she wants to see me." If she'd wanted moral support, she would have called. Wouldn't she?

"Well, do what you will with the information. I just wanted to let you know."

Clearly Josh didn't have a very high opinion of him, because he made an about face and headed right back to his truck again.

Dave frowned. In addition to finding his way in his new, active role as parent, he'd spent a lot of time thinking about Charlie. Mostly about how he'd hurt her. Mostly about what she'd said to him after they'd made love.

She'd been right. Being with her had scared him and he'd resorted to his fallback position: getting out of the way.

Maybe it was too late for them, but Josh had come to him for a reason. Charlie needed him—or perhaps just needed someone. He knew she felt very alone in Jewell Cove. He realized she spent most of her life looking after other people, but who looked after Charlie? No one. Not a damned soul. From what he gathered, she'd been looking out for herself for a long time now. Maybe it was time that changed.

Maybe it was time for him to be honest with himself about his feelings. And honest with her.

Chapter 13

Dave gripped the paper bag in one hand and wiped the other on his jeans.

Two police cars were still outside the clinic, along with an older model sedan and another newer, flashier car. Maybe this was a bad idea. He kept thinking that but then he also kept thinking about what Josh said.

So he opened the clinic door and stepped inside.

Robin was still working at the desk and looked up. "Hi, Dave. Sorry, our walk-in's closed for today."

"Josh found me," he said in a low voice. "I came to see Charlie."

"Oh." Her cheeks colored a bit. "Let me just check with her."

He waited, his toe tapping nervously, until Robin came back. "Come on in," she invited. When she started to lead him down the hall, he stopped her. "It's okay. I know which one is her office."

"Right. Okay." Robin looked a little flustered and Dave figured she wasn't used to this much excitement at the office. At the end of the hall, he gave Charlie's door a tap and poked his head inside.

"Hey," he said softly.

She looked up and his heart slammed against his ribs. She looked terrible and wonderful all at the same time. A few strands of hair were coming out of her bun, her eyes looked tired, and her shoulders were slumped. In short, she looked done in. But she was still his beautiful Charlie.

His. From the moment he'd first held her in his arms, he'd thought of her as his.

He wasn't sure why he'd fought it so hard. Now wasn't the time for that conversation, though. They could get into that later.

"You heard," she said wearily, leaning back in her chair and rubbing her temples.

"I heard. Are you okay?"

"Me?" Her brows lifted in surprise. "Of course I'm okay. But the girl in the next room is having a hell of a day." She tried a weak smile. "You might as well come in."

He stepped inside and lifted the bag of food. "I guessed you hadn't eaten yet, so I brought you dinner."

"Dave..."

"Don't." He lifted a hand. "Charlie, you've had a crazy day and you're exhausted. It's as simple as that."

She nodded, smiled wearily, then waggled her fingers. "Get it out then. I'm starving and that smells like Gus's handiwork."

It was. This close to Christmas Gus specialized in two things: oyster stew and roast turkey. Dave had opted for the turkey, thinking it would be better warmed up if she couldn't eat it now.

He presented two takeout containers, plastic forks and knives, napkins, salt and pepper packets, and a separate container with gravy. "Merry early Christmas," he murmured, handing her the gravy.

"To you too," she said quietly. She met his gaze. "Thank you for this, Dave. Really. It was very considerate."

"Can you tell me what happened? I mean, are you allowed?"

Charlie sprinkled pepper on her vegetables. "She wanted to make sure the baby was okay. I convinced her to turn herself in. She's just a young girl, Dave. Mixed up and afraid, who made a bad choice. She's not a bad kid." She paused, with her fork hovering over her potatoes. "I guess I still want to believe there's a happy ending in it for her."

Dave looked at her, felt a wave of love wash over him. God, she had such a generous and forgiving heart. He loved that about her. Hoped that her forgiveness extended to him, too, because he really wanted to start over with her. Make things right.

Charlie looked up, met his gaze. "I want to help her, Dave. Whatever shape she wants her life to take, I'd like to help her get pointed in the right direction. We were right. She chose the manger because she wanted him to be found, and she stayed nearby until she saw us take him. She didn't just dump him without a thought. That's got to count for something."

"Phew." Dave shook his head. "It's still crazy to think about that night, isn't it? I wonder why she didn't just leave him at a hospital, or police station."

"I don't know. I suppose she might have been worried about being seen. I got the impression it wasn't really thought out." She cut into her turkey and took a bite.

"Anyway," she finished, waving her fork in the air, "one good thing about it. The mystery of baby Daniel's mom is solved."

They ate in silence for a few moments until Dave couldn't take it anymore. "What does this mean for Daniel?"

She shrugged. "I don't know. I'm reminding myself to be realistic. He was never mine to begin with. I always knew I'd have to give him up eventually. With the break in the investigation, I suppose things will move forward a little faster." Her lips quivered for a second. "At least we'll have Christmas. I doubt anything will happen before then."

She was hurting and trying to cover. "You've been sick, Josh said."

"I didn't realize you and Josh were buddy buddy."

"We're not. He's worried about you. Seeing you today, so am I."

"I'm just tired. I had that nasty bug going around and so did everyone else in Jewell Cove, I think. We were putting in some long days. I'll be fine."

"I think, Charlene Yang, you tell everyone you're fine whether you are or not."

She stopped eating and stared at him. "What do you mean by that?"

"I just mean that...well, I've been doing a lot of thinking. You tell people you're fine, you give of yourself, but you never really let anyone in. You don't want to be any trouble. And you don't want to give someone the power to really hurt you, either. Because you've been disappointed a lot in your life. And it works but only a little because deep down you're lonely and you need someone to give all that love to. Being a doctor is perfect. You get to help people without becoming personally involved."

"Wow. That's some psychoanalysis."

"And that's exactly what I'd say if I wanted to avoid the issue and turn the tables. We're more alike than you think, Charlie."

"Except I did let someone in. You."

He hadn't expected her to admit it, and it took him by surprise.

"We don't have to talk about this now," he said. "On top of everything else."

"Or ever, right?" She picked up her fork again, and stabbed it into her mound of potatoes, her lips set in an angry line.

"I didn't come here to pile on, Charlie. Not after the day you've had."

"You pretty much said it all anyway," she reminded him, playing in the potatoes but not eating them.

"No, I didn't. I didn't say near enough. And I certainly didn't say the right things."

Her fork stopped moving. He might have imagined it, but he thought he saw her lower lip give another little quiver before she bit down on it.

"I went to see Nora," he explained. "And the whole time I was watching their family all together I was thinking about you, and the fun we had together, and how easy it is to talk to you, and how much I loved kissing you...and...and how much I missed you."

Her chin started quivering again.

"I was an idiot, Charlie. I let my fear of being tied down get in the way of what I really wanted. You. I told myself I didn't want to settle down, but the truth is I've moved around so much, I've never had much luck with romance that...well, I wasn't sure I was ready to put down roots. If I'd ever be ready." He swallowed. "I'm probably saying this all wrong..."

"You're doing okay."

She was looking at him with luminous eyes and he pushed forward. "I love you, Charlie."

Charlie hadn't been expecting those words. Not today, not ever. And damn him for getting to her on a day she was emotionally vulnerable to start with. She blinked to clear away the moisture that had sprung to her eyes. "Don't say that," she whispered, her voice hoarse.

"Why?" he asked. He walked around her desk and turned her steno chair so it was facing him, then squatted down in front of her, just like she'd done with Michelle earlier. "Why don't you want me to say it? Because you don't want to hear it or because you want to and you're afraid?"

"It's been barely a month of you and me doing a dance and...whatever." She fumbled the words, words that scared her to death. He was right. Because if he said them and didn't mean them she was bound to get her heart broken. And if he did mean them...

If he did...

"Do you believe in fate, Charlie?"

She swallowed. Hard. "I don't know."

"I do." His fingers dug into her knees as he held on to her. "I think I landed here in Jewell Cove for a reason. I think I came here because I needed to. That night at the tree lighting something happened. I turned around with that baby in my arms and saw you and nothing has been the same since."

She heard the echoes in her head, echoes from her past. *Make sure you keep up your marks, Charlene. Don't forget to wear your best dress, Charlene. This is important to the family, Charlene. Don't disappoint us, Charlene.*"

She was no better than he was for avoiding the truth. She had dreams of a family of her own but it turned out she was too chicken to act on it when she had the chance. And now here was the man of her dreams standing in front of her telling her he loved her and she was backing away. What the hell was wrong with her?

He lifted his hand and touched her cheek. "A month isn't very long. But it was long enough for me to come to my senses. Long enough for me to recognize that I'd met someone who made me smile again, made me laugh, made me actually look forward to the future rather than just going from day to day. Do you know how rare that is?"

She put her hand over his and drew it away from her face, down into her lap. "Dave," she said quietly, "it was barely a week ago when you stood in your kitchen and told me flat out that you couldn't give me what I wanted. What changed? Why should I trust that?"

He got up from his squatted position but held on to her hand, gave it a tug until she was out of the chair, and reversed positions so that he was in the chair and he pulled her into his lap.

His arm was strong as it circled her, his face utterly open and sincere as he looked up at her. "Charlene."

She waited. He seemed to be gathering his words, and there was a sense that whatever he said next was going to be of utmost importance. Butterflies winged through her stomach and her fingers trembled. It terrified her how much she wanted to believe him.

And then there it was, a look in his eyes that was so beautiful that it felt like her heart was melting right there in her chest. It made her breath catch and a strange sort of excitement pulse through her veins. "David," she whispered, and reached out and placed her hand along the side of his face, feeling the stubble against her skin.

He turned his head slightly, kissed the curve of her palm.

"There are so many things I might have done differently," he said, his arms still tight around her hips. "I might have not gotten together with Janice. I might have put off having kids, or stayed in the Navy. I realize that right now, I'm exactly where I'm supposed to be. In Jewell Cove. With you. And that I wouldn't be here if any of those things hadn't happened. They all led me to you, Charlie. You are where I'm meant to be. You make my world make sense."

"You really mean that, don't you?"

"With my life. I don't need to count weeks or months to figure it out. And it won't be perfect all the time. I know that. I just know I want to try."

It won't be perfect all the time. She rolled those words around in her head a few times, mulling them over. She thought about Michelle in the next room, struggling so hard to make decisions, thought about Josh, who'd lost his wife overseas mere weeks before she was due to return home. She thought about Lizzie's mom, and how she'd had to be put in full-time care. Truth was, there was no such thing as perfect all the time, and perhaps that was Charlie's problem. She'd built up this imaginary dream life to be so perfect that it was an impossible, unattainable goal.

Instead she had a wonderful, slightly damaged, sexy, beautiful man holding her tight and asking her to give them a shot. And it occurred to her that perhaps she'd been demanding too much, because what he was offering was everything. Himself. All he asked in return was that she meet him halfway.

"You really mean that you love me?"

She relaxed into his arms, curling into his embrace so that her face was nestled in the curve of his neck. "Oh yes," he answered softly. "Charlie, there was a moment. I know you remember it. You have to. A moment when we were making love and our eyes met and it was like lightning."

She did remember. It had been a magical, soul-deep connection beyond anything she'd ever known. It had been the moment that had given her hope that the life she longed for might be within her grasp.

Now he was telling her it was. And she could either choose to believe him or walk away.

She thought of what Lizzie would say right now and she laughed a little, holding onto him a bit tighter. Lizzie would tell her to stop being a chicken and take a chance, because if she didn't, she'd always regret it.

"Is that a good laugh or a bad one? Cripes, woman. I spill my guts to you, and you laugh?"

She pushed on his chest so that she was sitting up and could look him square in the face. "David Ricker, I am terrified of having my heart broken. But lucky for you I'm more afraid of what will become of me if I don't take a chance. So here it is. I fell in love with you too. Right about the time you turned around with a baby in your arms and told me we had a problem."

A smile bloomed on his face and he pulled her close, kissing her like she was a cool glass of water and he was a man dying of thirst. With a heart full of hope, she kissed him back, melting into him, loving the taste and feel of him until she realized someone was knocking on her office door.

Reluctantly she removed her lips from his and then felt heat rush to her face as she saw Josh standing in the doorway, his knuckles resting on the door frame and a goofy grin on his face.

"I hate to interrupt this reunion, but Michelle is getting ready to go now. She asked to see you first."

Charlie turned to Dave. "Do you want to meet her? She seemed very interested in knowing who found her baby."

"She brought us together, didn't she? Of course I'll meet her."

"I'll be right back."

Michelle agreed to meet Dave, and Charlie loved the way he smiled at the girl when she walked through the office door. He had a big heart too, whether he realized it or not.

"Thank you," Michelle said quietly. "For saving my baby."

"You're welcome," he answered, and he came forward and shook her hand. "Don't worry, okay? You've got Dr. Yang in your corner. And if I've learned anything, it's that when she's got your back, it's not the end. It's just the beginning. You're going to be just fine."

Michelle nodded, shouldering her backpack, and then she suddenly smiled.

"Oh!" She let the pack slide to the floor and hurriedly undid the zip. "I nearly forgot. I took this the night I left him in the manger. I didn't mean to steal it, I just wasn't sure..."

She stood up. It was the doll from the manger, still diapered and swaddled and wrapped in Dave's soft shirt.

Charlie started to laugh, and so did Dave. She put her arm around Michelle's shoulders. And in that moment, she knew that everything was going to work out exactly as it should. And it had nothing to do with facts or figures. It was all down to one simple thing: faith.

Chapter 14

Light snow fell on Christmas Eve. The tangle of lights Charlie had wrestled with the first day were twinkling from the shrubs throughout the church yard. A floodlight lit up the nativity, and together Charlie and Dave went forward and placed the original Baby Jesus on the straw.

"Back where he belongs," Dave said quietly, holding Charlie's hand.

"It seems like so long ago I was sitting here talking to him like he was my best friend. So silly..."

Dave shrugged. "Who knows? Maybe he was listening."

Charlie laughed a little, leaning against Dave's arm. "That's even more embarrassing. I was telling him about this guy I could see from the window at Breeze's on my lunch hour. How I'd made up this fantasy boyfriend..."

"I hope the reality surpasses your imagination."

"Oh, definitely."

The parking lot was filling up and many of the townspeople walked to the church for the Christmas Eve service. It wasn't generally Charlie's speed, but lots of things were changing this year, and for the better. As she and Dave stepped inside the vestibule together, with Daniel cradled in Dave's strong arms, she felt more a part of the community than ever.

"Merry Christmas, Charlene," called Gloria Henderson, who was bustling her way toward the front of the church to take her place at the organ.

"Merry Christmas," she called back. The same thing happened a half dozen more times as they hung up their coats and took the baby out of his snowsuit. Robin showed up with her sister, Todd Smith was there in uniform, still on duty but stopping in to take in part of the annual tradition just the same. Josh and his extended family and lots of people she recognized from businesses around town arrived, smiling and laughing and filled with Christmas spirit. She introduced Dave to several, and a warm glow filled her from head to toe as they finally made it to a pew near the back to enjoy the caroling and service.

A huge pine tree was at the front of the church, decorated in white lights and ornaments and exuding a festive piney smell throughout the sanctuary. But best of all were the candles, thick pillars of them, lit on every windowsill, the stained glass glowing in their light. Once the service was over, there was mingling again in the crowded entry, and a sense of peace and goodwill and happiness that Charlie wished she could bottle and carry with her forever. Meggie appropriated Daniel for a diaper change, and Charlie held on to Dave's hand feeling like everything was right in the world.

She looked at the door and saw Marissa Longfellow and to her surprise, Michelle was with her, dressed in a new winter coat, black leggings, and boots that came to just below her knees. She was quite pretty today, with her hair washed and falling easily over her shoulders, and a little hint of makeup. Charlie tugged on Dave's hand and led him to the entrance, where they stepped outside into the cool air peppered with fat, lazy snowflakes.

"Michelle. You look wonderful." Charlie, who usually shied away from physical intimacy, gave the girl a quick hug. "I didn't expect to see you here."

Michelle smiled shyly. "Ms. Longfellow is my new Santa Claus. I have a court date after Christmas, but she convinced the judge to let me stay with her in the meantime. Extenuating circumstances, she said. And then we paid a visit to the secondhand store and got me some new clothes."

Marissa smiled. "Michelle wants to make a new start. It won't be a fast process or an easy one. She could use a helping hand, that's all."

"I agree."

"Me too," Dave echoed.

"I know that what I did was so wrong." She smiled sadly at all of them. "But I want to build a better life and I want a better life for him, too. One that he'll find with a good family."

Charlie knew it had to be hard for Michelle to say. "That's very brave of you, sweetie."

"I hope one day I can be someone my son can be proud of. I'm thinking it might be like asking for a Christmas miracle, but who knows, right?"

"Stranger things have happened," Charlie confirmed, taking Dave's hand. "I happen to be a big believer in second chances."

"Me too," Dave confirmed, looking down into Charlie's eyes. For a long moment their gazes held, and Charlie felt like the luckiest woman in the world.

After they said their goodbyes, they collected Daniel and headed back to Charlie's for the night. She'd turned on her lights before leaving, and as they drove in the yard, cheery multi-colored bulbs glowed on the new snow. She realized that she'd come to love this cottage. Come to love Jewell Cove, especially once she started to let people in. It was home. When Dave took the keys from her hands and opened her front door, her heart gave a little pang. She took a moment and made a wish. A wish that Dave would maybe want to make it his home, too. When they stepped inside and shut the door, he pulled her close and kissed her; long, thorough, beautiful. She put her arms around his neck and squeezed. When he was here, it felt like a missing piece of the puzzle was finally in place.

She'd tucked Daniel into bed and poured them each a glass of wine as he built the fire, and she was ready to put on a Christmas movie when Dave took her hand.

"I have something for you."

He led her away from the entertainment center and to the front of the tree, where a few gifts already waited, tucked beneath the branches. Confused and a little excited, Charlie couldn't help the smile that curved her lips.

"What?" he asked. "You look like the cat that ate the canary."

"I'm just happy," she answered. "I've never spent Christmas with anyone like this. It's special."

"So are you." He reached into the middle of the tree and took out a box, about four inches square. "I tucked this in here before we left. I thought about waiting for tomorrow, but I want you to have it tonight."

He held it out, and she took the red foil-wrapped box into her hands. It was light, and with shaky fingers she undid the ribbon and slid her fingernail beneath the tape holding the paper in place.

She lifted the lid and found an ornament inside—the same one she'd found at the bookstore at the Evergreen Festival, a perfectly round ball covered with paper quotes.

"Oh, Dave. It's lovely." She held it in her fingers. "It's the Shakespeare one, right?"

His gaze was intent on her as he gave a slight nod. "Yes."

It was very thoughtful, and she remembered him being a little longer in the store that day. "You said that they were changing the register tape, but you were buying this, weren't you?"

"I was."

"I love it." She was so perfectly happy at this moment, she was positive life couldn't get any better. But then she picked it up by the loop and went to hang it on the tree and a splash of green caught her eye. Bright green, like from a highlighter pen. She drew her hand back and turned the orb so that she could examine the strip of paper.

I would not wish any companion in the world but you.

A lump grew in her throat and the text blurred for a second. "Oh, Dave." She drew in an emotional breath. "What's it from?"

He put his arm around her waist and drew her close. "I looked it up. It's from The Tempest."

She took one step forward and hung it on a branch right in the middle of the tree.

"I love you. You know that, right?"

"I do. So what do you say, Chuckles?"

"Say?"

He lifted her hand to his lips. She looked up at him, unsure of what he was asking, simply loving the sight of him there before her, knowing she loved him and was loved in return. Nothing could be sweeter.

"Companions. Partners. Lovers. I want it all. I want it all with you."

Okay, so she hadn't quite expected for her wish to be granted so quickly. But she was learning not to look a gift horse in the mouth. "I want that, too."

"I'm on a month-to-month lease with Tom."

"And there's more than enough room for us here," she added, feeling ridiculously starry-eyed.

"We can always put on an addition later..."

"For the kids. Are you okay with that? I don't know what's going to happen with Daniel, but I want children, Dave. At least a couple."

He grinned at her. "I'm more than okay with that." He kissed the tip of her nose. "We're really going to do this."

"Yeah," she said. "We are."

He reached for her, curled a hand around her neck, and pulled her close for a long, searing kiss that left her breathless. Charlie let out a moan as he pulled her earlobe into his mouth, sending a dart of pure desire to her core. She reached for his dress shirt and started unbuttoning it, but his hands got in the way as he touched her breasts and pulled her against his hard body.

It only seemed to take seconds and they were stretched out on the rug in front of the fire. Without saying a word, they slowed their hands, took their time, savored each second. There was no urgency; just the sweet rush of anticipation. Charlie looked up at Dave and saw more than just a man. She saw her future.

"Merry Christmas, sweetheart," he said, and kissed her tenderly.

"You're my favorite Christmas gift," she decreed, and then the rest of the world disappeared. It was just the two of them, a sweet little cottage on the bay, and a dream for forever.

THE END

Turn the page to begin the heartwarming CHRISTMAS AT EVERGREEN INN

Christmas at Evergreen Inn

DONNA ALWARD

Chapter 1

Todd Smith felt the back end of his SUV slide as he took the turn at barely more than a crawl. He was heading north toward Jewell Cove, a hot meal, and a warm bed.

Goddamn if this wasn't the worst Nor'easter they'd seen in years, with crazy high winds that took the heavy snowfall and whipped it around so you could hardly see. He had his four-way flashers on and his headlights slashed through the snow, but it was getting harder and harder to see where the road met the ditch. If he wasn't careful, he was going to be in it.

He might be off duty right now, but he'd gone into the station anyway, volunteering to help. His job was to help stranded travelers, not become one of them.

And to do that he had to stay on the road. A road filled with lots of curves and turns, as it happened. But this was his last run. Once he returned to town he'd check in at the office and then head home for the night. Thank God the road so far was clear of vehicles in the ditch.

He'd no longer got the thought through his head than he saw a dark hump on the right, and tire tracks leading down the embankment. "Shit," he muttered, and carefully slowed, pulled as far over to the side as he dared, left his headlights on to show him the way, and set his hazard lights flashing.

He hopped out of the truck and made his way through the snow to the car. From four feet away he saw a person inside. "Please don't be hurt," he prayed, pushing forward to knock on the window. Hopefully the driver had simply slid off the shoulder and into the ditch, because getting an ambulance out here was going to be a challenge.

He rapped on the glass. "Hello? Are you okay?"

The window rolled down to show a very anxious middle-aged man whose face sagged with relief at being found. "Oh, thank the Lord! I ran off the road a few minutes ago and I don't have any cell service, and everyone says that you should stay in your vehicle..."

"So you can be picked up safely," Todd said, nodding. He knew it couldn't have been long since the tracks leading to the car were still visible. "I'm Officer Todd Smith with the Jewell Cove Police Department. I've got a four-wheel drive up there, and I can give you a lift into town. You can make arrangements to come back for your car later."

The man nodded briskly. "That sounds wonderful, Officer. I just have this with me, can I bring it?"

Todd looked inside the car. A small overnight bag and a briefcase sat on the passenger seat. At least the guy travelled light.

"I don't see why not. Let's go, though. It's getting worse out here instead of better."

He helped the man get out of the car and climb the bank. "You don't have to tell me twice. I'm Jacob Sewell," the man explained. "I was headed here on business and thought I'd beat the storm up the coast. Stupid of me, really."

Todd wanted to agree with him, but there wasn't much sense in making the guy feel worse. "Well, Mr. Sewell, my guess is you'll be stuck in Jewell Cove for a day or two while this gets cleaned up. Hope you're not in any hurry." He reached for the man's arm, giving him a firm tug to get him over the bank. Overnight bag and briefcase shuttled forward and bumped his arm and then settled back again. Ridiculous man had driven up the coast in December in nothing more than a pair of leather dress shoes and a pea coat.

"Here's my truck. Hop in and we'll see about getting you a place to stay in town."

Thankfully, Mr. Sewell wasn't too interested in talking on the drive. Todd looked over once and noticed the man's fingers were gripped together so tightly the knuckles were white. Not much wonder. The roads were a mess, they were barely crawling along, and he was probably still reliving the sensation of sliding into the ditch and being stranded.

It didn't help when the back end of Todd's truck skidded from time to time, even with the four-wheel drive. For some reason a line from an old, animated Christmas special popped into Todd's mind: it wasn't a fit day for man nor beast. When the "Jewell Cove, 1 mi." sign appeared, Todd started to relax a bit. Once they got to town limits, hopefully the roads would be plowed and in a little bit better shape. The next question was where to go. He knew that the motel on the main drag was already full. When he'd left for this last run, the lot there and across the road at the service station already housed a few transport trucks where even the truckers had pulled off for the night. The best chance would be the Evergreen Inn. His chest tightened a little at the thought. Lainey Price ran the inn now. She'd always been beautiful, but now she was beautiful and successful, and Todd found that even more intimidating. Not that he'd ever own up to it, of course. The roads in town weren't much better, and Todd turned left off of Main and up the few blocks to connect with Oceanview Drive, feeling the tires grabbing in the snow that was getting deeper by the moment. The clock on the dash said eight forty-nine.

Surely anyone else would be off the roads by now if they had any sense at all.

"I'm going to park at the back lot of the church, and we'll walk over," Todd said to Mr. Sewell. "I don't imagine the inn has much space for vehicles at the moment and there's no parking on the streets tonight."

"Thank you so much, Officer Smith." Mr. Sewell sighed heavily. "I'm just so relieved to be here safe and sound. I don't know what I'd have done if you hadn't come along."

The wind was so sharp that the little snowflakes bit at their faces as they crossed the parking lot and then the street to reach the inn. At some point, someone must have shoveled the front walk and steps, because the snow wasn't as deep there as elsewhere. Regardless, it still drifted over the path and they had to stomp their way through it.

When Todd reached the front door, he tried the knob and found it locked. He knocked then, good and hard. Someone would hear, surely. But he was worried that the locked door meant they were full for the night. The second knock got results. The door opened and Lainey stood to the side, leaving the door only open a crack. "Todd?" "I've got a stranded motorist out here, Lainey. Any room at the inn?"

Her brows pulled together. "Not really. But come inside out of that weather while I help you sort something out."

He and Mr. Sewell stomped their way inside, out of the blowing snow. Sewell looked so utterly relieved to be somewhere warm and dry that it was almost comical.

Todd half expected the man to kneel and kiss the ground. Todd merely stayed on the welcome mat and removed his gloves. He had to get this guy settled and get home. His time on the roads wasn't quite done yet. "This is Mr. Sewell." He performed a basic introduction. "Found him just the other side of Fiddler's Cove, car in the ditch. He needs a place to stay for the night."

"Of course. We're packed in pretty tightly here, Mr. Sewell, and I'm not sure I can guarantee you your own room. The motel is full up, though, and even if you did want to go somewhere else, there's not much chance of it. It's only supposed to get worse out there before it gets better. We'll find a way to squeeze you in somewhere."

She smiled reassuringly.

Lainey looked up at Todd. "You've been out on patrol?" Her pretty face showed concern. "The roads must be terrible."

"They are, but I'm done now. If anyone was out there, we've picked them up."

"And not much chance of anyone starting out. They've closed the highway, you know." Damn. That put Todd in a bind, but he'd have to get Sewell situated first. "Busy night for you, I take it," he said, noticing a little strain behind her smile and warm cinnamon eyes. Lainey had always been beautiful. Her ancestors had come to Jewell Cove as freed slaves during the Civil War, but in the '60s her grandfather had married a white woman from New Brunswick, giving the town gossips lots to talk about. Mixed marriages were not the done thing back then. Now, two generations later, her heritage showed in her honeyed skin and jet-black hair. Todd had always found her simply stunning.

She was dressed in black trousers and a soft gray sweater, her curls caught up in a ponytail. Always professional on the job, he thought. Used to be Lainey was a bit of a party girl. Not lately, though. He tucked his gloves in his jacket pocket. No, for the last few years they'd all calmed down and taken on real-life responsibilities. She took Mr. Sewell's coat and hung it in the closet. "Lots of people are stranded, that's for sure. Mr. Sewell, can I offer you a cup of coffee and something to eat? I'm afraid we don't generally serve dinner, but today's a special circumstance. It's mostly breakfast food I have on hand, but I can make you some eggs and toast or offer you muffins and fruit."

"I'm not fussy," Mr. Sewell replied. "Whatever is easiest is fine."

"Then please, head into the parlor and make yourself comfortable. I shouldn't be long." A grateful Mr. Sewell disappeared into the parlor. Lainey sighed and looked up at Todd. "Phew. Well, the storm is causing a sensation. No shortage of conversation topics in there tonight. But I hope no one else shows up. I was already full when you knocked on the door."

"I can try to find another place for him to stay." It was a polite offer; they both knew that going anywhere now was impossible.

"There is no other place, Todd." Lainey reached for his coat. "Come on, take this off and have a coffee. You look dead on your feet. It must have been nerve-wracking, out there on the roads."

It was true. He'd been out most of the day, and the intense attention it had taken for him to drive had left him exhausted. Particularly now that he was done, out of the storm, and relaxed. It was like it all caught up with him at once.

He let her hang up his coat while he took off his boots and placed them neatly by the front door. She smiled at him and led the way to the kitchen. Todd watched the gentle sway of her hips and wondered—not for the first time—why he'd never bothered to ask her out. He'd never been the shy type. Maybe it was the sense that Lainey was out of his league. When she did something, she did it all the way. As teens she'd partied hard and got straight A's and was school council president. Now she'd taken over the inn and was making a great success of it. As far as Todd knew, she'd never failed at anything.

The kitchen of the inn was an old-fashioned monstrosity, lined with solid wood cupboards and a big oak table and chairs at one end by several windows. A butcher block provided a working area in the middle of the room, and there was a hutch made for the back corner—a triangle-shaped piece painted a brick red and then distressed to make it look antique. A red tablecloth covered the table, and in the middle was a beautiful pine and candle centerpiece. Christmas-themed serving dishes lined the hutch as well, giving the room an appropriately festive look.

Despite the old-fashioned country décor, the appliances were stainless steel, shiny, and large.

"You know, I've never been inside here before."

"Really?" Lainey turned on the coffee machine to heat the water. "It's generally not so busy this time of year. Sure, it fills up during the weekend of the Christmas festival, but once that's over, we're pretty quiet until at least Easter." She busied herself around, taking out muffins and pastries and two coffee mugs. "I let the seasonal staff go after Thanksgiving." She laughed. "So it's just me here. I certainly didn't expect a full house this close to Christmas. I'll have my hands full tomorrow morning."

She popped a coffee pod in the machine and hit the button. "What do you take?"

"What?" Todd had been watching her efficient movements, marveling at the change in her. The girl he used to know had been a little bit of a hell-raiser. Nothing too serious, but definitely good for a beach party or whatever was happening after the sun went down. Now, though, she'd gotten all respectable and...domestic, with her coffee and home-baked muffins and homey kitchen. But when she smiled at him, there was a sparkle in her eye that told him the girl he'd known growing up was still in there.

"In your coffee," she said, and grinned. "Which you'd know if you quit staring at my ass."

He coughed. "Jesus, Lainey."

That was the girl he remembered. She'd say what was on her mind and then laugh about it.

"You take it black, don't you?" she asked, tilting her head.

"Don't all cops?"

She laughed again and reached for a plate for the muffins. "Yeah, well you becoming a cop was a big surprise, that's for sure. Mr. Straight and Narrow. Besides, I try not to think too much about law enforcement." She angled him a look that he understood all too well. As much as he hated to admit it, it was the truth that not everyone got treated the same...even in Jewell Cove.

"Truce," he said, offering a genuine smile. "Yes. I was staring at your ass. It's a mighty fine one, as it happens. And yes, I take my coffee black. And finally, you, Miss Lainey Price, still have an awfully smart mouth. I see that much hasn't changed." He sobered for a moment, though. "But I'm glad you're comfortable enough with me to call me out."

"We go back a long time. Seems to me we attended an awful lot of the same parties not that long ago."

His grin reappeared. "A guy's gotta grow up sometime."

She winked at him, then shoved a muffin in his hand. "I bet you didn't eat dinner. Have a muffin."

Lainey disappeared with a tray containing Mr. Sewell's coffee, muffins, a bowl of fruit, cream, sugar, and butter. While she was gone, Todd's coffee finished brewing and he reached for the cup. God, it was good. Hot and rich and soothing. The muffin was good, too, some sort of carrot nut thing with a crumb topping. Since she was taking her time coming back, he reached into the container for another. He'd missed dinner, and once he started eating, he realized how hungry he was.

Lainey came back to the kitchen and put her hands on her hips as she saw him reach for a third. "If you'd waited two minutes, I would have made you an omelet or something. Heated you some soup...I don't have much in this kitchen, but in the cottage my fridge is pretty well stocked."

"Cottage?"

She nodded. "I like my own space. When I took over the inn, I hired Tom Arseneault to convert the storage building at the back into a little apartment for me. It leaves another room open for guests in the house, too."

"You've done a great job with it since Joan and Roger retired," he said, referring to the previous owners.

"Thanks." She looked absurdly pleased at the compliment. "Are you sure I can't fix you something?"

"This is fine. Fills the hole. I need to call in, anyway. And be on my way."

Lainey raised one doubtful eyebrow at him, but he ignored it. Instead he pulled out his cell and dialed the office and dispatch.

When he hung up, he looked at her, eyebrow still raised, and sighed. "Okay, so you were right. The roads out of town are all closed." As much as he hated to ask, he did anyway. "Is there room at the inn for me, too?"

Lainey stared up at Todd. Room at the inn? What was this, some sort of weird Christmas play or something? Not only that, the place was filled to the gills. All the rooms were taken. She was going to have to put the last fold-out cot in one of the rooms for Mr. Sewell, if one of the male guests consented to sharing space for the night.

The father and son duo had already volunteered to give up their room to a pair of sisters on their way to Boston for a girl's weekend. The men would be bunking on the sofa and loveseat in the parlor, once everyone went to bed.

"You can't get out to your place at all?"

"Nope. The highway's shut down and the chief just ordered us to stay put, wherever we are. Particularly if we're in town, because he'll need us in the morning."

Bryce Arseneault might be the youngest chief Jewell Cove had ever had, but no one doubted his authority, either. If he said, "stay where you are," you stayed. There wasn't anything Lainey could do about it. Besides, having Todd Smith at the inn was no big deal. They were all adults. This was her *job*.

But stay the night? As much as she hated to admit it, Lainey'd had a thing for him long before he became a cop, which was why she trusted him so much. She certainly wasn't going to tell him. The hot and sexy police officer was never at a loss for dates, but he'd never asked her out. Not once. It was hard not to feel slighted.

The only available space for him to stay wasn't at the inn at all. It was in the cottage. In her quarters. The very thought sent a strange sort of swirling through her stomach, a combination of nervousness and desire.

"You can sleep on my couch," she told him, hoping he couldn't see the heat that had risen in her cheeks. "It's the only space left, but it's comfortable enough."

"On your couch. You mean over there." He hooked his thumb to the right, gesturing out the back.

"Yes, over there." She would keep this businesslike. Like everyone else, he was a casualty of the storm. Besides, he'd been out there trying to help people. The very least she could do was give him some food and a blanket for the night.

"I guess it'll have to do."

The words were blandly said, but Lainey saw a twinkle in his eye. When Todd looked like that, it was hard to remember to resist his charm.

"You," she said, pointing a finger, "are incorrigible."

"So they say." He tilted his coffee cup; it was nearly empty.

Lainey sighed. "Listen, do you want to join everyone in the parlor or anything? I've got to finish making sure the rooms are done up and everyone has enough towels and stuff. Flashlights, too, in case the power goes out."

"Let's hope not. That'd be fun. Not."

"We've got a generator. But I'd rather not have to worry about it."

He lifted his cup. "I might have another of these. Go do what you need to do, Lainey. You don't need to entertain me. I'm just glad to have a place to hole up for the night."

She left him there in the kitchen and busied herself in the remaining guest rooms, checking supplies and testing flashlights. She took extra blankets from the linen closet in case they did lose power and it got cold, and took the last fold-out cot out of storage and put it in the Captain's room for Mr. Sewell since one of the guests had kindly offered the space. The one good thing to come out of the storm was that she was incredibly busy, and it took her mind off things. Namely, Christmas.

It was always her favorite holiday, but this year she just couldn't seem to get in the holiday spirit. Last year had been such a disaster that now the goodwill to men and warm holiday glow just seemed to bring her down.

It wasn't even that her heart was still broken. She'd moved on; started putting the pieces back together. It was more that the decorations and songs and sappy TV programs reminded her of how she'd felt last year. Of how much she'd hurt. Yes, it was the reminders that hurt now. She'd loved Jason with everything she had. He'd been The One. And a week before Christmas he'd broken their engagement.

Now Todd Smith was in her kitchen and for the first time in months she felt the delicious, unexpected stirrings of attraction. In a way it was scary as hell. Love hurt. But this wasn't love; far from it. Besides, Todd didn't do love, and that made her feel tons better. Because in another way, it came as a great relief to know she actually *could* feel like this again.

Back downstairs, she checked on the guests congregated in the parlor. Todd wasn't there, but she spent several minutes chatting, letting them know where she'd be in the night if anything happened. They checked the weather report and before long the first of the group decided to go up to bed.

Lainey took the tray of dirty cups and plates and went to the kitchen, expecting to see Todd there, but the room was empty. She heard a strange, rhythmic grating sound and looked out the back window. He'd found a shovel and was clearing the walk between the main house and the cottage.

She stopped and smiled for a moment. She could say all she wanted about him and his sexy smile and flirtatious ways, but he was a good man when it came right down to it. Hardworking and honest. And right now, his seeming lack of desire to settle down worked in his favor rather than against. The last thing Lainey wanted to think about was romance. A relationship. She wrapped her arms around her middle and watched him in the dim circle of the porch light. Nope, she certainly wasn't interested in a boyfriend. Scratching an itch with a guy like Todd, though? That thought had its attractions.

She was twenty-six. What was she going to do, stay celibate the rest of her life?

Todd moved around to the front of the house, wading through the drifts until he was out of sight. With a sigh, Lainey put the dishes in the dishwasher and then went back to the parlor to set up the hide-a-bed and lay out blankets for the father and son. She wouldn't go to her own quarters until everyone was settled.

Todd came back inside through the back door. His jacket and hat were covered in snow, his cheeks ruddy from the cold wind. Lainey took one look at him and knew it would be stupid to make him wait here. She handed him the key to her door. "Go on over. I'll be there soon. I'm just waiting for everyone to get settled in case they need anything."

"Are you sure?"

"Look at you. It doesn't make any sense for you to take off your boots and coat and then have to put them back on again. Besides, you can turn on the TV, kick your feet up for a bit. I won't be long."

He took the key. "Sold."

He opened the door again and Lainey called after him, "Don't snoop through my stuff."

His eyes snapped to hers, and she wondered how in the world they could seem like they were twinkling all the damn time.

"Now Lainey, that would be an invasion of privacy. I'm offended you'd think I'd do such a thing." He put a hand to his heart.

Her lips twitched. She walked over to him, not caring about the draft, and looked up into his face. "You forget, I've known you for a long time, Todd Smith. I *know* you'd do such a thing."

"Lainey."

"I'm just glad it's too cold for you to run my underwear up the flagpole."

He nearly choked on his laugh and she raised an eyebrow. How the boys from the baseball team had gotten the principal's underwear, no one knew. But they'd run it up the school flagpole on a Saturday and it had stayed there until the custodian had taken the rather large sized panties down on Monday morning. It had never been proven who did it, but Lainey had known. It had Todd written all over it.

"Go on," she said. "I'm not paying to heat the outdoors."

With a mock salute he pulled the door closed and she watched him make his way to the guest house. Moments later the outside light came on over there, too, and she knew he was inside.

In her private space.

Despite her words, she actually did trust him not to snoop. Because Todd had kept his sense of humor, but she knew one thing for sure. He'd grown up and acquired a sense of honor and fairness, too.

It made for one hell of a potent combination.

Chapter 2

Lainey finally turned off the lights and headed out the back door to the small cottage.

She loved her little space. It was close enough to be onsite if she were needed, but it gave her some privacy, too. She'd had Tom do the heavy renovations, but she'd decorated it last summer, choosing the color, painting the walls, and purchasing some new furniture.

The snow stung her cheeks as she hustled along the shoveled path. It wasn't far, but even so, she was covered with white when she turned the knob and opened the door. She closed it quickly, not wanting to let out the heat or let the snow blow in.

Todd was kneeling before her fireplace, jabbing at the flaming wood with a poker.

Mercy, he was hot. Always had been. He was tall, a good six feet, with dark hair and brown eyes that were warm as melted chocolate and twice as sinful. Being a cop in a place as small as Jewell Cove wasn't all that physically demanding, but he kept himself in good shape. Today, off duty, he wore jeans and a plain black hoodie. Even so, the slim line of his hips and the width of his shoulders was evident.

"I thought I'd build a fire," he said, picking up a small log and placing it on the flames that were licking along the smaller bits of kindling he'd arranged.

She finally moved instead of staring. She took off her coat and boots and stowed them away, then shivered. She turned the heat down during the day and she hadn't been back over since the storm started and people had begun arriving.

"I forgot I'd left the heat down," she apologized. "Sorry about that."

"No problem. This gave me something to do, anyway." He hadn't turned on the TV or anything. The room was completely quiet other than the odd snap from the fire.

"Do you want something to drink?" She smiled, reminded herself to relax. She'd known Todd for years. And yes, she'd had a big crush, but nothing had ever happened between them and it wouldn't now either, right?

"I wouldn't say no." Todd brushed off his hands and stood, sending her a smile.

"It's been a long day. For both of us, I expect."

She went to the kitchen—really just a working area off the main room—and opened a cupboard. "I don't have an extensive liquor cabinet," she said, rooting around. "There's some vodka here, I think. And something pink...God, I think Cindy brought this over in the summer." She found a square-ish type bottle and took it out. "Aha. And whiskey. That might do the trick on a cold night like tonight."

"Works for me."

She took down two short glasses. "Ice?"

"Please."

"Mix?"

Lainey nearly laughed when he looked horrified at the idea. "Okay, then." She poured a couple of fingers worth in each glass and went back to the living room, then handed him a glass before sitting down on the sofa.

He sank down beside her, not too close, but not at the opposite corner, either.

Her pulse throbbed at her wrist at the simple nearness of him. She lifted her glass for a sip, hoping her fingers weren't shaking. It wasn't like her to be nervous like this.

"Don't you want to toast?" he asked.

"Oh." Heat rushed to her face. "Well, go ahead." She smiled brightly. He thought for a minute, his brow puckering in the middle, while Lainey wondered what the heck he was thinking. Then his face brightened, and he smiled at her and lifted his glass.

"Here's to the girl who lives up the hill. If she won't, her sister will. Here's to her sister."

He winked, saluted with his glass, and took a healthy drink while she burst out laughing.

"Where in the world did you hear that?" She sipped at the amber liquid, felt the warmth of it slide down her throat and into her belly, leaving a fiery trail. Gorgeous.

He shrugged. "Have you met my grandmother? She's got a saying for damned near everything. I always think I've heard them all and then she'll come out with another one."

Lainey relaxed against the sofa cushions. "Well, that's funny. Cheers. It's been a long day."

"Amen to that." Todd took another drink. "This isn't half-bad. And look at you, drinking it straight."

"Because I'm a girl?"

He laughed. "You are? When did that happen?"

She swatted at his arm and his laugh settled around them, warm and sexy. Oh my. Maybe whiskey to ward off the chill wasn't such a good idea. Because things were feeling warm all right...

They sat in the quiet for a few minutes, both of them sitting back with their heads against the cushions. Todd turned his lazily to look at her, a thoughtful expression on his face. "Hey Lainey? How come we never dated, huh?"

Inside she felt like her tongue was about it be tied into knots, and butterflies swooped and swirled in her stomach. But that was inside. Outwardly she kept her composure and looked back at him. "Probably because you never asked me."

"Hmm. Clearly an oversight on my part. You're not as intimidating as you used to be."

She snorted. After all this time, she doubted he was really interested. Just because she felt like a silly girl around him didn't mean she'd lost her mind. "Me, scary? What's the matter, have you exhausted the inventory in town?"

"Ouch." He got up and retrieved the bottle from the kitchen counter, brought it back, and added a splash to his glass before putting it on the coffee table in front of them. "Jeez, I'm not *that* much of a player."

A smile twisted her lips, a silent laugh. "Of course you're not." She added the tiniest bit of whiskey to her glass, too.

"Hey. That's sarcasm."

"Oh, well done!"

"That was too," he mumbled.

She snickered.

"Okay, smarty-pants." He sat up a bit. "You said because I never asked you. Does that mean you would have said yes if I had?"

"Only in a weak moment," she fired back with a cheeky grin, feeling immensely proud of how quick on the draw she was tonight. What were they doing? Flirting? Passing the time? What would happen next, a game of Truth or Dare?

Todd looked around her small living room and tilted his head a bit, then looked at her curiously. "Hey. I just realized something. You don't have any Christmas decorations in here."

And just like that, the whiskey soured in her stomach. "Gee, would you look at the time," she replied dryly, turning her wrist to look at her watch. Only she wasn't wearing one because like most people, she relied on the clock on her phone.

"Interesting." Todd relaxed and crossed one ankle over his knee, holding the glass negligently. "I think what we have here is a big ol' Scrooge. Or Grinch." He grinned. "Naw, you're too cute to be a Grinch. And you're not even green."

"You're a pain in the ass."

"But I'm right, aren't I? Just what have you got against Christmas, anyway?"

She gulped some of the whiskey, letting the heat burn the back of her throat. "You were at the inn. There are lots of decorations over there. There's even a big Christmas tree in the parlor. But wait...you didn't go in there, did you? You were being anti-social."

He frowned, and her little jab didn't deter him in the least. "The inn isn't here, though, is it? Of course you'd decorate for guests. But *you* don't have a tree, and here it is, the...what date is it today, anyway?"

The whiskey was starting to take a toll, softening the edges of her mind. She had to think for a moment. "The twentieth."

"That's right. December twentieth and no tree. No lights. No...you know, those big red flowers. Or pine boughs. Or presents."

"Nothing wrong with your powers of observation, Officer Smith. When do you make detective?" She made her voice syrupy sweet. She took back all the nice thoughts she'd had about him being a cop. He was far too observant and nosy right now.

He leaned forward now, peering into her face. "Come on, Lainey. Don't you celebrate? Are you, uh, a different religion or something?"

"No, I'm not. I just haven't been in the mood this year, that's all."

She got up from the sofa and went to the kitchen, took the last gulp of liquor, and put the dirty glass in the sink.

It was time to get Todd a blanket and a pillow and go to bed.

She marched past him to go back to the door, reached inside her coat and took out a small bag. "Here," she said, tossing it toward him. "Emergency packet. We keep them in a cupboard in the main house."

He removed the tape from the bag and peered inside. It contained a foldable toothbrush, travel-sized toothpaste, little bottles of body wash and shampoo, and mouthwash.

"Hey, thanks," he replied, finishing his drink. "This is handy."

"I'll get you some blankets and stuff."

She disappeared into the bedroom and went to the closet to get out a spare quilt and a soft pillow. The living room would stay warm, particularly if Todd put another few logs on the fire. When she marched back out, Todd had put his glass in the kitchen and was now standing in front of the fire, one hand on the mantel, staring into the flames.

"Here you go," she murmured. "There's an extra throw on the back of the sofa if you get cold."

"I'll be fine."

He turned around and their gazes met. The alcohol had mellowed her quite a bit, reinforcing some of her barriers but breaking down others. She shouldn't be staring at him so boldly. She'd deflected his questions, but she knew she hadn't fooled him at all.

"Lainey?"

"Yes?"

"Why aren't you in the mood this year? The real reason. Because most people at least put up a little table-top tree or a wreath on the door or something."

She swallowed against a lump in her throat. Damn him. He wasn't teasing now, and it made him harder to put off. "It's just...well, I don't know if you remember or not, but last year this time Jason broke off our engagement. It kind of ruined Christmas for me."

"Right." His eyebrows pulled together as he frowned. "Why did he do that again?"

She shrugged. "He said he'd found someone else. That it wouldn't be fair... Oh, I'm not getting into the gory details. Let's just say it tainted my view of the holidays."

Todd nodded. "Well, if it helps, I think he's an idiot. And because he's an idiot, you're better off without him."

She stared into the fire. "Intellectually, I know you're right. If he was in love with someone else, getting married would have been a disaster. It's just that last year I felt so terrible. My heart was broken. In the middle of all the

Christmas joy and happiness, I was cancelling wedding plans. And so, every time I see all the decorations and hear the carols and all that, it just reminds me of all that stuff and it brings me down."

"Then we need to bring you back up."

"I tried. A girl can only eat so many cupcakes before her pants get a little too tight." She sighed. "You know what the worst part is, Todd?" She didn't quite know why she was confiding in him so much, except that maybe she'd had a little too much whiskey and the fact that she no longer felt like she could vent to her girlfriends, who'd been so supportive in the early days. She knew they'd all expect her to be fine now and had probably gotten sick of her being such a downer. "The worst is that for the longest time I kept asking myself what she had that I didn't. Was she prettier? Smarter? Funnier? Sexier?" She shook her head. "Man, I sound so stupid saying that."

He took a step toward her. "Not stupid. Human. You are pretty, and smart, and funny."

"Yeah, my door's being beaten down daily by men looking for the perfect woman."

"I didn't say perfect." He smiled. "Know what else you are?"

She looked at him, waiting for him to continue.

"Sexy. Sexy as hell."

It wasn't fair how he said those words and her whole body seemed to respond. Something was simmering between them, and it wasn't just in her head. "I wasn't fishing for compliments, you know." Her voice sounded a little hoarse. She hated that he could have this kind of an effect on her...and loved it at the same time. She'd needed the boost so badly.

"I know that. I thought it needed saying anyway."

He was really close now, so close she could reach out and press her hand against the breadth of his chest if she wanted. She did want, but fear of making the first move held her back. Her breath was shallow, her body taut with anticipation as he lifted his hand and put it along the side of her face.

"Todd," she warned, and made the mistake of looking up into his eyes.

"Shh," he responded. "Let me show you. Don't move."

She didn't fight it, even though she knew she should. His lips touched hers, gently at first, soft and tasting like warm whiskey. They teased and nipped at her mouth until her lips opened on a glorious sigh.

As soon as she melted just a little, he slid his other arm around her back and pulled her close. At the same time, he deepened the kiss, his tongue tangling with hers.

Lainey didn't think. Instead, she disobeyed his order to remain still and slid her hands inside the hoodie, up over the warm, smooth skin of his back. Her fingers played over the firm muscles and she felt them shift as he tightened his embrace. His mouth slid away from hers and swept along the curve of her jaw, right to the sensitive point on her neck, just below her ear. A sound came from her throat, half-moan, half-gasp, and she felt him smile against her skin.

"So. Damn. Hot." He breathed it against her neck as she tilted her head to give him better access, and his left hand slid under her sweater to cup her breast, his thumb rubbing against the hard tip.

She wasn't sure how much longer she could stand up.

As if he read her mind, he moved his hand down, over her hip, and bent quickly to catch her up into his arms. Never in her life had a man done that, and it made her all swoony just thinking about it. But it wasn't just that. The teasing expression that usually marked his face was gone, replaced by an intensity that made her toes curl. He was one hundred percent focused on her, and never in her life had she felt so desired and so desirable.

He laid her gently on the sofa, then followed her down, his weight pressing her into the soft cushions, his hard body sliding against hers seductively. She arched up with her hips, desperate to meet him, and he kissed her again with an urgency that stole her breath.

And yet...despite the passion that throbbed between them, he made no move to remove any of her clothing. He wasn't pushing, or rushing, or taking anything for granted, and she found an unexpected sweetness in that. He just kept kissing her, and kissing her, until she thought she might die from the bliss of it.

Todd. He was everything she'd always imagined he'd be... and more. *How come we never dated,* he'd asked. Now she was asking herself the same question because by God, the chemistry was certainly there between them.

She ran her hand over his hip, over the back pocket of his jeans, holding him close. With a growl, Todd reared up enough to pull her part way to sitting and pulled on her sweater, tugging it off with haste so that it was wrong side out and twisted and then lying on the floor. *So much for not removing clothes...*

The excitement had her quivering against him. She loved the heat of his wide hand on the skin of her ribs, just below her breasts. The way his thumb grazed the underwire of her bra, then expertly flicked open the front clasp. Still he said nothing, but she didn't want him to. All she wanted was the feel of his mouth on her, and once it happened she cried out in pleasured shock.

"Mmm," he finally murmured against the sensitive nipple. "Sweet. A little salty. So good."

She was relatively sure he had her so hot now that her jeans were going to start melting. The air felt blissfully cool on all the spots where he'd kissed or licked her, but she pushed him away for a few seconds so she could reach the hem of his hoodie and pull it over his head.

Todd Smith without a shirt on was a beautiful sight. "Oh," she said, admiring, and ran her fingertips down over his breastbone, over the pebbled nipple and the texture of the sprinkling of dark hair. He braced his hands on either side of her head and lowered himself down so their chests were pressed together and the feel of skin on skin was surprisingly intimate.

It would only take a minute to take this to the next step. He'd undo her jeans, slide them down over her legs, then remove his own. They'd make love...slowly, then faster as need overtook them...

Todd began the journey, and his fingers found the button on her jeans. And as much as she wanted to, as much as her whole body was crying out for this, it was threatening to overwhelm her, and she knew they had to stop. What had begun as him proving a point had turned into something bigger than she'd expected. It didn't matter that she was a grown woman, or that she'd known him for years and had fantasized about this very thing more times than she'd like to admit. The truth was, she didn't have sex on the first date. If she wanted to prove to herself that she could still feel, still desire, still be desired...mission accomplished. But there was a fine line between where they were now and making a mistake that they'd regret in the morning.

"I can't," she breathed, not wanting this to end but knowing it should. "Todd..."

"Okay." He moved his hand, and she thought that was the end. But instead, he simply kept kissing her, kept her senses drugged with him, his taste, his touch, the scent of his skin and the cologne he wore. He lavished attention on her lips, her breasts, all the while rhythmically grinding against her. She was helpless to stop him, and lost herself in the sensations until she could take no more. It was too much, and need took over, pushing all other thoughts from her mind. She ground back, harder and faster, and when he lightly bit her nipple her muscles tightened into a glorious, surprising climax.

Her eyes were closed. She heard her harsh breath echo through the room, followed by his own as he rested on his elbows, still above her.

He moved slightly; she felt his lips touch her shoulder in a light, tender kiss.

When she opened her eyes, she saw the slight gleam of sweat on their skin. The firelight flickered shadows through the room, setting off the bits of gold in his gorgeous eyes.

"God, you're beautiful," he whispered, brushing a piece of hair off her forehead and tucking it behind her ear. "So, so beautiful."

It was a heck of a time to feel bashful, but she did. Now that she wasn't lost in desire and passion, modesty came rushing back. She was glad he was still pressed against her so that her breasts weren't just *out there*. "You are too," she murmured, biting down on her lip. "I didn't, uh, expect that."

"Me either." He grinned at her. "I was just going to kiss you. It seemed like the right thing to do at the time. But then...wow. I think I lost my mind."

"And took mine with you. About before, I have a thing about—" She stopped.

Could she even call this a first date? It almost sounded like she presumed there'd be a second, which she didn't. They were stuck together during a snowstorm, that was all.

They'd had a few drinks. Played around...

She cleared her throat a little. "About one nighters."

He didn't seem too upset about it. "Hey, it was probably good you stopped. I don't have any protection with me anyway."

"Oh? I figured a guy like you would always be prepared."

He sat up, frowned a little. "A guy like me? What's that supposed to mean?"

Now she was exposed and she hurried to cover herself. "I just meant that you aren't often hurting for female company."

For the first time that evening she couldn't tell what he was thinking. She'd seen him teasing, seen him so serious and focused on her, but this look was impenetrable.

Had she offended him? Or more unbelievably—hurt his feelings?

"I see."

She *had* offended him. She had enough of her wits back about her to realize that.

"That didn't come out right. Todd, that's not how I meant it. You just date a lot, that's all."

He frowned. "Just because I date doesn't mean we...ah, hell." He ran a hand over his face. "Is that how everyone sees me? As some sort of player? Or is it just you?"

She shook her head quickly. "No, I'm sure they don't. *I* don't. I mean...everyone likes you, okay? No one thinks you're playing anybody." She huffed out a frustrated sigh. "Me and my big mouth. Look. I haven't dated at all since last Christmas, so of the two of us, you were the most likely candidate to, you know, be prepared."

He stared at her for a moment, and then his expression softened a little. "Sorry," he said quietly, and reached for her sweater. "I guess you hit a nerve."

He handed it to her and then grabbed his hoodie. While he was turning it right side out and putting it on, she reconnected the clasp of her bra in record time and pulled her sweater over her head. "Let's just forget about it," she suggested.

"We kind of got carried away, didn't we?" Todd asked. Now that they were dressed, a little of the awkwardness had passed, but not all.

"A little." She tried to smile at him. "I...well. Let's just say today has been full of surprises."

He chuckled, the warm smile she liked returning to his lips. "It has been that. And this was a good way to end it, I think."

And speaking of ending it...

"Todd..." Never in a million years had she ever thought she'd say these words, but they were coming out of her mouth now. "I'm not really in a relationship kind of place right now. So tonight should probably be it for us. I don't know what you had in mind, and maybe you weren't thinking of asking me out at all, which means I feel really ridiculous right now for making that assumption. I just want to be honest, and clear."

"As long as you don't say 'It's not you, it's me' we're okay," he replied. "And as long as you don't have regrets. Because that was pretty amazing."

It was. She hadn't had that many partners, but she could honestly say that having an orgasm with her pants on had never happened to her before.

"Maybe we should call it a night. Get some rest. Tomorrow's going to be another crazy day."

She got up from the sofa. There was a certain amount of dissatisfaction in the movement, because what she really wanted was to curl up in his arms, be warm and cozy, and fall asleep. For that reason alone, she needed to put some distance between them.

"Maybe you're right." He smiled up at her. "Should I apologize?"

She thought about it. "For what? Todd, you were there. Clearly I was having a good time."

"If I'd known it would be like that, well, I would have made sure we dated earlier." His smile was so big now a dimple popped in his cheek. It should have looked ridiculous and instead it was stupidly alluring.

She kind of wished he had too, but what good did that do them now? Maybe in another time, another place, but Lainey wasn't in that place now.

"I'll see you in the morning, okay? Maybe put a few extra logs on the fire before you turn in. It'll help with the heat. Sometimes the baseboards don't throw as much warmth as I'd like."

"You got it," he replied.

She had no idea how to make a graceful exit, so she gave a weak smile and disappeared into the bathroom to brush her teeth and wash her face. When she came out he was putting wood on the fire and she slipped into her bedroom and shut the door.

Once she was in bed she listened to the sounds punctuating the silence. There were the bumps and thumps of Todd getting ready for bed, the click of the light switch flicking off, the muffled sound of him settling on the sofa with his blanket. The wind gusted around the windows, creating a whoosh and rattle that was far from comforting, and the stinging snow pelted against the window as the storm raged on.

And she was in here, and he was out there, and she was wishing she didn't care so much about guarding herself that she couldn't take advantage of a gorgeous, sexy, willing man when she had the chance.

Chapter 3

Todd rolled over, blinked, squinted, and reached up to rub the grit from the corner of his eyes.

His first sensation was the realization that he was on Lainey's couch, still in his hoodie and jeans from yesterday, curled up and covered by a thick quilted blanket. The second thing he realized was that the storm had ended overnight, and sun was filtering weakly through the curtains as day began to break.

He sighed, staring up at the ceiling.

Last night had been unexpected.

There was a reason why he'd never asked Lainey out. Even when they were teenagers, he'd kind of felt like she was out of his league. He couldn't explain why.

Maybe it was that she had always seemed to have it all together. She'd been popular too, never hurting for a date, always invited to parties. He'd seen her at a lot of those parties.

It wasn't that he'd been hurting for company, either. He knew that. Lainey was just...different. And Todd had always been a little afraid that he'd be shut down if he made a move.

Then, when she'd come home from college, she'd been joined at the hip with that Jason guy. Sure, he'd had a fun social life for a lot of years, and he'd confess he was guilty of laying on the charm a bit now and again. But he wouldn't make a move on another guy's girl. Even if he'd finally had the courage to ask her out, by that point she was strictly off limits.

Last night though...nothing had stood in their way. They'd both grown up. His fast and loose days had been over for a while now, and she was most definitely single.

Plus she was feeling really down about the holidays, and he'd wanted to cheer her up.

Give her back some of her confidence, see her smile.

Wow, had that backfired.

Not the confidence thing—that had been cleared up the moment she'd melted in his arms. It was *his* reaction that had kept him from falling asleep. From the moment he'd taken her in his arms, he'd known this was something different. Something special that he couldn't take lightly or laugh away in the morning. Something that had never happened to him before, ever.

It went deeper than simply fooling around to pass the time. It was stronger than simple physical desire and need. He cared for Lainey. Maybe he always had, which was why he'd never gotten up the nerve to ask her on a date. And why it had taken a couple of whiskeys and a blazing fire to give him the nerve to kiss her like he'd wanted to for years.

Lying under a blanket on her couch, he considered the unlikely truth that she mattered more than he'd realized. And last night hadn't felt like a one-off; it had been a first step to something new.

The question was, did he want to pursue it? Did she?

And when the hell had he started thinking about stuff like this, anyway?

"Good morning," she said, her voice soft and a little timid. He pushed himself to sitting and saw her standing in her bedroom doorway, dressed in baggy gray sweatpants and an oversized T-shirt. She looked adorable, warm, and still sleepy.

"Looks like the storm's over," he said, thinking that probably wasn't what he should have said at this moment but at a loss for anything else.

"Now it's time for clean up," she answered, and moved away from the door. "I've got to get over to the main house to get breakfast for that crew. Take your time and come over when you're ready."

She disappeared into the bathroom and he flopped back on the sofa. Hardly a smile from her this morning, definitely no mention of last night. It was like nothing had ever happened. A few minutes later she emerged, her hair gathered up in some sort of knot and he noticed a sheen to her lips that hadn't been there before. She went straight to her bedroom and popped back out in no time flat, dressed in jeans and an oversized sweater.

"I'm late," she said, going to the door for her coat and boots. "I can't really hang around. But in twenty minutes or so there'll be scrambled eggs and pancakes if you're hungry."

He was. Starving. The few muffins he'd had last night, coupled with the alcohol had left his stomach raw and rumbling this morning.

"I'll be over soon," he replied, getting up from the sofa. He picked up the blanket and started folding it. "I'll start some of the shoveling, too."

"You don't have to do that. You're probably wanted at work."

Wow. Talk about wanting to get rid of him.

"Well, I kind of have to shovel out so I can get to my car, don't I?"

Lainey shoved her arms into her coat sleeves. "Oh, right. We'll just have to figure it out one thing at a time, won't we?" She opened the door and stopped. "Oh," she said.

He went up behind her and started to laugh. A good two feet of snow had been packed against the door and now formed a semi-wall.

"Give me two minutes and I'll shovel you a path."

"Don't be silly. I'll do it."

The shovel was still stuck in the snowbank beside the door, and he watched as she reached for it, trying not to touch the wall of snow and knock it indoors. She managed it, but when she stuck the shove in the first time, the drift started to collapse on itself. Powdery snow fell back inside the doorway.

"Dammit."

Todd was going to offer to help again, but he saw the determined set to her jaw and let her be. Instead, while she began clearing a path to the back door of the inn, he finished tidying his bedding and went to the bathroom to brush his teeth and clean up a bit. There was a lot of snow. She'd be sick of it by the time she reached the back, and he'd take the shovel and do the front walks down to the parking lot.

By the time he got outside, she was three-quarters of the way to the back door, clearing a two-foot-wide path that would have to be widened later. When he reached her, he took the shovel from her hands and started throwing snow in big scoops.

"You didn't take long," she said, stepping back.

"You're going to be busy, and I figured I should earn my breakfast," he replied, turning around and smiling for a moment, wanting to leave things on a friendlier note than this morning's cool reception. "At least it's not heavy, wet stuff."

"There's enough of it though that moving it will be an adventure. The plows are going to be busy for a day or two."

He got to the back step and started clearing the entire width. "I'm sure the main highways will be open. You won't have to worry about putting up with me for a second night."

"That's not what I meant."

The fact that he wouldn't have minded being stranded another night was probably bad news. From all the signs, he was pretty sure that she regretted what had happened between them. He was more sorry about that than he expected.

Todd started on the next step but paused when Lainey put her hand on his arm.

He looked down at the thick mitten and swallowed tightly. She'd hardly looked at him since getting up, let alone touching him. He lifted his gaze and found her eyes steady on him, her cheeks bright pink. That could have been caused by the cold and the physical exertion of shoveling, though.

"Todd, I really don't know what to say this morning. And I'm responsible for what happens for about a dozen people today, and maybe after today, too, so my mind is running overtime, and I don't want this to be awkward, you know?"

Maybe not regret then. Maybe Lainey was just overwhelmed. She was running this place single-handedly, which normally would be okay in the off season, but she was full up right now. She didn't have time to think about him or them or what had happened last night.

"It's okay." He smiled down at her. "You've got a lot on your plate this morning. Let's tackle that first."

"First?" She looked unsure, so he let go of the shovel and cupped her chin in his gloved hand, just lightly, but enough that it held her still as he dropped the lightest of kisses on her surprised lips.

"Yes, first," he replied. He let go and went back to throwing snow off the steps until a path was cleared to the door. "Go on in and warm up," he ordered, "and I'll be in as soon as I can."

She nodded quickly and passed him on her way to the door. He couldn't resist. On her way by, he gave her bum a tap with his hand, and she yelped and scooted forward. When she looked back at him, a scowl on her face, he laughed and winked at her. One of them needed to do something to lighten the atmosphere around here.

When her lips twitched just a little, he knew he'd succeeded. And when she shut the door, he started to whistle as he began working his way around the house to the front door.

Lainey stomped the snow from her boots and pulled off her gloves, lifting her cold hands to her flaming cheeks.

The last fifteen minutes had been excruciating.

It wasn't bad enough that she'd had a terrible time trying to sleep, but she'd stood in her bedroom doorway for a good ten or fifteen seconds, watching Todd before he realized she was there. He was so sexy, so...wonderful. He was the total package, and guys like that never hung around for long. But she had last night to remember, and she'd indulged in a little daydreaming for a few seconds. Like what it might be like to crawl under that blanket with him and wake him up with a kiss.

Once she'd said good morning, though, she'd gotten so bashful. Last night she'd been sprawled on that sofa beneath him, half-undressed, probably sounding like an idiot. The only way to keep her composure at all was to focus on getting over to the inn and looking after the guests.

And then he'd kissed her. And swatted her butt and winked at her and she'd gotten all giggly and flustered again. Stupid man.

"Good morning, Ms. Price," Mr. Sewell said, entering the room.

"Good morning." She banished her thoughts and smiled at him. "Sorry I'm a little late getting things started. I had to shovel the walk."

"I think I'm the first one up, except for the pair in the living room. I think I heard voices there on my way past. I was just going to see if I could find some coffee first."

"Give me two minutes, and I'll have it brewing." She took off her boots and slipped on a pair of shoes she kept for indoors. "I hope you slept well."

"It was just fine. And way better than being stuck in my car." He laughed lightly at his own quip. "Speaking of, I hope that police officer got home okay. The roads were a mess last night."

Lainey focused on scooping coffee into the filter. "Actually, by the time you got here, they'd closed the highways. He ended up on my couch last night, and he's kindly offered to shovel the front walk in lieu of board and breakfast."

There. That sounded businesslike enough, didn't it?

"You really did have a full house last night."

She poured water into the reservoir. "Fullest I can ever remember, and I've been here a few years now." She looked over at him and smiled. He was a pleasant looking sort of man, and she wondered what sort of business brought him here this close to the holiday. "So you're a lawyer," she said, taking out mugs. "What brings you to Jewell Cove in a bitterly cold December?"

"I'm working with Ian Martin on the Aquteg Island case," he said, grinning. It lit his face up considerably and made him look much younger. "The details are so unique that it's been fun. Very different from any other property deal I've worked on."

Lainey knew some of the details; everyone in Jewell Cove did. Aquteg Island—commonly known as Lovers' Island—had been a waypoint for the underground railroad during the Civil War. Mystique had surrounded it for decades, but lately the pieces had come together. The rumors of treasure had been true after all. Some pieces of it had been distributed in antique jewelry pieces now owned by descendants of the Foster and Arseneault families. Then Josh Collins had discovered coins over the summer and had donated them to the Historical Society. But the biggest discovery had happened in the fall, when a relative of Edward Jewell, the town's founder, had taken an interest. Rich in his own right, Christopher Jewell had funded a treasure hunt that had netted articles more valuable, at least in Lainey's mind, than any gold pieces or ruby necklaces.

He'd found documents. Records. Ship manifests and names of slaves who traveled through the island, aided by privateer-turned-abolitionist Charles Arseneault and his future wife, Constance Arnold. It was particularly important to Lainey, because her ancestors, Isaiah and Jerusha Price, had been aboard Charles's ship during one of those trips.

There was a move now to have the island classified as a national historic site, and she smiled at Sewell. "What an exciting thing to be involved in," she said, handing him a cup of hot coffee. He sat at the table and she put cream and sugar in front of him. "You know, my great-great-grandparents traveled that railroad. They stayed here in Maine, though, rather than travel on to Canada."

"Good heavens." Sewell looked up at her. "That's amazing."

She nodded, understanding the confusion when he looked at her skin, which was more the color of the bottle of whiskey from last night rather than black. "My grandfather married my grandmother in the sixties. It was pretty unusual to have a mixed marriage here at the time, and they caused a pretty big sensation. Then my dad married my mom, and she's Irish – red hair and freckles and all. So I'm kind of a melting pot kid. Still, I love that the history of the island is part of my heritage."

"You've seen the books? The ones they found?"

She nodded. The books were in bad shape, having been preserved in a sea chest deep in a cave on the island. But the names had been unmistakable.

The back door opened and Todd came in, stamping his feet on the mat. "Well. That's the start of a morning workout." He grinned at Lainey, his cheeks ruddy beneath his hat. "It's going to be a while before the streets are clean. Hope you have lots of food."

"Any chance of me getting out to Refuge Point today, do you think?" Mr. Sewell spoke up and Todd shook his head.

"I doubt it."

"I guess I'll have to phone Ian and let him know," Sewell said with a sigh.

"Tomorrow for sure, I would think," Todd told him as he unzipped his jacket. "You're going out there to see Ian?"

"Mr. Sewell is part of the deal with the island," Lainey said. She went to the fridge and started taking out ingredients.

"That mystery has kept this town guessing for years," Todd confirmed. "I know some people think it should be left as is, but I think it should be preserved as a historic site. It's important and shouldn't be forgotten."

Lainey looked over her shoulder at him. He was completely serious, and her admiration for him went up another notch. She felt that way, too.

"Todd, help yourself to some coffee. If neither of you mind, I'm going to get breakfast going. People are going to be hungry soon."

Todd and Sewell chatted easily over coffee while she sliced ham to fry, whipped eggs for scrambling and stirred up pancakes with a healthy helping of Maine blueberries in the batter. As everything started cooking, she took a pretty plate from the cupboard and filled it with mini croissants and danishes from the bakery and put a dish of whipped butter beside it. For several minutes she was busy watching the food as it cooked. While she didn't usually have to cook for this many at once, she enjoyed this part of the job. She'd always been comfortable in the kitchen.

"That smells amazing," Todd said, standing at her shoulder. She hadn't heard him get up from the table, and she jumped a little in surprise.

"Thanks."

"Do you want help with anything?"

The door to the kitchen opened and the two sisters stuck their heads in. "Good morning," one of them said.

A pancake was ready to be flipped and the eggs were setting up nicely, so Lainey let out a breath. "Actually, you could help. If you could pour the coffee into that carafe and take it and the cream and sugar to the dining room, that'd be great. There are mugs on the buffet that everyone can use."

"No problem."

Once he was headed for the dining room, she started another pot brewing and heated water for a pot of tea for those who preferred it. The ham was lightly browned, the eggs at a delicate point and a warming tray was filled with pancakes. Lainey transferred everything to warming dishes and made her way to the dining room, putting everything out so guests could serve themselves buffet-style. Lastly, she grabbed a bottle of maple syrup, a glass pitcher of juice, and a bowl of strawberries and the meal was ready.

The table seated twelve, which left no room for Lainey, who usually made a point of eating with her guests. Instead, she refilled coffee and tea, fetched more cream, replaced the empty strawberry bowl with sliced oranges. Neither was there room for Todd, but he snagged a bar stool from the kitchen and perched upon it, holding his plate on his knee. He talked and laughed with the guests, answering questions about the town and the storm with ease. Once he caught her eye and gave a little wink, which made her blush. She covered it by fussing with the plate of pastries. It was clear that Todd had all the guests in the palm of his hand, particularly the ladies. His good looks and easy charm had everyone smiling and laughing and she started to wonder if he had any flaws at all.

As the meal wound down, Lainey made sure to remind the guests of the DVD shelf in the living room, or the library in the parlor where they might find a book to their liking. Todd also mentioned that the town streets would likely be cleared later in the afternoon, and that he'd keep everyone posted.

"Does that mean you're hanging around?" Lainey asked, stacking plates as the guests began to rise."

"I called Bryce this morning. He wanted to know if I could stay in town today, help out. Not much going on now, with everyone snowed in, but with the potential for accidents and how slow we're probably going to be to respond, I'm kind of on call. I'm going to head to the station in a bit."

"Be careful out there," she cautioned, frowning. "It looks so beautiful and sunny, but the roads are probably terrible."

"Don't worry." He looked down at her and she felt that warm, melty sensation again.

"I'd better get this cleaned up," she said, stepping away. "I'm guessing I'll have people to feed for lunch and probably dinner too, depending on whether or not other restaurants are open and if people want to brave the sidewalks."

"Are you set for groceries?"

She thought for a minute. "I am for lunch. I'll worry about dinner after that's over."

He went to the buffet and grabbed a clean plate. "What, going for second breakfast?" she joked.

He loaded it with ham, eggs, and two pancakes and then shoved it into her hands. "You didn't eat. And you need to. I don't have to check in until ten. Sit down for five minutes and fuel up."

There wasn't much in the way of sentimentality in his words, but Lainey felt her throat tighten at the attention he gave her. It wasn't just that he'd noticed. He'd also fixed her a plate and pulled out a chair for her. She sat, and he handed her the syrup.

"It's a damned fine breakfast," he said, pouring her some coffee. "You should enjoy it, too."

"Thanks, Todd. For everything today. You were really a hit with the guests."

"It's my sparkling personality." To her continued surprise, he started stacking plates and put them on a tray to go to the kitchen.

"Well, it is, actually," she agreed. "But then you always were charming. Almost too charming."

He grinned. "I know."

"And so modest, too, and humble."

He laughed. "See? This is why I never asked you out before. You're too quick. A man's ego could be sliced to shreds before he even knew what was happening. And mine's more fragile than you might think."

She put down her fork. "Is it all an act, then?"

"Maybe not all." He stopped by her chair and knelt down a little. "But I don't show people the real me that often. Come on, you must know that a lot of people hide behind humor and charm."

"It's deliberate then."

"Sometimes. Not always. If I'm really comfortable with someone, it's easier."

"And you're comfortable with me?"

He gave her a piercing look. "More than I'm comfortable with."

Something stirred within her. She got the feeling that last night she'd seen the real Todd, at least for a few minutes. His guard had been let down in those moments before she'd dashed off to bed, abashed at what had happened at the same time as she'd been beautifully relaxed and sated. And he was being real now. He had to be, to admit such a thing.

"So, Miss Price, if I were to ask you out on an actual date, would you go?"

The invitation surprised her. And flustered her, too. Last night had been one thing. An accident. A special circumstance. But if they made plans, had a real date, it would be acknowledging that there was really something going on that went beyond being in the right place at the right time. Lainey really wasn't sure she was ready for that. The very idea scared her, because of where it might lead. One date could lead to two, or three, and before long feelings were involved and she wasn't at all interested in getting those trampled on again.

It felt like it was too soon. Rationally she told herself it had been a year, so how long was she going to wait, anyway?

"It's pretty hard for me to get away right now," she replied. "I've got guests booked in until the twenty-third. I'm closed the twenty-fourth through the twenty-sixth, but that's Christmas."

He stood back up. "I see," he said, standing back. "I'm on the schedule from the twenty-second through Christmas, too. I work the holiday so the guys with family can be home with their kids and stuff."

Why didn't she want to date him again? Because right now he seemed quite perfect.

Maybe that was it. He was too perfect. And she knew very well that too perfect didn't actually exist.

"Well, I'd better get going. I'll stop in later with a road update, okay? Thanks for putting me up last night."

His voice was merely friendly now, lacking the soft warmth she'd heard in it before, and she felt a shaft of regret knowing it was because she'd refused his invitation.

"You're welcome. You more than earned your room and board with the shoveling and stuff. Take care out there today."

"I will."

She stayed in the dining room and listened for the moment he went out the back door. Then she let out a deep breath, wondering if she'd done the right thing.

Then she remembered all the events where she'd seen Todd, a new girl on his arm, that lopsided smile and sparkle in his eyes just for her, and knew she wasn't equipped to deal with a man that potently sexy.

Chapter 4

By five o'clock Lainey felt run off her feet.

She'd cleaned up the breakfast mess and then started the batch of soup she was planning on feeding the group for lunch, knowing it needed to simmer for a couple of hours. Once the kitchen was spotless, she went through the house and tidied as much as she could, replacing towels and bedding and cleaning bathrooms. She answered questions about the town, made phone calls to determine what was open and what wasn't, updated guests on road conditions, fed them lunch, made more phone calls since the only two guests to leave were the father and son, who'd decided to try their luck on the highway south. That still left her with all rooms full for the night and a sofa open for Mr. Sewell if he chose it.

It also meant feeding everyone dinner, which usually wasn't part of the inn's service. The Rusty Fern was open but the grill was closed, Breezes Café informed her that they were run off their feet and short staffed, and that only really left Gino's Italian.

Gino, bless him, said that he could supply her with baked ziti, garlic bread, and salad for fifteen. The only problem was getting it to her. The walkway from the road to the inn was shoveled, but the roads above Main still hadn't been touched by a plow. When Lainey went out at three o'clock, she could still see where Todd's SUV had left deep tracks in the snow. They, along with the ones from the men who'd left an hour earlier, were the only set of tire tracks on the street. Everyone else was staying put.

She ordered the food anyway, saying she'd figure out something for delivery.

At five there was a knock on the front door and when she answered it, Todd was there with a truck that was not his. "What are you doing here?" she asked, looking behind him at the monstrosity. It was a diesel, fitted out with a wedge blade on the front. "Don't tell me you're clearing snow."

He grinned. "And having a great time. It's one of Tom Arseneault's rigs. The road crews are so busy on main streets and highways that a bunch of us are helping clear some places in town. I wanted to see if you needed anything."

Lainey looked at him, pondering. Why had he come back? She hadn't really been overly kind this morning, and when she'd taken a few moments to breathe she'd felt guilty about that. She wasn't usually cold or rude. She'd been... afraid. Todd was so dynamic, almost larger than life. She could easily get swept up in fancy...and fantasy.

Now here he was, asking if she needed a helping hand—again.

"Todd, has anyone ever told you you're too good to be true?"

He laughed. "Nope. Never."

She shook her head, disbelieving. "I'm sorry about this morning. I wasn't very nice. To be honest, I wasn't sure how to act, and I was overwhelmed."

"You have a full house. I get it."

"No, not that. Well, not entirely that," she amended. Determined not to blush, she looked up at him. "What happened between us...well, it was unexpected and I didn't know how to handle the morning after. It wasn't you, though, it was me."

He smiled at her again, and she let out a sigh. "I know. Oldest line in the book."

"It's okay. Let's not worry about it now. Seriously, is there anything you need?"

He was so easy going that she had to blink to switch gears. "I have an order for dinner at Gino's. I was trying to get in touch with a cab to deliver it for me, but..."

"But Hal's only got two taxis and both are busy?"

"I wish. He's not running them at all."

"I think I could handle it in the truck. Anything else?"

Just like that, her problem was solved. She thought for a moment. If they were going down to Main, she could use some things from the bakery for tomorrow. "Is the bakery open? That would help me a lot."

"It might be. Get your coat and shut the door. I'll run you down."

"Give me one minute."

She dashed inside, popped her head into the parlor and said she'd be back in thirty minutes. Normally the room was empty this time of day, and she could lock up and put a sign on the door stating the time she'd reopen. But desperate times...

A minute later she had her purse and was bundled up to her neck in warm clothes. "Let's go," she said, stepping on the running board so she could hop up into the cab.

"I never thought. You're leaving the inn unattended."

"I know. Honestly, the bed-and-breakfast kind of guest is usually pretty honorable. That being said, I'm hoping this is a quick trip. It feels weird."

"If you want I can pick things up and you can stay."

It was a generous offer, but she had the business credit card to pay for things and it would just be easier this way. "It's fine. Truly." She shrugged. "Something about a storm and being stranded makes people band together. I had one couple who made their bed and offered to replenish towels for me today. The sisters who are staying asked if I needed help cleaning up from lunch." She smiled. "Which is actually one of the things I love about running this sort of business."

He took her to the bakery first, clearing the end of the street with the plow as they went. The sign on the bakery storefront said "Open" but the place was empty of customers. Todd waited in the truck while she popped in, selected a variety of breads and sweets and dashed back out again. Main Street had at least been cleared, so driving to Gino's wasn't difficult. Todd went in with her, and they left again with two boxes—one filled with foil-covered pans of ziti and another holding huge containers of salad and loaves of garlic bread.

The interior of the truck smelled delectable, like garlic and tomatoes and fresh bread and rich cheese. "Thank you so much for this, Todd." He lowered the plow blade again as they made their way slowly up the hill toward Oceanview Drive, pushing snow to the side of the road. "I couldn't have gotten through with my car."

"I had trouble with my four-wheel drive this morning," he admitted, watching the road carefully as the snow furled away from the blade. "Tom's truck is much better. Anyway, I'm glad I could help."

She knew spending more time with him might not be the wisest course. She'd thought of him all day, even during her busiest times. She'd thought about Jason, too, and how she'd opened her heart to him only to have him stomp on it. The truth was, Todd reminded her of Jason and that made her put up her guard automatically. He was good looking, popular, personable; naturally social and the kind of person who attracted others to them. She hadn't been able to hold her own with Jason, and he'd found someone else who could. It wasn't just the fact that Todd was the first man she'd kissed since her engagement ended; it was also that she was fairly certain that she wouldn't be able to hold on to him, either, if they pursued anything.

And yet he'd done her a favor yet again and out of the goodness of his heart. It would be rude to accept his help and then send him on his way. Besides, like this morning, they'd be surrounded by people. The least she could do was feed him dinner.

"You'll stay for dinner, won't you?" She unbuckled her seatbelt and turned toward him. "There's plenty."

"I need to get the truck back to Tom, but thanks for the invitation."

"Are you sure? There's lots."

He hesitated, then shook his head. "Honestly, it's already nearly dark and I haven't been home yet. I know the main road has been cleared, and I'd like to get home and get myself cleared out before it gets too late and cold."

Of course. She reached for her purse and hooked it over her shoulder, then opened the door to the cab. "I never thought of that. Of course you want to check on your own place." She reached for the bags of goods from the bakery and hefted one of the restaurant boxes.

He hopped out and came around the front of the truck, carrying the other box.

"Thanks for the invite, though," he said, following her up the walk. "Maybe I'll take a raincheck?"

At the door she paused. Her keys were in her coat pocket and her hands were full. She put everything down carefully and reached for the ring, surprised when his strong hand circled her wrist.

"Lainey? A raincheck, maybe some night when it can be just the two of us? Would you like to have dinner with me?"

He was repeating his invitation of earlier. She nodded. Perhaps a bit too quickly, because the idea scared her to death and was exhilarating all at the same time. She wasn't ready for this. And yet she wouldn't say no.

"I'll call you," he said, giving her wrist a squeeze.

"Okay." The word came out like she'd been holding her breath and suddenly let it out. Breathless.

Her fingers fumbled with the keys but she finally got the right one in the lock and opened the door. Then she picked up the food and stepped inside, Todd following her in and shutting the door behind him. For a few minutes they were busy taking everything to the kitchen, and all too soon they were back at the front door and she was seeing him off.

"Thanks again for the help today. I really appreciate it."

"It was no problem. I'd say we're even." When her cheeks heated, he smiled, popping a dimple in his cheek. "You make a mean breakfast, Lainey."

Lord, he was a tease. He leaned forward and placed a light kiss on her cheek. "I'll call you."

She nodded, unable to speak. The days' worth of stubble on his face scraped her cheek and his lips were soft and warm. She was tempted to turn her head, just a bit, and kiss his lips. But the door was open and guests were around and so she took a step back.

"Drive carefully," she cautioned.

"I will."

He jogged down the steps and walkway to the truck, got in, and started the engine with a rumble. He lifted one hand in a wave and then he was gone.

She shut the door and turned around to find one of the sisters—Christine, if Lainey remembered right—grinning at her.

"Phew," Christine said. "A man like that would make a girl want to commit a crime just so he could put her in handcuffs."

Lainey burst out laughing, horrified and amused all at once. There was no sense in denying anything, not with that farewell kiss in plain view. "He's something, all right." She fanned her hot face. "And he's also a heartbreaker."

"A good man and a heartbreaker? That's a lethal combination."

"Which is why I've stayed away."

"Until now."

She laughed. "Oh, nothing's going to come of it. I'm sure of that." Todd might have shown some interest in the last twenty-four hours, but he'd avoided her plenty in the decade or so. This was probably nothing more than a game to him. A flirtation, to use an old-fashioned term. "Now, let's get dinner on the table. Gino's cooking is amazing."

The evening passed quickly, and by eleven Lainey retired to her quarters again.

But this time it was different. Tonight she could see Todd there, sitting on her sofa, kissing her by the fire, the light of the flames flickering in the amber whiskey in his glass.

She let out a sigh. The silly thing was that one night was all it took for him to invade her thoughts and fantasies.

He was right about one thing, though. All through dinner tonight she'd heard the guests talking about their holiday plans, and then they'd gathered in the parlor next to the Christmas tree and watched *It's a Wonderful Life* on TV. She'd thought about her little house, naked of all Christmas decorations and cheer. Maybe Jason had ruined last Christmas for her, but their relationship was over. She shouldn't be giving him the power to ruin this holiday when he probably wasn't thinking about her at all.

Even though it was late, Lainey went to the storage room and rummaged around for a green and red storage box at the bottom of the stack. Once she found it, she dragged it out to the living room and opened it. She took out a clean and folded tablecloth in red and green plaid and put it on her little table. Next came a small but weighty box that she handled carefully; nestled into stiff Styrofoam was a beautifully crafted snow globe that played Silent Night when wound up. Silk holly boughs, berries, and pinecones soon graced the mantel above the fireplace, and she found two stockings folded in the bottom of the box—hers and Jason's. He hadn't taken his with him last year, and she remembered taking it down from the stocking hanger and putting it in the box. Somehow she'd fooled herself into thinking he'd be back. That disillusion had only lasted a few weeks but by that time the decorations had been packed away, and she'd forgotten about it until just now.

She sat on the sofa and held the stocking in her hands, her fingers tracing the quilting on the soft fabric. He'd hurt her so badly, not just breaking her heart but shaking her confidence in herself.

It wasn't right that he was still ruining things. Lainey got up, went to the fireplace, and tossed the stocking on the flames. It took a while for the fabric to catch, and it smoked and smoldered a lot, but eventually it was enveloped by flame and melted against the logs and ashes.

It was nearly midnight now, but Lainey looked around the room and liked what she saw. Oh, there was no tree, but she could remedy that. Still, the cheery decorations made her feel positive and hopeful and happy, so she put on the kettle and made herself a cup of instant hot chocolate in a goofy-looking Santa mug that she'd unearthed from the box and rinsed out.

As she sipped and basked in the warmth of the fire, she realized that over the past year she'd started over probably half a dozen times. It also occurred to her that each time she hadn't been going back to square one; instead, she'd been starting by increments, each new beginning a new step forward. Last night she'd made a giant step forward, and tonight she'd made another.

Maybe with each step, the next one got a little bit easier. In any case, tonight she felt better than she had in a year. And that was saying something.

Chapter 5

Todd skirted around the inn and went to the back, his hand clutched tightly around the waxy paper containing the flowers he'd bought. It was just dinner. It's not like there was any big reason to be nervous, but he was. Incredibly.

He still couldn't believe Lainey had said yes.

It was cold out and had been since the storm front had cleared. The wind off the sea was bitter and harsh, and Todd's breath made big puffs in the air as he paused in front of her door. Swallowing hard, he lifted his hand and knocked, then took a step back. Maybe if he took a deep breath, he'd find his confidence again. The last thing he wanted was for Lainey to know how nervous he was. He still couldn't believe how honest he was with her over breakfast the other day. But that was Lainey. She was kind and nurturing and...easy to be with. Before you knew it, you were sharing things.

She opened the door and his breath caught in his chest. She looked beautiful, in a little black dress that dipped and flowed in all the right places, hugging tightly to her hips, showcasing her long, gorgeous legs. The neckline was scooped and draped in folds somehow, making the effect feminine, modest, and still incredibly sexy.

"Come in while I get my coat," she suggested. "It's cold."

He unglued his tongue from the top of his mouth and stepped inside, then held out the flowers. "For you."

Her eyes met his and the attraction he'd felt that first night, in front of the fire, came rushing back with a vengeance.

"You brought me flowers." She sounded so surprised, so pleased, that he was glad he'd thought to stop. Almost everything had been red and white, too, for the holidays. He'd had a heck of a time finding something non-Christmassy in consideration of her earlier confession, finally settling for pink rosebuds.

And then he realized that Lainey had been busy. There were Christmas decorations and...and a *tree*. What the heck?

"You decorated," he said, shoving his hands into his jacket pockets, not knowing what else to do with them. After all her scrooginess, there was a definite festive flair to the little cottage.

She smiled as she filled a vase with water. "I did. After the storm I got thinking that it wasn't right to let something that happened a year ago ruin the holidays for me. I just got the tree this morning. Do you like it?"

It wasn't big, probably only five feet tall, but she'd decorated it with miniature white lights, wide red ribbon, and gold and red ornaments. "It's pretty," he replied. He hadn't put one up at his house either, but that was because he always spent Christmas at his folks' place. Honestly, after going to the effort of not being Christmassy for her benefit, he was feeling a little off balance.

"These are really beautiful, Todd." She put the vase on the table, the pink looking out of place on top of the red and green plaid of her tablecloth.

"To be honest, I was kind of surprised you said yes when I called."

She stepped back from the table and looked up at him. "Me too. But the inn is empty, and no bookings now until after Christmas, and you're off for the evening, and tomorrow night is Christmas Eve, so..."

"So you find yourself at loose ends?"

"I suppose I am. And maybe a little tired of being alone."

The air between them seemed suddenly heavy and charged. He had the overwhelming urge to kiss her, to see what was beneath that dress and pick up where they'd left off the other night. But he figured that would scare her off, so he tamped down the need that had flared up and focused on the initial agenda. Dinner.

"Well, I made us reservations at a place in Freeport. I thought since you had Gino's the other night—"

"—and the café really isn't the atmosphere you were going for?"

"Unless you're really craving one of Gus's turkey specials. Besides, everyone's too nosy in there."

She laughed lightly, and the sound rippled through him. Damn, she was something.

"Freeport sounds perfect, now that the roads are much better. Just let me grab my coat and purse."

She slipped away to the bedroom and came back carrying a little black purse with no strap and a long coat. He stepped forward and helped her slip her arms into the coat, resting his hands on her shoulders for a fleeting second. Then she reached back to take her hair out from beneath the collar and the moment passed.

She wore ridiculous heels, and he might have said something about them if they hadn't made her legs look so damned good. Instead he took her elbow as they went down the walk, and he made sure she was inside his SUV safe and sound before shutting the door. Once inside, he checked to ensure the heat was blowing on her feet before setting out.

It was already dark. Only two days past the solstice, the days were short, and it had been twilight before Todd had even left the station after his shift. He had satellite radio in the car, and it was set to a current hits station. The music filled the silence as they headed through Jewell Cove and toward the highway.

Lainey tried to relax against the back of the seat, but she could still feel the light pressure of Todd's hands on her shoulders when he'd helped her on with her coat. The tension had been so thick back at her place she could have cut it with a knife, but it hadn't been a bad sort of tension. Oh no. It had been the delicious, anticipatory kind.

For a second she'd thought he was going to take a step forward and kiss her, but he hadn't. She couldn't decide if she was relieved or disappointed.

He had brought her flowers, though. Roses. She generally preferred mixed flowers, but she appreciated something specific in the gesture. Mixed flowers were kind of...casual. But roses...roses were romantic. And he'd brought her half a dozen, interspersed with white baby's breath. It had reinforced the message that this wasn't just dinner, it was a date.

A *date*-date.

"You're back at work, then?" she asked, breaking up the silence, trying to break up her thoughts, too, before she got carried away.

"Until Boxing Day. I was day shift today. Tomorrow I'll work four until midnight, and then Christmas Day until six. Bryce'll be able to be home with Mary and the kids for Christmas Eve and Christmas morning."

"That's really good of you."

"It's no big deal. My folks are waiting to have Christmas dinner around seven, so everyone is there." He looked over at her briefly. "You know my sister, Emma? She's home with her husband and their baby. Mom and Dad will be plenty busy on the day."

He merged on to the highway, checking his blind spot. "What about you? What are your plans?"

Lonely, that's what. She almost wished she had work to keep her busy. "Oh, I'll probably go to the Christmas Eve service with my parents. Then Mom is having her dinner around one or two, I guess. It's just the three of us this year."

They talked during the rest of the drive, keeping to the light and harmless topic of family Christmas traditions and the odd memory, and before Lainey knew it, they'd arrived at a little restaurant right on Main Street. Todd helped her out of the car and once more took her elbow as they walked to the entrance, the warmth of his hand burning through her coat and making the nerves flutter through her stomach again.

Once inside, he helped her with her coat, which the hostess solicitously hung up for her, and Lainey caught Todd staring appreciatively at her dress.

She'd always liked this dress and didn't have much occasion to wear it. But she liked how it fit, and how the silky black fabric looked against her skin. She'd left her hair down, too, let the black curls tumble freely to her shoulders. She felt pretty tonight, and the way he was looking at her, it seemed he approved, too.

The hostess showed them to their table, a little table for two set with a trio of flickering tea lights. It wasn't until they'd ordered drinks that Todd spoke again, making Lainey's pulse leap.

"Damn," he said quietly. "You're beautiful, Lainey."

She shyly met his gaze. "You're not so bad yourself," she replied. He hadn't worn a suit, but he was in black trousers, a crisp white shirt, and a flawlessly knotted tie.

She wasn't the only one who'd noticed, either. Over his shoulder she saw the hostess and a waitress, their heads together, looking their way. Todd didn't even have to try. He had this innate sexiness that women responded to.

The waitress came back with their drinks and listed the specials, her gaze flicking occasionally to Lainey but mostly she spoke to Todd. Lainey smiled to herself a little.

Todd gave the woman his full attention and she started to blush. She made it through the description of the lobster risotto okay, but when she got to the veal marsala she started to stumble under his direct gaze. When she was gone again, Lainey started to laugh.

"What's so funny?"

"You. That poor girl had her tongue tied in knots by the end."

"What did I do?" He adopted an innocent expression which only made Lainey laugh more.

"You know very well, giving her your undivided attention and then rubbing your finger along your lower lip." She shook her head.

"I did that?"

She nodded. "Yes, you did. And if you didn't do it on purpose that's even worse. I never pegged you as someone who's unaware."

He leaned forward. "Aren't you just a little bit jealous, Lainey?" His dark eyes held hers, and she knew exactly how that waitress had been feeling. Flustered, nervous, excited.

She leaned forward a little too. "Not a bit."

He looked so disappointed she laughed out loud, then put her fingers to her lips, abashed at the sudden noise. His grin returned and she thought once more how much she actually enjoyed him. Todd Smith was anything but dull. But then, he never had been.

"Not even just a little?" He lifted his hand and moved his thumb and forefinger only about a half-inch apart.

She shook her head, but her smile softened as a warm feeling of tenderness came over her. "I don't because you know who you came with, and I know you're a gentleman. I don't feel jealous, Todd. I feel lucky."

His gaze warmed and he slid his hand across the table, linking his fingers with her. "Wow, Lainey."

She gave a tiny shrug. "Just don't let it go to your head," she murmured, loving the feel of his thumb rubbing over the top of hers.

The moment was interrupted by the return of the waitress who brought Lainey a glass of pinot grigio and Todd his iced tea and left a basket of bread on the table, along with a small plate of olive oil and balsamic vinegar for dipping.

"I love dipping my bread." she said, pulling her fingers away from his and grabbing a slice of baguette. She dunked it in the oil and vinegar and took a bite, closing her eyes with appreciation at the smooth flavor of the oil matched with the sharp tang of the aged vinegar.

The bread was followed by fresh caprese salad, then their entrees. They chatted constantly about things happening in the town, memories of grade school, hopes for the future. Lainey told him she'd wanted to take over the inn after Joan and Roger retired, and that it was a huge responsibility but one she was proud of. Todd said he'd once had dreams of joining the FBI but now he was enjoying working as a small-town cop.

"Really?" Lainey said, picking at her side of parmesan risotto. They'd barely eaten anything; they'd been talking non-stop.

"I like knowing most of the people I see each day. Even with the storm, I was out helping people, you know? It's nice to be able to do that in my own community."

Lainey nodded. "I know. Which sounds funny because at the inn I deal with strangers each day, but I get to help them see how great the cove is. The businesses all promote each other, and it's nice. It keeps people connected."

He laughed, cutting into his chicken. "It's kind of funny, thinking of the two of us who used to party all the time, being all civic-minded now."

"People change," she mused. "Grow up."

"Yeah," he said, "They do. And we get wiser, and sometimes more scared, and sometimes being a grownup isn't all that we thought it would be."

"We really didn't have a clue, did we?" she asked, smiling wistfully.

"No. But I wouldn't go back. I think things truly turn out the way they're supposed to, you know? Like you and me, here tonight. Everything up to this point has brought us to this moment. And I don't know about you, but I think this date is going okay."

It was more than okay. It was going so well that Lainey
kept forgetting that she was supposed to keep her guard up.
The more he smiled, the more they talked, the more smitten
she became. He'd always been unfairly good-looking. But
tonight she was discovering a new side. A deeply caring,
mature side that made her feel safe and strong when she was
with him.

When their plates were taken away, Todd asked about
dessert. She was already quite full, but she told him to order
some if he wanted. He did, along with two spoons and two
coffees. As the evening wore on, Lainey sipped on rich
coffee and, when Todd gave her a spoon, she dipped into the
vanilla bean cheesecake. It was heaven.

He paid the bill and held her coat for her once more, then
when they walked to the car, he took her hand in his.
Lainey's senses were on high alert, even from something as
simple as an innocent handclasp. It was a point of
connection   between   them;   a   chaste   yet   clear
acknowledgement of their attraction and a tacit promise
that there was more to come. On the drive back to Jewell
Cove, the conversation turned to the meal, their favorite
parts, and other favorite spots to dine on the midcoast. As
they got closer to town, though, the interior of his SUV
turned quiet. They were nearly to the inn, and the silent
question kept repeating in Lainey's mind: should she end
the date or ask him in?

She knew what she wanted. She just didn't know if it was
a smart idea.

He pulled in behind her car in the narrow space allotted
for the cottage, put the vehicle in park, and turned off the
engine. Lainey gathered up her purse and opened her door,
and Todd did the same on his side. The air was spectacularly
clear and cold tonight, and the sky was full of thousands of
pinpoints of light. Lainey's feet, in nothing but her heels,
were cold instantly, and her breath formed a cloud in front
of her face.

She reached inside her purse for her key and put it in the lock, then turned to face Todd.

She still hadn't made up her mind. But she did know that she wanted a goodnight kiss.

"Thank you for dinner," she said softly. "I had a really nice time."

"Me too."

Their eyes met, clung. Time seemed to hesitate as the moment held, weighted with anticipation and questions. Then Todd took a half-step forward, lowered his head, and placed his lips on hers.

Beguiling, she thought. Odd that such a strange word should pop into her head at this moment, but that was the only way she could think of to describe his kiss.

Beguiling. Fascinating, soft, sweet, luring her in for something bigger and grander. With a delighted sigh she put her hand on his shoulder and kissed him back. It felt... perfect.

Their lips parted but they remained standing close, touching each other, letting the effect of the kiss linger.

"Mmm," he hummed, and she felt the tip of his nose nuzzling her temple, urging her toward a second sampling.

"Mmm," she agreed, lifting her chin a little, indulging in the kiss foreplay. "Do you want to come in?"

"I thought you'd never ask."

His reply was so quick and sure that her pulse gave a solid thump. Her hand trembled as she turned the key in the lock and opened the door. He shut it behind them as she turned on a lamp then kicked off her heels.

It was warmer inside, and without saying a word they took off their coats and hung them by the door. Her arms were bare and the dress only came down her thighs about two-thirds of the way to her knees, but she wasn't cold. The goosebumps on her skin were from excitement rather than temperature. Todd came forward and gathered her in his arms, kissing her with an intensity that had been absent outside. But they were inside now. In private. And they had all night if they wanted.

His hand skimmed over her hip. She wanted.

She took a step back and put a hand on his chest. "What's your rush?" she asked, her voice low, and he smiled at her, a little smile full of wicked promise.

"No rush," he replied. Then, to her surprise, he spread his arms wide. "I'm all yours, Lainey. Do what you'd like." His dark eyes glittered at her dangerously. "Take all the time you want."

Oh. My.

"Stay right there," she murmured, moving towards him. "And put your hands here." She dropped them to his sides. Her heart beat fast, caught up in the seductive feeling of control. She first reached for his tie, shimmying the knot down until it came undone and the silky fabric fell over her fingers like water. She ran it through her hands, watched his eyes widen, and then she dropped it on the floor. Next, she went to work on the buttons of his shirt, taking her time undoing each one, revealing the warm, firm skin of his chest inch by inch. She pushed the fabric off his shoulders, but she didn't undo the cuffs on his sleeves. With one hand she gathered the material together and effectively pulled his arms slightly behind him, gently tethered together by his own clothing. It left his chest bare, and she pushed away any lingering nerves and did what she wanted right in this moment. She slid her lips over the hard plane of his pecs and flicked her tongue on his nipple.

"God, Lainey." The words came out choked and she smiled against his skin.

"You taste good," she said, kissing his breastbone.

"You're playing with fire, here," he warned her. Then he groaned and she smiled again. She knew exactly what he meant. All this was well and good, but he was promising that she could expect the same from him.

"Oh, I hope so," she replied, and with her one free hand she found his belt and began slipping it through the buckle.

He was stronger than her. It didn't take much for him to get his hands free, and she heard a button pop as he pulled at the sleeves of his shirt. Thrilling at the sound, Lainey reached back and undid the hook-and-eye at the nape of her neck. The drape of fabric drooped and fell to her waist.

She hadn't worn a bra beneath the dress. The back was low, and the folds of the fabric concealed a lot. Now she stood before him, the material pooled at her waist, her breasts open to his gaze which had gone from blank surprise to heated desire.

But for all the tension simmering between them now, Todd still took his time.

His hands gathered the material at her waist and tugged it down over her hips, leaving her in skimpy black panties and matching stockings. Lainey closed her eyes, luxuriating in the feel of his fingers trailing over her skin, the touch of his mouth at the curve of her shoulder, the feel of his hair in her fingers as she held on to him. His body was so hard, so strong, and she twined herself around him, desperate to feel closer, yearning to crawl into his skin if that were even possible.

Lips and hands explored until Lainey's knees felt weak and she didn't want to stand anymore. Slipping out of his embrace, she took his hand in hers and led him to her bedroom, her heartbeat pulsing in parts of her body that were begging for his touch.

She left the lamp off, but the moonlight sifted through the slats of the blinds, creating a pale glow around the bed, leaving the corners dark and mysterious.

"Lainey," he murmured, saying her name again, almost like he needed confirmation that she was here and that this was all right. In response she turned to him, lifted his hand, placed it on her breast. His palm was wide and warm, and she knew without a single doubt that she didn't just want him tonight. She needed him.

Him. No one else.

So she gave herself over to each sensation, vocalizing her pleasure as he laid her on the bed and explored every single inch of her body with his hands and lips. She writhed on the bedspread, gripping the soft coverlet in her fingers, her breaths heavy and punctuated with delighted gasps. When she could hardly stand it a moment longer, she turned the tables and rolled him over so he was flat on his back. The only clothing she wore now were her black stockings, and she unbuckled his trousers and slid them down over his hips, his legs, his feet. And then she did exactly what he'd done to her: drove him to the breaking point as she explored his warm, hard body.

They were both more than ready when Todd climbed off the bed and reached for his pants. Flushed with desire, Lainey watched as he retrieved a condom from his pocket and tore it open. He looked down at her and she didn't say a word. She simply opened her knees in invitation.

She'd thought she was prepared, but the moment he slipped inside her something changed. He hesitated, braced above her, his dark eyes nearly black in the washed-out light of the bedroom. They were joined in two places now; their bodies, his filling hers, and, she realized with awe and a little bit of fear, their hearts. This wasn't just physical. There was a connection between them, strong, and true.

And then he started moving.

Lainey couldn't fight against the assault on her senses. He was everywhere, within and without, the scent of his cologne mingled with the smell of sweat and sex, the sight of his muscles bunching with each rhythmic thrust, the sound of his seductive moan against the softness of her ear. She offered herself up for his pleasure, finding her own in his sublime command of her body, until he fastened his mouth on the tip of her breast and she came apart beneath him with a cry of release.

As her muscles went limp, he kissed her, long and slow, and she closed her eyes, unable to think straight through the blissful fog of post-climax.

But it was his turn now, and she gathered up what energy she had left and looped her legs around his back, linking her ankles.

He swore, a curse of what sounded like rough gratitude, and all she could do was hold on and marvel at his power and beauty.

Moments later they lay on the bed, the sheen of sweat drying on their skin.

Lainey's limbs were gloriously weak and she knew she should move but lacked all will to do so. Todd lay beside her, and her heart turned over a little when he reached over and found her hand, folding it inside his own. He was a man capable of great power but also incredible tenderness.

"Wow," he said softly, and she heard his sated chuckle in the darkness.

"Really? You think?" She couldn't help it, she had to tease him right now or else she'd let her emotions take over and find herself in far too deep.

He rolled to his side and she turned her head to look at him. He wasn't smiling, though, and she wondered if she'd miscalculated by being deliberately light.

"Lainey," he said, his gaze holding hers. "I...You..." He sighed. "Damn. You blew my mind."

She might have laughed except she could tell he actually meant it. There was an awe in his voice that reached in and challenged her innermost insecurities. "It was pretty incredible," she admitted, and she rolled to her side, too, so they were facing each other. No secrets. No hiding.

They lay that way, simply looking at each other, for long minutes until they got cold. "Climb in," she offered, getting up and turning down the covers. Maybe she should insist that he go. But she'd spent so many nights alone and she had the opportunity to have someone beside her tonight.

"You're sure?"

She swallowed tightly. "If you don't want to stay, that's okay. But if you do...you can. No pressure."

He got under the covers. "Come here," he said firmly, and she got in between the sheets as well. The moment the blankets were pulled up, he reached out and looped his arm around her waist and pulled her close, fitting his body around hers so that they were spooning.

"You feel so good," he said. "Warm and soft and naked." She could feel his lips turn up in a smile as he pressed his face to her shoulder.

She closed her eyes. "You feel good too," she answered, focusing on how his hand felt splayed against the slightly softer skin of her belly, how warm his breath was against her hair.

Lainey had missed this. Missed the closeness, the intimacy of being with a partner, trusting them to hold you through the night. That's what tonight was, she realized. Not just sex, but *intimacy*.

She wasn't sure she was ready for it, but she craved it all the same.

He kissed the back of her head and she relaxed in his arms. There was time to figure everything out tomorrow.

Chapter 6

Todd woke before Lainey.

The room was still dark, with just enough light from the streetlight half a block away to cast shadows and let him see the angles and curves of Lainey's face. God, she was beautiful. Her ink-black hair tumbled on the pillow. Her nose was slim and fine, even elegant, and her lips looked kissable and soft. She looked so peaceful sleeping. So trusting and innocent. As he watched, she let out a sigh and stirred a little, then tucked her hand under her cheek and slid back into oblivion, her long dark lashes resting on the very top of her cheeks.

Todd swallowed. He was hooked and he knew it. Last night had been unlike anything he'd ever experienced. It wasn't just sex for fun. He didn't just like Lainey; he'd experienced a real and honest connection. Now he was in her bed, and the biggest surprise of all was that he didn't want to leave.

It just felt...right.

He didn't want to wake her, so he simply watched her sleep for a long time, until his eyes grew tired and he drifted off to sleep again. As drowsiness crept in like a harbor fog, he was thinking about how today was Christmas Eve and that he'd like to spend it with her.

Lainey's chest cramped and she couldn't breathe.

She struggled to come out of the dream, but it wouldn't let her go. On some level she knew she was dreaming, but it was so vivid, so real, that the emotional turmoil made her feel sick to her stomach and tears streaked down her cheeks. She was standing in her living room, and Jason was there.

Christmas decorations were up and the lights twinkled on the tree. There were presents beneath it, too, foil wrapped boxes with big bows, waiting to be opened. Stockings hanging from the mantel, plump with surprises, and a fire crackling in the fireplace.

You're cold, he said. *I can't get through to you and I need more.*

She grabbed at his arm, clawing at it with her fingers. *No,* she cried. *Don't leave me.*

I can't marry you, Lainey. Stop it. You're embarrassing yourself.

Her heart was breaking. She couldn't have stopped the panic if she'd tried. As it was she could hardly breathe, and her sobs came on gulps of air.

Jason, please, please, she begged. *Don't do this.*

For Christ's sake, he growled, and looked at her with such distaste that it felt like she was withering before his eyes, becoming smaller and smaller, unlovable and insignificant.

There's someone else, she said, weeping uncontrollably. *Someone thinner and prettier and smarter than me. There's someone else, isn't there?*

Yes, he answered, only this time she looked up and it was Todd standing there, glaring at her with disgust all over his face.

"No!" She sat up in the bed, breath coming hard. Sweat had popped out on her forehead and she realized the covers had fallen to her hips, leaving her upper body bare. When she looked over, she saw Todd coming awake at her outburst, rising up on an elbow with a deep frown marking his normally flawless face.

"What is it?" he asked, sitting up. "Hell. Look at you. It's okay, Lainey. It was just a dream."

He slid over and tried to put his arms around her, but the end of the dream was still so fresh and so prescient that she shied away from his touch. She could still see him in the dream, looking at her like she was stupid and a nuisance.

Just like Jason had a year ago, leaving her with that bottomless ache in her heart. Instead, she scrubbed away at her tears and hastily pulled the covers up under her armpits.

His frown deepened if that were possible. "It was that bad, huh."

She couldn't talk to him about it. The last thing he'd want to hear about is how she was dreaming about her ex in the hours after she'd made love with him. Or how Jason had turned into Todd at the end.

"I'll be fine. I just need to wake up," she replied. "I'll be back in a minute."

She slid out of bed and hurried to the bedroom door, where she grabbed a robe from a hook and hastily wrapped it around herself. Then she disappeared to the bathroom, using the toilet and then splashing cold water on her face to try to wash away the ugly, heavy feelings left in the dream's wake. She brushed her teeth and dragged her fingers through her hair. Finally, when she couldn't put it off any longer, she left the bathroom and went to the kitchen. She couldn't think about going back to bed and pretending everything was okay. It wasn't. And she was so confused she needed some space to clear her head and sort it out.

By the time she had the water in the coffee maker reservoir, Todd had slipped on his pants and had come to the bedroom doorway. "You're not coming back to bed?" He sounded disappointed, and part of Lainey wanted nothing more than to go back and crawl beneath the covers and imagine that those feelings and memories hadn't happened. But she couldn't. They were too fresh. Too real.

"I thought I'd make us some coffee," she replied, avoiding his gaze. "What would you like for breakfast?"

He pushed away from the doorway and came forward. "Lainey, what the hell happened? What's wrong?"

She smiled brightly. "Nothing! Everything's great. I'm hungry. Do you want eggs? Or I could make pancakes or something."

He hadn't put a shirt on, and the sight of him shirtless—even in her peripheral vision—made her pulse jump. But then, physical attraction had never been the issue, had it? He reached out and gripped her wrist in his fingers. "I don't give a good damn about breakfast," he grumbled. "But something's happened. Last night you asked me to stay and cuddled so close to me I was like a human blanket. This morning you're avoiding me and can't even look me in the eye. What the hell did you dream about, anyway?"

He was right, so she lifted her gaze. What she saw in his eyes surprised and dismayed her. He looked *hurt.* Annoyed too, but hurt, and maybe even a little afraid.

It would be so easy to love him. To let it overtake her. All she had to do was think of last night, and how she'd felt like both smiling and weeping at the end of making love. She'd been so happy, and so full of emotions she couldn't even name.

Feelings that transcended description. Feelings she hadn't had since those early, infatuation-soaked days when she and Jason had started dating.

But her dream had showed her one thing that she'd suspected all along and had ignored. She wasn't ready. And they should move on now before they really got emotionally involved and people got hurt.

"Todd, last night was..." She swallowed against the lump in her throat, wondering if she could possibly be a good liar. She'd never really tried it before, not beyond telling her parents she'd been studying at someone's house and then going to a party or out with a boy. This was different because she was an adult now. The real question was whether or not to be honest. Spare his feelings or just lay it out there and watch him walk away? Because that was surely what was going to happen.

"I'm just not ready," she said honestly. He deserved that much. He'd been the steady one, patient with her, understanding of her past relationship and her need to go slowly. She was the one giving out mixed signals and it wasn't fair to him. To either of them.

"Ready for what?" he asked, but he stood very still, as if he were guarding himself against something unpleasant.

She felt strangely like crying, which was stupid. They'd gone out on a few dates. Let their hormones get the better of them. But neither of them was invested, were they?

It had only been a few days.

Except it was more than that. They'd known each other forever. It wasn't like Todd was some stranger. If anything, it hit her harder because she'd gotten a good look at the man he was inside.

"Ready for a relationship. After last night...please, don't tell me it was just sex." She looked at him, hoping he understood. "Maybe it would be easier to say that and walk away, but it would be a lie, and I want to be honest with you."

And that was a big revelation. She cared enough about him, respected him enough to be truthful even when it wasn't the easiest or most convenient thing she could say.

"It wasn't just sex," he said quietly. But he still stood on the other side of the counter from her, not coming any closer. "It was something more than that for me. I care about you, Lainey. We can take it slower if you want. I didn't mean to scare you."

She frowned. "I didn't say I was scared."

His dark eyes pinned her with the truth, though. "Yeah, but you are. You're terrified. And maybe it's my fault. You told me from the beginning that you were still in a bad place emotionally. I just thought..."

He took a step back, sighed and gave his head a shake. "I'm an idiot, I guess."

"You thought what?"

He met her gaze. "I thought if I asked you out again, and you saw how *not* scary it could be, it'd be okay. It was so easy to be with you, to laugh and tease each other and stuff. Last night wasn't just sex, you're right. But maybe it was too soon."

He was being so sweet that her heart hurt. "You deserve much better than I can give you, Todd. Truly."

"Oh, for God's sake," he replied, a trace of annoyance threading through his voice. "That's right up there with *it's not you, it's me*. You know what that is? That's when someone would rather quit than deal with their own shit."

She swallowed against a lump in her throat. He was so right, but that didn't mean she could change what was. "Maybe I am dealing," she retorted. "Maybe I just can't do it on your schedule, okay?"

He sighed again, rubbed his hand over his face. "You think I don't know you still have a thing for him? Come on, Lainey. Let's be totally honest here. You were crying in your dream and you said his name."

Her face flamed. She hadn't realized she'd actually said Jason's name. And how could she possibly say that it had been Todd in her dream in the end? She was so messed up and that's what she was going to go with.

"Look, I'm messed up. I've never denied that. Why are you even here? Why did you even want to try?"

"Because I like you. I've always liked you. And I thought if you got out of your own head for five minutes, you'd realize that you still had a life to live."

Quiet fell over the room. He was angry; she got that. But if he thought she'd been oblivious or self-pitying all these months, he was sorely mistaken.

"Living my life? Look around you. I run a business that, from Easter through Thanksgiving, keeps me run off my feet. I'm with people all day, making sure their needs are met and their days are full and enjoyable. Meanwhile I go home to my little cottage at night by myself because the man I loved decided I wasn't enough. Yeah, my confidence took a beating. And it takes a while to bounce back from that. Know what else?"

He looked as if he were going to interrupt her, so she plowed on. "While I'm busy looking after everyone else's needs, no one looks after mine but me. And sometimes there's not a lot of me left over. I had my heart broken, Todd. *Broken*. I had to cancel my own wedding. My friends got tired of hearing me cry about it and I was always a third wheel in couples' things, so I stopped going out as much. I had to deal with thinking about my fiancé being with someone else while we were together those last few months. Do you have any idea how sick and dirty that made me feel? So if I don't bounce back the moment you waltz in and get me out of my own head, I'm okay with that. Someone has to give me a break and it might as well be me."

He stared at her for a long moment, then acknowledged her speech with a slight nod. "Okay," he said, "okay. Fair enough, Lainey. I'm just saying that at some point you have to decide to move on. After last night I thought we had a chance, that's all."

She was going to say something more, but he took another step back and away from her. "I'll get my stuff," he said, and turned and walked away.

It was hard to breathe. She knew she had been honest, but she also knew that didn't equate to being fair. He was a good man and she'd let loose all of her pent-up feelings and frustrations. She hadn't even really considered the whole thing about no one caring about her needs until she'd actually said the words and had known they were true. And maybe that was why she hadn't moved on. She'd kept herself busy caring for everyone else, caring for the business and her clientele that she hadn't had time to really look at what was going on with herself.

He came back out of the bedroom with his shirt on. He stopped in the living room and picked up the tie that she'd dropped there last night and went to the door to get his jacket and shoes. Her chest constricted as she watched him, feeling like a failure and like this was all her fault.

"Todd..." She finally moved forward, jolted into action as he was nearly ready to walk out the door. "I'm sorry, I wish I wasn't so screwed up. I wish I had my shit together."

"Don't sweat it. I get it," he said, his voice dull. He was going to leave and this was final. She could hear it in his tone, see it in the brisk way he shoved his arms into his jacket. Added to her feelings of inadequacy was a real sense of regret.

"Please, don't..." she started, but the sentence trailed off into silence. Don't leave? Don't give up? Don't call me? She had no idea what she wanted. And when she looked up at him, his expression was closed off.

For a prolonged moment they looked at each other, and finally his eyes softened just a bit. "Take care, Lainey."

"You, too."

With one last, long look, he opened the door and slipped outside.

It was barely seven a.m.

Lainey heard his truck start, the sound of it fading as he drove away. She turned around, feeling strangely adrift. No guests to distract her. No errands to run. Nothing except an empty cottage.

The tree sat in a corner, the lights off, the garland dull in the faded morning light.

The decorations on the mantel were lifeless without a fire crackling at the grate.

Another Christmas and another romantic disaster. She should have known better than to put up a tree. To get her hopes up.

Maybe it was just time to give up. On Christmas and on love.

Chapter 7

S he couldn't stand the sight of the Christmas decorations.

Lainey fought back tears as she dug out the boxes again and started putting everything away. Damn him. And damn her, too, for allowing herself to have hope. To get sucked into the holiday, buying into the idea of Christmas spirit or miracles or whatever. She'd been right in the beginning, leaving that stuff packed away. Instead of getting her hopes up, she should have left well enough alone, not gone out to dinner with him, not slept with him, for God's sake.

Tablecloth, centerpiece, boughs of holly and pinecones from the mantel—all back in the box. The angel on the top of the tree packed away, ornaments pulled off and dropped into their box, garland rolled up and stuffed in a corner, mangled and twisted.

She didn't care. She just wanted it gone. She shoved it all back in the storage closet, a sheen of sweat on her forehead from both lugging the boxes and the speed with which she'd completed the task. Then she stripped her bed and put the sheets in the washer.

The last thing she wanted was to smell him in her sheets tonight. Instead, the scent of his cologne plus the unique scent of him rose up from the cotton and hot water, making her eyes burn.

He'd looked so hurt. But not angry. No, he'd put up a wall as soon as he'd realized she was shutting them down; a barrier to protect his feelings.

He'd had feelings for her.

He'd made no secret of that.

She was the one who'd said that anything between them was impossible.

The smell of the sheets was too much for her now and she closed the lid on the washing machine and escaped to the living room where she sat on the sofa, put her elbows on her knees, and rested her head in her hands. Normally she didn't remember dreams the morning after, but she remembered last night's with crystal-clear clarity.

Nothing had hurt her the way Jason's betrayal had. She'd loved him. She'd believed in him. She'd believed in *them*. He'd destroyed all of that, but more than that he'd ruined her confidence and he'd made her afraid. Only a fool would put themselves in a position to be hurt like that again.

Except the alternative was that she would be alone forever. At twenty-six, she just couldn't quite see herself living alone for the rest of her life. She wanted to find that special someone. She wanted children. For the first time in several months, she stopped feeling badly about it and felt mad.

Angry at Jason for doing this to her. And angry at herself for letting him. She was a hot mess of anger and sadness and yearning. Through her tears she gave a short laugh. What sort of man would be crazy enough to take that on?

The phone rang. Lainey jumped, then looked at the display. It was her mom, and Lainey knew that if she didn't answer her mom would come over to see what was going on. She worried about Lainey, particularly since Lainey hadn't made a secret of her anti-holiday sentiments. There'd already been several calls about Christmas plans and her mom's not-so-subtle attempts to get Lainey involved in local festivities.

Lainey gave a mighty sniff, cleared her throat, and pressed the talk button.

"Hello?"

"Good morning, sweetheart."

"Hi, Mom."

"Just checking to see if you're coming for dinner before church tonight."

Oh God, that's right. Christmas Eve was always her mom's oyster stew and fresh rolls and yule log for dessert. Just the thought of it right now was enough to turn Lainey's stomach. "Sorry, Mom, I've got some stuff to do at the inn today while it's empty of guests." It was the best excuse she could come up with on a moment's notice. "But I'll meet you at the church tonight." There was no way she'd get out of the Christmas Eve service. It was tradition, even more than the oyster stew.

"Are you okay? You sound congested." There was worry in her mom's tone. "With the storm and everything, maybe you've been working too hard. I know you were swamped."

She prepared to lie for the second time in five minutes. "Just a bit of a cold, I guess. Nothing major." *Just going through an emotional hurricane*, she thought, closing her eyes and shaking her head a little. She sighed. Were men really worth all this trouble?

Then she thought of how Todd had looked at her last night, the moment he'd slipped inside her, and it stole her breath, even now. She wished she could say they weren't worth it...

"Lainey? Are you still there?"

"Yes, of course. What did you say?"

"I said you should take something and go have a nap instead. Do you want me to bring over some soup or tea or something?"

The last thing she wanted was her mom here. She'd comment on the dearth of decorations—a move that Lainey was already regretting—and then she'd start her well-meaning prying into what was going on. Lainey really didn't want to spill her guts today, and her mother was terrifyingly good at getting to the bottom of trouble. It was a mom thing, Lainey supposed.

"No, I'm fine, really. I've got stuff here anyway. I'll make some mint tea and take a nap, okay?"

"If you're sure..."

"I'm sure. And I promise I'll see you tonight." One good thing was that she knew Todd was on shift tonight. He'd told her he worked so other guys could spend the time with their families. She could go to church and not worry about running into him at all.

Then she'd come home and wallow all she wanted.

Hell, she'd faked being okay often enough over the past year that getting through tonight was no big deal. A little makeup, a deep breath, a pasted-on smile and she'd be good to go.

"All right, honey. I'll see you later, then. And I'll save you some stew."

Her stomach rolled thinking about it, a by-product of her emotional distress and the fact she'd had coffee and nothing else this morning. "Thanks, Mom. I'll see you later."

She hung up the phone and sat back against the cushions. This was what she had to look forward to, then. A quiet, terribly empty day ahead of her, followed by an hour and a half of community togetherness and holiday spirit ending with going to bed alone again.

Merry flipping Christmas.

***

In Todd's experience, working on Christmas Eve generally went one of two ways.

Either he got a lot of calls, or things were quiet. Tonight, however, had been a mixture of both. He attended a small car accident where someone was rear-ended at a stop sign and responded to a report of a suspicious person which turned out to be nothing more than someone waiting for a drive who was late. Calls through dispatch were few. He found that the night before Christmas found most people in a peaceful, happy frame of mind. Of course, there was a smaller percentage that was unhappy, stressed, and angry and sometimes that didn't turn out so well for those families. He always dreaded responding to a domestic disturbance, but even more so at the holidays. As much as he'd like to think that sort of thing didn't happen in and around Jewell Cove, of course they did. Heck, it was just a little over a year ago when Jess Collins's ex had come back to town and caused trouble.

Mostly, though, people were just lonely.

He kept his radio turned down low as he parked the cruiser and walked toward the church. The service had already started, and he was planning to slip in the back and leave again if he needed to. Snowbanks were high on either side of the concrete walk, the result of the storm earlier in the week. When he opened the door to the vestibule, the sound of the congregation singing "O Come All Ye Faithful" rang out.

He didn't even go inside the sanctuary. He stood out of sight, over by the coat racks, listening. Absorbing the positive, happy vibe that surrounded him.

The truth was, he'd been miserable all day.

It was hard to be happy about the fact that Lainey had dreamed of someone else in the hours after they'd made love. But under the circumstances, he'd been willing to move past it, because he understood. She thought he didn't, but he did. She'd been hurt so badly, and they'd really connected last night. The dream had been prompted by fear.

If he could see things that clearly, why couldn't she?

He sighed, leaning against the wall as another carol began, this time "Hark the Herald Angels Sing." The bass line in the organ was triumphantly robust, but Todd just couldn't seem to gear himself up to enter the sanctuary and sing along. The reason he'd left Lainey alone this morning wasn't because she'd dreamed of Jason but because she couldn't move past it. The plain truth was she looked at

Todd and saw her ex. And Todd simply couldn't be accountable for some other guy's mistakes or actions. Until she realized that, she was going to be alone.

Sounded reasonable enough. Except...except he'd really thought they were starting something great. He wasn't looking for a casual hookup. He was looking for something meaningful, and he thought they'd had a chance. He'd wanted them to have a chance... He really liked her. Maybe more than that.

Maybe, hell. He really cared about her. He couldn't have slept with her otherwise.

Damn. He shouldn't have come here tonight. All it did was make him feel worse.

He turned to leave just as the minister began to read the first scripture of the service, but a movement at the sanctuary door caught his eye and he turned his head.

Lainey stood there, her eyes wide as she stared at him.

He swallowed.

"Lainey," he said, down low, wanting to keep his voice quiet so no one inside could hear.

"Hi," she said softly, and he saw her throat bob as she swallowed too, as if there were a lump caught there. He knew how that felt. It was a like a big ball of bitter disappointment that wouldn't move.

She was so beautiful. Was it possible that he'd fallen completely under her spell in only a few dates? He knew it was. It had to be, because looking at her now he got that strange heavy feeling in his chest, like a rock of uncertainty.

"You look pretty," he said, not knowing what else to say. It was true, anyway.

She wore black leggings and boots and a long red sweater that was the perfect color next to her warm skin and dark hair. She wore it down tonight, the black curls tumbling over her shoulders.

"So do you," she replied, and he saw color rise to her cheeks. He smiled a little.

He was in his uniform after all—trousers, shirt, jacket, and the belt at his waist that held all his gear and was heavier than most people realized.

"I was just leaving." His eyes never left hers, but he gestured towards the door with his thumb.

"Oh. Right. I came out to..." She never finished the sentence. It trailed off and she held his gaze, almost like she wanted to say more but couldn't.

The moment drew out, and she stayed silent, and Todd let out the breath he'd been holding. "Right. Well, Merry Christmas."

He turned to go. It felt wrong to walk away but what else was he supposed to do?

His hand was on the handle of the metal door when her voice called after him.

"Todd...wait."

He hesitated, his hand still on the handle, his insides quaking. He turned his head and saw she was grabbing a coat from the rack, shoving her arms into the sleeves.

A man with an ounce of self-respect would just leave. But he was a man who desperately wanted her to change her mind. And if there was any hope that she might do that...

He'd do what she asked. He'd wait.

Lainey's heart was beating so fast it felt like it was up in her throat. He looked so strong and fierce and delectable in his uniform. Worse, she knew what he looked like out of it.

There was no denying the power of her physical attraction. But was it enough?

She pushed her arms through the sleeves of the coat, hurrying in case he decided he didn't want to wait. She'd been thinking all day. All through the long afternoon, wiping her eyes and nose until they were red. While she showered and carefully applied makeup to cover her red-rimmed eyes and nose. While she heated a lonely can of soup for her dinner and realized that this was possibly the most pathetic Christmas Eve she'd ever had.

And as she'd thrown the rest of the soup down the garburator, she concluded that the only person to blame for that was herself. Not Todd. Not Jason. Just her.

He opened the door and a gust of wind blew inside the vestibule, but they clearly couldn't talk inside. As she followed him out, the open lawn of the church grounds provided them with lots of privacy. Without speaking, they started walking down the path. The snow was deep enough that they couldn't venture on to the lawn area, not until they got closer to the nativity scene that went up every year. The caretaker had cleared a path through to the manger and a new bench that was nearby.

Lainey looked down at the doll wrapped in a blanket and set on top of thick yellow straw. "Last year Charlie and Dave found a baby here. It seems like yesterday."

The discovery of the mystery baby boy had been the talk of the town.

Todd nodded, a smile touching his lips. "He was a cute little thing. Barely a few weeks old. I answered the police call, you know."

"I didn't know that."

"I kind of thought this Christmas Eve was going to be dull in comparison." He looked over at her, his breath forming a puffy white cloud in front of his face. "But I don't think so. I'm here with you. And that seems plenty complicated."

She walked away, just a few steps to the empty bench. When she sat down, the cold seeped through her leggings. Todd came and sat beside her, his coat making a rustling sound as he settled on to the bench.

"I'm sorry I'm such hard work," she said, shoving her hands in the jacket. She found a pair of gloves inside and realized that in her hurry she'd grabbed the wrong coat. She started to laugh then. The whole week had been incredibly surreal. Taking the wrong coat seemed somehow perfect.

"What's so funny?"

She looked over at him and couldn't help but smile. "This isn't my coat."

He chuckled, a deep sound that rode deliciously along her nerve endings. "It's been one of those days."

"You've been distracted too?"

"More than I should be."

She paused. Thought about what she wanted to say. Thought about what she felt and what she wanted to do about it. In the end she resorted to thinking aloud. "You know, no one really knows what they're doing. Everything's a crap shoot. We make decisions and they could be wrong or they could be right and we have to live with them and sometimes that really sucks."

He leaned against the back of the bench and crossed one ankle over his knee.

"Are you talking about this morning or last year?"

She was scared. Terrified. But she looked over at him and admitted, "Maybe both?"

"I'm not him, Lainey. I know you're afraid of being hurt, but you can't put that on me."

"I know that. It's just easier to say than to do. I'm so afraid of getting my heart broken." If she were going to be honest, she should be honest all the way. "And you might have the ability to do that, Todd. What happened between us this week...it's scared the shit out of me."

He turned on the bench and reached out for her hand, pulling it out of the pocket and cradling it between his own. "It wasn't just sex for me, Lainey. I'm not seventeen anymore, or even twenty-one. I'm a grown man. I want something more. If you believe nothing else, believe that this was never me amusing myself."

"I know that. And maybe that's what scares me so much." His hands felt so good over hers. "It wasn't just playing around for either of us. It could have been. The chemistry is certainly there." Just admitting it made her insides curl. "But unless I'm mistaken, there was more, too."

"Definitely more," he agreed.

Lainey sighed. "I'm scared, Todd. Scared of letting myself really care for someone again only to be disappointed. Scared of not being able to bounce back a second time when I haven't done very well the first."

"You know there's a chance that you wouldn't have to bounce back, right?"

As thrilling as that sounded, a part of her found it impossible to believe. "The thing is, if there's a chance it might work out, there's a chance it might not. And I'm terrified of taking that risk."

He sighed. And she knew he thought this conversation was going to end the same way as this morning.

But she didn't want it to. She wanted to be stronger. She wanted to reach out and grab at a chance at happiness. It was just so hard. The wounds ran deep.

"Todd, it might have been easier if he'd just changed his mind. But he'd found someone else. He'd been seeing her for a few months before he broke off our engagement. It wasn't just cancelling the wedding, though that was a horrible experience and really humiliating. It was more... making me doubt everything about myself. What did she give him that I didn't? What if I'm not the kind of woman who..."

She frowned, unsure of how to word what she was feeling. "Not the kind to keep a man, I don't mean that. But what if I'm never The One but always The One Before The One?"

"He's an idiot," Todd stated baldly, and she laughed a little despite herself.

"I know," she admitted. "Deep down, I know I shouldn't listen to that little voice. What I'm trying to say is that it's hard to ignore it. And this morning, after that dream..."

She might as well tell him the ending. Maybe it would make more sense if she did.

"I didn't want to tell you this before because it was all too fresh and overwhelming. But hey, I've got nothing to lose now, do I?" She put her free hand over top of their joined ones, ignoring the cold. "I dreamed he was laughing at me, and being so cruel. And then at the end it wasn't him laughing, it was you, and it hurt so bad."

"It was me?"

She nodded, biting down on her lip. "Yeah. And when I woke up, and you were there, I was so afraid that you'd eventually turn into that guy that I ran. I ditched you first because I'm a coward."

To her surprise, he reached out and pulled her close into the circle of his arms.

"You're not a coward. Lainey, in my job I see all sorts of people. You know what you are?"

She shook her head.

"You're hurting. Despite what you may think, you pulled yourself up and kept going. Look at yourself. You've taken on the inn and it's no small thing to run a business. And yet you do it and do it well. Your guests love you. You make them feel like they're at a home away from home. You make them feel like they're family even for the night or two they're with you. Your business is a huge success in this town. Yeah, you might struggle on a personal level, but who doesn't? You just have to realize there is more to you than that. You're kind, and caring, and nurturing. You know how to make people feel special. Maybe Jason wasn't smart enough to see that, but don't ever let him take it away from you."

She blinked against the tears that gathered in her eyes, and burrowed closer against his jacket. "Thank you. I don't want him to, you know. I want to be brave and fearless."

He leaned back and put a finger beneath her chin. "Look," he said, his face grave. "I can't promise you that we'll last forever. It's too early for that. But I can make some promises, okay? Like I will never, ever cheat on you. I will always be honest, and I will never be cruel. But I can only promise those things if you'll meet me halfway, Lainey."

He was giving her a second chance. All she had to do was reach out and take it. Meet him in the middle. And she knew one thing for sure: if she didn't at least try, she'd regret it. She'd always wonder what might have been.

She had enough regrets. She didn't want to add another.

"Maybe if you could add one more thing to that list?" she asked, loving the way he was looking at her right now. Like there was no one else in the world. Yes, part of it was the uniform. But mostly it was the man she knew was beneath the uniform. A man who could make her laugh. Could make her sigh with satisfaction. And who was far more honorable than she'd ever given him credit for.

"One thing?" He raised his eyebrows.

"Be patient with me? I can't promise to get over my insecurities overnight, but I can promise to try. Because despite what I said this morning, I don't want this to be the end. I want to try again. I know there aren't any guarantees, but I want to try. And I want to try with you, Todd."

He leaned forward and touched his lips to hers, a light, whisper of a kiss that was far more devastating than any they'd shared before. It was new and deliberate and not just about the moment but about the future.

"I was miserable all day," he admitted.

"Me too. I wallowed and ate soup and went through a lot of tissues."

"You did?"

She nodded. "Yes. But you can't use that against me."

He smiled. "I won't. Come here."

This kiss lasted longer, and by the time it ended Lainey couldn't feel the cold in her hands or feet or on the tip of her nose; she was warm all over.

The radio crackled at his hip. He listened intently—Lainey couldn't make out the words, but he seemed to understand.

"I probably need to go," he said, looking disappointed. "But I'm done at midnight."

"I'll be at home. If you want to come over, that is."

His eyes flared. "Just try to stop me."

He walked her back to the doors of the church, and nudged her with an elbow. "You'd better put that coat back. I don't want to have to arrest you for theft."

Happier than she could remember being in months, she turned around and looped her arms around his neck. "If you do, will you put me in cuffs?"

"Why Miss Price," he said softly. "You're sassy tonight."

"I'm happy," she corrected.

He kissed the tip of her nose. "I gotta run. I'll see you after my shift."

He left her there at the doors, and once he drove away in the cruiser she went back inside. The congregation was at the point in the service where they all lit candles as they sang "Silent Night." But Lainey hung up the coat and stayed in the vestibule, simply watching, and feeling a contentment she hadn't felt in a long, long time.

She was going to be all right.

And she had to re-do Christmas. In three hours.

Chapter 8

Lainey thought she'd never escape the church.

First off, she met Ian Martin, the lawyer working on the Aquteg Island project. He said that Mr. Sewell had sung the inn's praises and that it looked like the island was destined to become a historic site, which they both knew would please the majority of people in the town. The artifacts, too, were being restored thanks to Edward Jewell's ancestor, and the hope was that there'd be a visitor's center on the island where the documents and bits of treasure would be securely showcased.

Ian squeezed her arm and to her surprise, said, "This might sound odd, Lainey, but I think your great-great-grandparents would be proud of you. I think it's wonderful how you've made the Evergreen Inn such a key part of the town."

"Thanks, Ian," she replied, flushing a little. "That's high praise."

"You earned it," he said. "I'll see you at the next Chamber of Commerce breakfast?"

She nodded. "I wouldn't miss it."

Once Ian had gone, she met up with her parents, who noted her rosy cheeks and bright eyes.

"I don't know what had you so glum earlier, or why you skipped out on most of the service, but you look much better." Her mom searched Lainey's face as if looking for clues.

"If I tell you it's a guy, will you let it go or grill me for hours?" she asked.

Her mom's face lit up. "A man? Really?"

"Yes, really. But it's early yet. We're just taking it day by day."

"Who?"

Lainey's chest tightened. This would be the first time saying it out loud...

"Todd Smith."

Her mom's expression turned knowing. "It's about time! I always knew you had good taste."

Lainey raised a skeptical eyebrow. "Really?"

"Well, everyone makes mistakes."

Lainey knew she was referring to Jason and she laughed. "Just don't make a big deal of it, okay?"

"Whatever you say. If you want to bring him along tomorrow, he's welcome, but no pressure."

"Thank you, Mom." Lainey leaned in and hugged her mom, loving the feel of the warm arms around her.

"We just want to see you happy."

Lainey turned to her dad. "Merry Christmas, Dad."

"You too, honey. Good to see you smile again." He gave her a warm hug and Lainey realized something else. No matter how old you got, there was something about a father's hug that you never outgrew.

Honestly, she was starting to feel as if she might burst from all the happiness.

"I'll see you both tomorrow, yeah?"

"As soon as you like."

Lainey nodded. "Love you both."

A few more greetings prevented her leaving right away, and it was nine-fifteen before she finally managed to walk home, wearing the correct coat this time. Once inside, though, she rushed to the storage closet and dug out the boxes—again. Racing against the clock, she replaced the mantel decorations, the centerpieces, set up the tree and decorated, though the garland wasn't quite as precise as before. She shoved the empty boxes away, dashed around and tidied the cottage, started a fire in the fireplace, redid her makeup, took out a bottle of wine, and uncorked it to breathe.

At eleven-forty-five she fluffed her hair, took a breath, and went to the fridge to put together a plate of crackers, brie, and red pepper jelly, as well as fresh, crisp grapes and strawberries.

At twelve-sixteen he knocked on the door.

She opened it, stepped aside for him to come in, disappointed that he was out of uniform but so insanely happy to see him that she got over her disappointment in a flash.

"It's after midnight," he said softly, unwinding his scarf and taking off his jacket.

"Then I guess it's the perfect time to say Merry Christmas," she replied, moving into his arms where she belonged.

And it was.

Read on for the first chapter in SOMEBODY LIKE YOU, the first book in Donna's DARLING, VT series, and don't forget to follow Donna on Bookbub at https://www.bookbub.com/profile/donna-alward for her latest release news, preorders, and special deals!

SOMEBODY LIKE YOU CHAPTER 1

E very single terra-cotta pot was smashed.

Laurel Stone blinked quickly, annoyed at the sting at the back of her eyes as she stared the mess. She was angry. Furious. Most people would rant or turn red in the face. But not Laurel. When she got mad, she angry cried. And right now she was so infuriated that she could barely see through the hot tears.

She'd come in early to do some watering and deadheading before starting the weekly stock order, but discovered the gate hanging limply from its hinges, its lock busted. She immediately took out her cell and called the cops, working extra hard to keep her voice from shaking. Falling apart was not an option. She'd made it through a lot of life changes lately and had kept it together. This time was no different.

Now, as she waited for the police, she swiped at her face and bit down on her lip. It was only six thirty in the morning and she hadn't even had her first coffee yet. The brew sat cooling, forgotten in her ladybug print travel mug. Normally she hummed away to herself, unwinding the hose in the cool morning air. Not today. Today she had to deal with the fact that crime actually happened in quiet, idyllic Darling, Vermont.

And that left her shaken.

The Ladybug Garden Center was her pride and joy, her foray into building a new life for herself. There'd been little incidents in her first few weeks of opening, but she hadn't thought much of them. The parking lot had been messed up a bit where someone had pulled doughnuts with their car. Two lilac bushes from the bed by the store sign had been stolen. She'd sighed at the inconvenience but chalked it up to simple mischief.

This time the intent was obvious. Deliberate. And it felt personal.

All the pottery was in shards on the floor. Six-packs of annuals had been pushed off their tables, spilling dirt and crushed blossoms. Hanging baskets had been carelessly dropped, so that the planters cracked and split. Tomato and pepper plants were strewn everywhere, broken and wilting. The lock on the little safe had been smashed, and they'd taken the small amount of money set aside for a float.

Laurel was sweeping shards of pottery into a dustpan when she heard the gritty crunch of tires on gravel. She stood up and braced her hand on her hip as the cruiser crept slowly up the drive and into the parking lot. Might as well get the report over with, and then get on with the cleanup and the call to the insurance agent.

The cruiser door opened.

Damn, damn, damn.

She'd forgotten, though she wasn't quite sure how she could have since Darling was such a small town. Aiden Gallagher. One of Darling's finest, complete with a crisp navy uniform, black shoes, and a belt on his hip that lent him a certain gravity and sexiness she wished she didn't appreciate.

The last time she'd seen Aiden, she'd been home from school, barely twenty-one, and he'd flashed her a cocky take-a-good-look grin, all the while parading around the Suds and Spuds pub with some girl on his arm. Not that she'd expected any other sort of behavior from him. But still. Ugh.

Aiden approached the gate and she took a deep breath. He was a cop answering a call. Nothing more. And that was how she'd treat him. She definitely wouldn't acknowledge that they'd known each other since they were five years old. Or that he'd once had her half-naked in the backseat of his car.

"Laurel," he greeted, sliding through the gap in the fence. "Looks like you've had some trouble."

She would do this. She would not cry again, especially not in front of Aiden. She had too much pride.

"A break-in last night." She opened the gate a bit wider so he could get through. He passed close by her, his scent wafting in his wake. She swallowed. After all these years, he still wore the same cologne, and nostalgia hit her right in the solar plexus. He took off his cap and she saw his hair was still the same burnished copper, only shorter and without the natural waves, and his skin showed signs of freckles, but nowhere near as pronounced as they'd been. He wasn't a boy any longer; he was a man.

He looked over his shoulder, his gray-blue eyes meeting hers.

Definitely a man.

"Wow." He stopped and stared at the carnage. "They made a real mess. Was anything taken?"

She shrugged, focusing on the issue at hand once more. "Inventory-wise, I won't know until I get things cleaned up and do a count. But I doubt it. The float for the cash is gone, but that's only a few hundred dollars. Mostly they just made a mess."

Laurel bent over and righted a half-barrel of colorful begonias, purple lobelia, and million bells. Her gaze blurred as she noticed the crushed, fragile blossoms and pile of dirt left on the floor.

"Laurel?"

She clenched her teeth. If he saw her with tears in her eyes . . . today was upsetting enough without adding humiliation to the mix.

"Laurel," he said, softer now. "Are you okay?"

"I'm fine." She bit out the words and pushed past him, going to the counter area. She could stand behind it and the counter would provide a barrier between them. "You don't need to worry about me, or take that soothing-the-victim tone. What do you need for facts?"

She sensed his withdrawal as he straightened his shoulders, and she felt momentarily sheepish for taking such a sharp tone. But she was angry, dammit. Hell, she was angry most of the time, and starting to get tired of hiding it with a smile. This was truly the last thing she needed.

"Do you have a slip or anything with the amount of the float?" Now he was all business. It was a relief.

She took a piece of paper from beneath the cash drawer in the register. "This is our rundown for what goes in the float each night. It's put in a zip bag in the safe. Like a pencil case."

He came around the counter, invading her space, and knelt down in front of the cupboard. "This is the safe?"

"I know. It's not heavy-duty . . ."

"It looks like they just beat it open with a hammer."

Great. Now she was feeling stupid, too. "It's Darling. I didn't expect something like this to happen here."

He stood up and gave her a look that telegraphed "Are you serious?" before stepping back beyond the counter again. "Something like this happens everywhere, Laurel. What, you didn't think crime happened in Darling?"

Well, no. Or at least, not until today. The fact that she'd already come to this disappointing conclusion, and then he'd repeated it, just made her angrier.

Coming home was supposed to be peaceful. Happy. The town was small, friendly, neighborly. Even after years away, many of her customers remembered her from her school years and recalled stories from those days. Darling even had a special "Kissing Bridge" in the park. There were several stories around how the bridge got the name, so no one really knew for sure. But the stone bridge and the quaint little legend to go with it brought tourists to the area and made Darling's claim to fame a very romantic one. In a nutshell, those who stood on the bridge and sealed their love with a kiss would be together forever.

She should know all about it. Her picture—and Aiden's —hung in the town offices to advertise the attraction. Just because they'd only been five years old at the time didn't make it less of an embarrassment.

"I'm not naïve," she replied sharply. "Is there anything else you need or can I get back to cleaning up?"

"Can you think of anyone who might want to give you trouble? Someone with a grudge or ax to grind?"

Other than you? she thought darkly. This was the first time they'd actually spoken since she'd poured vanilla milkshake over his head in the school cafeteria in their senior year. "No," she replied. "I can't imagine who'd want to do this."

"I don't suppose you have any video cameras installed."

She shook her head, feeling inept and slightly stupid. Maybe she was a little naïve after all. She hadn't lived in Darling since she was nineteen—nine years. Things had changed in her absence. New people, new businesses.

"I'll have another look around. It looks like a case of vandalism more than anything. Probably some teenagers thinking it's funny, or after the cash for booze or pot, and smashed some stuff for show." His gaze touched hers. "Kids can be really dumb at that age."

Her cheeks heated. He hadn't had to say the actual words for her to catch his meaning. "You never know. They might have been dared to do it. Or some sort of stupid bet."

He held her gaze a few seconds longer, and she could tell by the look in his eyes that he acknowledged the hit. He'd kissed her because of one of those bets . . . more than kissed her. They'd been parking in his car and he'd rounded second base and had been headed for third. And then she'd found out about the wager and lost her cool. Publicly. With the milkshake.

The only thing she regretted was saying yes to going on that drive in the first place.

"So you still haven't forgiven me for that."

Laurel lifted her chin. "To my recollection, you haven't asked for forgiveness."

Aiden frowned, his brows pulling together. "We were seventeen. Kids. That was years ago."

Which didn't sound much like an apology at all.

"Yes, it was. Now, I have a lot of mess to clean up. Is there any more information you need or are we done here?"

He stared at her for a long minute. Long enough that she started to squirm a bit at his continued attention. Finally, when she was so uncomfortable she thought she might burst, she turned away and retrieved the broom and dustpan from where she'd left them.

"Do you want some help with this?"

She didn't want him to offer. The idea of spending more time with him was so unsettling that she immediately refused. "No. Don't you have to get back to work? Besides, I have someone coming in at eight. You go do what you need to do, Officer Gallagher."

"Officer Galla . . . oh, for Crissakes, Laurel. Is that necessary?"

She pinned him with a glare. He was standing with his weight on one hip, accentuating his lean, muscular physique, one perfect eyebrow arched in response to her acid tone.

She wasn't the kind to hold a grudge. Not generally. Heck, she'd forgiven Dan months ago, and that was for something far bigger than a silly teenage bet. Why did Aiden get under her skin so easily?

Maybe it was because he'd been so callous, even after the fact. If he'd shown any remorse at all . . . but he hadn't. He'd taken the paper cup the milkshake had been in, and fired it across the cafeteria floor before charging out. And he'd never once spoken to her again.

Until today. And despite the change in circumstances, she felt much the same as she had that night in the backseat of his car. Out of her depth, over her head, and at a distinct disadvantage.

She looked away. "Sorry. I just want to clean this up and get ready to open."

She picked up the broom and began sweeping the little bits of broken pots and dirt into the dustpan. She saw his shoes first; big sturdy black ones that stopped in front of her. Then his hand, warm and reassuring, touched her shoulder. She'd been rude and brusque, and he was being kind. Damn him. Emotion threatened to overwhelm again. Couldn't he see that gentle compassion was harder for her to handle than cool efficiency?

"Are you afraid to stay here alone this morning?"

Her throat tightened. "No, of course not."

"I'm on duty until this afternoon. I can check in from time to time."

"I'm fine." She looked up at him and set her jaw. "I can take care of myself. I'm a big girl."

He stepped back. "All right. But if you think of anything or anything else happens, call right away."

"Okay."

She kept sweeping and listened to his footsteps walk away across the concrete floor. The building always smelled delicious thanks to the flowers, but this morning the scent was even more pungent because many had been crushed and mangled. She sighed and rested her weight on the broom handle. He was just doing his job. And she was pissed off—at the state of the garden center and the fact that the one person in Darling she didn't really care to see was the one who'd been sent to help.

"Aiden?"

He turned when she called his name, but his expression was neutral. She wished she could be that way. Unfortunately she always seemed to wear her emotions all over her face.

"Thanks for your help this morning."

He nodded. "Just doing my job."

He walked to his cruiser and got in while Laurel stood there with a flaming-hot face. Once he'd turned to exit the driveway, she kicked a plastic bucket that had been abandoned in the middle of an aisle, sending it spinning away with a loud clatter. No sooner had she decided to extend an olive branch than he came back with a line that deflated any sort of possibility of amity. He was just doing his job, like he'd do for anyone else. She was no one special. Never had been. The knowledge shouldn't have cut, but it did.

Anyway, the bigger issue was the problem at hand—getting the store ready to open in just a few hours. The Ladybug Garden Center was her baby now. She'd invested all of herself into it, and she was determined to see it succeed, not only this spring and summer but into the fall and winter. In order for that to happen she would have to take steps to ensure this sort of thing didn't happen again.

Just as soon as she cleaned up the mess.

And stopped thinking about how Aiden hadn't changed that much, either. In good ways and in bad.

T hanks for picking up *A Jewell Cove Christmas*, my two Jewell Cove series holiday stories!

I really loved writing this entire series, threading in a little family mystery and some cozy small-town neighbors and businesses. I'll confess that the town of Jewell Cove was inspired by the feel of several little coastal small towns in Nova Scotia, where I live, and the Evergreen Festival is inspired by the annual Father Christmas Festival that takes place in Mahone Bay every holiday season. It was a delight to bring you Charlie's story, and to re-introduce Todd Smith in his own happy ending as well.

If you enjoyed this book, I'd love it if you left a review and shared your thoughts with other readers! It's an excellent way to help your favorite authors reach new readers who might enjoy their books.

Thank you for reading, and stay tuned! There are more Jewell Cove books coming soon!

Best wishes,

Donna

About the Author

While bestselling author Donna Alward was busy studying Austen, Eliot and Shakespeare, she was also losing herself in the breathtaking stories created by romance novelists like LaVyrle Spencer and Judith McNaught. Several years after completing her degree she decided to write a romance of her own and it was true love! Five years and ten manuscripts later she sold her first book and launched a new career. While her heartwarming stories of love, hope, and homecoming have been translated into several languages, hit bestseller lists, and won awards, her very favorite thing is when she hears from happy readers.

Donna lives on Canada's east coast. When she's not writing she enjoys reading (of course!), knitting, gardening, cooking...and is a Masterpiece Theater addict. You can visit her on the web at www.DonnaAlward.com and join her mailing list at www.DonnaAlward.com/newsletter .

CPSIA information can be obtained
at www.ICGtesting.com
Printed in the USA
LVHW112126120821
695175LV00004B/48